A MAN TO RIDE WITH

BY JACK FARRIS:

A Man to Ride With

Ramey

A Man to Ride With

By JACK FARRIS

J. B. LIPPINCOTT COMPANY
PHILADELPHIA AND NEW YORK

For Mother
with love

PART I

THE STRANGER

Which of us has known his brother? Which of us has looked into his father's heart? Which of us has not remained forever prison-pent? Which of us is not forever a stranger and alone?

——THOMAS WOLFE

PROLOGUE

As the first grey light of dawn streaked the sky above the eastern foothills, the screech of night sounds along the river ceased, and with curious suddenness a hush fell across the entire valley; a period of grace that lasted less than a minute. Somewhere, beyond the giant water oaks that hung dense and lifeless along the river, a dog barked—a sad, interminable wail that echoed and re-echoed in the stillness. Another moment of quiet, again the bark of the dog.

In the still, grey morning light the house took form, a flat, weather-washed structure situated on the crest of a long, low ridge, three hundred yards or more from the river bend. The house had been strongly built; the yard was neat and clean, reflecting order and industry.

It had been wisely planned, for it was built far enough up the ridge to catch the infrequent breezes that stirred across the valley, but not so far that the barn and lot in the flat were inaccessible. Unlike the old gumbo shacks, some of which still stood in the upper basin, the house on the rise had been built to stand for many years.

The back door of the house opened and a man walked across the yard and down the rocky footpath that led to the barn lot. He was tall and angular, his face dark and stolid. When he reached the lot gate, he stopped and stood for several minutes, looking out across the valley. The high, prominent cheekbones, the straight black hair, the lack of expression in his face gave evidence to the Indian blood that flowed through his veins. Chad was not ashamed of his Indian mother; neither was he proud. It had been a great handicap, for there had been no other Indians in the river country when he came. From the first the gumbo people had resented him; had resented his Indian blood, his remote, stoical nature, his impersonal acceptance of drought and high water and the buckleweed that eternally threatened the crops; had, indeed, resented even his industry. Perhaps in time these things would have passed; but in time he had loved and married one of the gumbo women. They could not forgive him for that.

Now, twelve years later, Emma was going away. The gumbo rats were no longer there to see it; some of them would never know that the marriage had failed. But these things were not important, had never been important, for he had always lived apart from the river people, as he had lived apart from other men in other times.

After a while he walked across the lot to the barn. He stopped at the harness shed and took down two halters, then went to the stalls out back; a moment later he returned to the shed, leading a team of mules. He harnessed them carefully, then hitched them to the wagon that stood nearby. As he worked his face was bland and expressionless; when he had finished, he turned slowly and looked toward the house on the ridge. Only then, for an instant, did his eyes reflect the turmoil in his soul.

Sunstreaks of yellow and red were etching the sky above the knob when he drove through the lot gate and turned up the rocky wagon lane that led to the house. As he crossed the crest of the hill, he saw her, waiting beneath the mulberry tree beside the house. She was standing very still, looking across the valley toward the sunrise. She was prim and pretty in the new gingham dress she had pressed the night before; the big sunbonnet gave her the appearance of being even smaller than she really was. As he drew closer she turned her head slightly. Now he could see her face, as dark as his own, her lips pressed together in a straight line. She has put something between us, he thought, and even she does not understand what it is; but it is there, beyond words, and we cannot talk of it.

Last night, lying beside her in the big bed, knowing that she too waited sleepless for the dawn, he had thought: perhaps she will not go; perhaps now, tonight, she will work out the hurt her own way and it will be better that she did it alone. But she had endured the agony of waiting, had somehow grown strong in her suffering; now the memory of Timmy was locked inside her and he knew that she would not speak of it; never, to him.

She did not move when he stopped the wagon beside her. She waited until he climbed down and took the suitcase from her hand, then she walked away from him, to the other side of the wagon, and climbed up to the seat, using the wheel hub for a step. She sat down and carefully smoothed the folds of her dress; then she looked again out across the valley.

Chad wanted to speak to her, to say the things that he knew wanted saying, but he could not find words to express himself. He stood looking up at her, sensing the animal dumbness that stood between them. After a time he lifted the suitcase and laid it on the clean straw that he had spread out in the back of the wagon. He stood a moment longer, looking first at the empty barn lot, then, slowly, back toward the house. Already he could feel the loneliness of living without her, the meaning of what they had shared together.

He turned back to the wagon. "Is there anything else?" he asked.

"No. That's everything." She spoke softly, looking away from him.

He climbed up beside her and sat down; he picked up the reins and shook them; the mules leaned heavily against their collars, and the wagon creaked slowly down the hill.

They rode in silence down the rise, across the meadow strip that stretched away to the river, then on across the first piney ridges beyond. At the edge of the basin, they turned west, down the old river road that led to Gipson.

The sun rose slowly above the trees, driving out the river mist that hung dense and heavy along the stream. The soft drone of insects filled the air, muted and distant against the bright chatter of birds in the oaks above them. The metal rims of the wagon wheels ground against the sandy road.

Chad glanced at Emma, then away, remembering that day so long ago when he had taken her, his new bride, to the house his father had built for the Indian woman on the ridge.

CHAPTER 1

THE STORY OF Delton Walters became at last a kind of legend in the river bottom country. Like all legends it was told and retold a thousand times, and with each new telling something was added or something taken away. In the end it was impossible to say exactly where truth left off and fancy began.

The man himself was by temperament well suited to legendary attainments; for legend prospers best where there is no real information, and Delton Walters had, to an extreme degree, the faculty of silence. By nature an inturned and brooding man, he spoke not once of his past, and by this simple omission gave the legend-makers reason to believe that he was hiding something. Then, later, there was the sudden tragedy in his life, at which time his silence became unaccountably heroic and his resentments somehow justified. At such moments are legends born.

The story began one cold, rainy day in the winter of 1871 when Walters drove into Gipson in an open buckboard. A huge, bearded man with deepset, glowering eyes, there was in his very appearance an aspect of mystery and untold tales. The mystery was somehow confirmed by the pretty Indian woman who sat beside him on the spring seat. Although Walters called the Indian woman his wife, and even conferred an added dignity upon her by addressing her as "Mrs. Walters," people in Gipson could never quite bring themselves to believe that the relationship was altogether proper.

After making certain inquiries, Walters drove to the Chekow County Bank. Leaving the Indian woman seated alone in the rain, he went inside and purchased from the

Chekow County Land Commission a hundred acre tract of land in the upper basin of Big River Bottom. The river basin was in those days a wild, unsettled region, and it was said that Walters bought the land for almost nothing. The transaction was completed within an hour and Walters paid the title out in gold. He then returned to the buckboard and climbed back up beside the Indian woman; witnesses reported that they exchanged not a word. Before leaving town they stopped at the commissary and bought a supply of feed and groceries; then they drove away, heading west toward the river country.

It was at this point that the seeds of legend began to take root. During the next four years people in Gipson saw almost nothing of the Walters'. They came into town only rarely to buy supplies, and with each trip Walters seemed to view the village and everyone in it with mounting distrust. For her part, the Indian woman did not once enter a store or speak to anyone.

As to what their life in the basin was like, no one could with any degree of certainty say. It was true that an occasional story was brought out by a fisherman who had wandered into the region, but these stories simply confirmed what everyone knew already, for they always told of a suspicious, deeply resentful man who would not bow his head to speak courteously even to a passing fisherman.

One thing however was known; Walters was an extremely industrious man. By late spring he had cleared and planted twenty acres of land along the south bank of the river, and sometime during the following winter he completed an eight room log house as fine as any in Chekow County.

The next summer, sometime in August it was believed, the Indian woman gave birth to a son. Whether she died in childbirth or later that year was not known, for Walters buried her himself, leaving the grave unmarked.

Around the death of the Indian woman, and the two years following it, literally hundreds of stories sprang up. One of them had to do with a Mrs. Dora Adams, the wife of a Gipson minister, who went into the river bottom and offered to bring the child out for adoption. Exactly what happened to Mrs. Adams in the basin was hard to say, for she was by nature a capricious and rather imaginative woman; but one thing was certain, she had been most uncharitably dealt with. When Walters learned the purpose of her visit (the philanthropic Mrs. Adams reported) he had become absolutely violent and had conducted himself so insanely that the good lady actually feared for her life. The experience left Mrs. Adams in a state of shock which put her to bed for several days, and her report aroused so much indignation among the townsfolk of Gipson that there was for a time talk of legal action to separate the child from its mad father. A church committee was formed and meetings were held regularly for almost a month; but it appeared that no one was willing to undertake a return trip to the basin and the movement finally dissipated itself in a flurry of meaningless oratory.

Another story, told by a fisherman named Dolph Bellcraft, had to do with the Indian woman's burial. It seemed that Dolph was fishing at a point below the Walters house one night late in October when he saw a fire high up on the bluff. He at first assumed that it was Walters, burning brush, but decided after watching for a time that "something funny was going on." He surreptitiously worked his way up the bluff and from a secluded spot saw Walters standing before the fire with the body of the Indian woman in his arms. As Dolph watched, Walters flung the lifeless body into the blaze and stood silently by while it burned. It was a horrible sight to see, Dolph said.

There were, however, two or three unsatisfactory aspects to this story. First of all, Dolph drank a good deal, and from time to time (in various states of intoxication) his accounts of the incident took on the flavor of contradiction. Then, too, he had neglected to mention the weird scene until two or three months later, when it was known for sure that the Indian woman had died. Such inconsistencies were rather too obvious to ignore, and it was only after time had divorced the story from its original source that it was repeated for gospel truth.

14

Whatever abuses Walters may have suffered at the hands of the legend-makers, it was known that he continued to live for a time in the basin. After the death of his wife, he came into town even less frequently than before; and if he had been previously noncommital, he was now positively mute. When he drove into Gipson for supplies, the child was always with him, carried at first awkwardly in his arms, and later seated beside him in the buckboard. The child was rather more like his father than his mother; a dark, solemn little fellow who, except for the tragic circumstances surrounding his life, would have seemed ludicrously grave.

1877 was the year of the last big flood. Those who remembered it said that God's very wrath had been provoked. Rain fell steadily through May and most of June. The sky, grey and leaden, seemed to hang just above the treetops and the wind howled its way across the valley like the voice of doom. Big River at last thundered out of her banks and poured over the entire lowland region; for a brief spell the citizens of Gipson forgot about Delton Walters, for, as the waters continued to rise, it appeared that the village itself was in jeopardy. At last, toward the end of June, the sky cleared and the sun shone through. Only then did people think again of Walters, and it was commonly believed that he could not possibly have survived the flood. However, Walters had built his house high up the ridge leading to the bluff and those who knew the basin later said that the high water would never have reached its foundation.

In any case, Walters did survive the flood, although his crops were of course destroyed. And the experience had taken something else from Delton Walters: his will to stay on. On the first day of July, he drove into Gipson; the boy was with him and what few possessions remained were piled on the buckboard. Walters, it was said, had aged twenty years during those last bitter months; his black hair was now flecked with grey and the tragedy of his life was stamped in deep lines along his face; his once arrogant eyes had lost their fire, and he spoke brokenly, as one who had endured a shock from which he would not soon recover. He stopped at the Chekow County Bank and deposited three thousand dollars in the boy's name, requesting that the money be used to pay off accumulating taxes on the farm. Then he climbed back into the buckboard and drove away, as unceremoniously as he had come.

People in Gipson never saw Delton Walters again. The years passed and the story of his brief and ill-fated life in the basin was magnified, romanticized, elegized, and related in one form or another to every stranger who came to Chekow County.

There the story would have ended, except for the appearance, almost thirty years later, of another stranger in the river bottom country. The stranger was Delton Walter's son, who had returned to claim the land that his father had left him.

CHAPTER 2

AT A BEND in the river known as Pledger's Point, a bandy-legged little man with dark, leathery features and the lean, wiry body of a trained fighter stood precariously balanced on a distended tree trunk, his fishing line dangling in a patch of sunken brush eight or ten feet off the bank. He stared intently at the water, his teeth tightly clamped on the stem of a blackened corncob pipe and his eyes narrowed to slits; under a dirty panama hat tiny beads of perspiration glistened on his forehead. At last he slowly raised the fishing line, leaning slightly forward as the hook broke the surface; seeing the untouched bait, he looked at it meditatively for a long moment, then he lowered it again into the water, at exactly the spot where it had been before.

The fisherman was Will Kelly, the land agent of Chekow County. He had left his office in Gipson shortly after eleven o'clock that morning; it had been his intention to drive to the upper basin of Big River Bottom and run out some corner sections for a man named "Such" Farnsworth, who had recently purchased a tract of land farther down the river. It was not until Will was driving past Pledger's Point that his good intentions went astray. As it happened, he remembered that a sizable catfish (who had twice eluded him already) made his home in a brushy cove thirty or forty yards below the river bend; and at almost the same moment he discovered that he had by chance brought along his fishing tackle. Will did not give in to his strongest impulse without a small, inward struggle. In the first place, he had given "Such" his word that he would run out the corner sections that day, and, to Will, a man's promise was never to be taken lightly. He also

17

knew that the bend in the river would remain exactly where it was, and that it was impossible to reach the basin without driving past it, and that the temptation to stop and put down a line would be as strong one day as another. After turning the matter over in his mind for several minutes, he had hit upon what seemed to him a simple solution: remove the temptation by catching the catfish. Promising himself that he would spend no more than an hour at the point, he pulled his buggy-mare, Dandy, off the main road, tied her in the shade of a persimmon thicket, and took up his vigil on the distended tree trunk.

It was now mid-afternoon. As matters turned out, the catfish had warily kept his distance; he had not, in fact, so much as nudged the bait. But now and then, always it seemed at the moment when Will had decided to secure his tackle and try his luck another day, a sudden trickle of bubbles rising to the surface, or a quick stir of mud underneath the brush heap, would convince him that the quarry was there, ready to strike. Somehow the time had slipped away.

The sun was dipping low in the western sky when Will at last pulled in his line and looked at his watch. It was five minutes past four. He briefly considered driving on to the basin as a gesture of good faith, but he was still five miles from Carley's Crossing and knew that by the time he arrived there it would be too late to get any work done. Finally, he decided to return to Gipson and come back the following day.

Dandy, a thick-chested little bay, stood in the persimmon thicket, her head drooping abjectly. The air was hot and muggy under the trees and swarms of deer flies buzzed persistently around her head. Seeing Will, she tossed her head wearily at the flies and gave him a long, doleful look.

Will grinned. "Dandy, you're like a lot of people I know," he said, rubbing his hand along her nose.

After putting his fishing tackle in the catch-box at the rear of the buggy, he walked back to the mare and slipped on her bridle. "If you'll just stay on your feet another five minutes," he told her, "we'll be out of here."

It was drawing on toward sundown when Will reached Gipson, although the distance from Pledger's Point was less than six miles. The delay was due partly to the fact that Dandy, who had just passed her twelfth birthday, had developed rather set opinions about the speed at which in her dotage she should be expected to move; and also to the fact that Will had stopped again at Bear Creek, a mile west of town, and fished out a small hole there which he had been for some time neglecting.

When he arrived at the land office, a few minutes past six, a sweat-stained sorrel mare was tied to the front hitch rail and a man was sitting on the front porch. Even someone less familiar with the river bottom country than Will would have seen that the man was a stranger. He was dressed in dusty western levis and wore boots and spurs; a large black hat lay on the bench beside him. The man appeared to be asleep; his head leaned back against the window-facing and his eyes were closed.

As Will pulled Dandy in to the hitch rail, he could not help noticing the butt of a carbine protruding from a saddle holster on the mare's back; that confirmed his suspicions, a saddle gun was not standard equipment in the river country.

When Will glanced again at the porch, the stranger had raised his head and was looking directly at him. The look gave Will a slight inward start. The man's eyes, which were almost black, had a curiously piercing quality. He was very dark, his cheekbones high and prominent, his features rather gaunt. Mixed blood, Will thought; Mexican, maybe.

"Waiting for me?" he asked, climbing out of the buggy. He tried to make the words as amiable as possible for he somehow suspected that the man had been waiting for some time and he could not escape a slight twinge of guilt at having spent the afternoon so unofficially occupied.

"Are you the land agent?" The stranger spoke quietly, with no trace of an accent, but there was a directness in his tone which made the question seem more important than it really was.

"Well, I was when I left town this morning," Will replied,

smiling. "It's my guess that I still am . . . nobody else around here would have this job."

For an instant the stranger's dark features changed; the shadow of a smile touched the corners of his mouth, but it seemed an acknowledgment of Will's attempt at humor rather than an indication that the stranger was genuinely amused. Will had the uneasy feeling that he was being put on the defensive, and the sensation was particularly annoying because there was no real reason for it.

"Then it's you I'm waiting for," the man said.

Will finished securing Dandy's tether rope, then turned back to the porch. "Been waiting long?"

"Since noon." The answer was matter of fact, even genial, but somehow it added to Will's uneasiness.

"That's a long time in this heat," Will said, walking up the front steps.

The man stood up.

"As a rule, I'm around here," Will went on, "but today I had some work to do in the river basin . . . fellow down there brought some land last month, wanted me to run out the corner sections . . . should have got down that way before today . . . just kept putting it off, you know how that goes. . . ."

"That's all right," the man said. "I didn't mind waiting." He was looking directly at Will, his eyes faintly amused, and it was the look more than the interruption that brought Will up short. Suddenly he felt a little foolish. There was something about the stranger, a kind of intuition, that gave him an advantage. With men like this, Will thought, pretences are at best a dangerous business.

"The truth is, I didn't make it to the basin at all," he said. "Stopped off at Pledger's Point and spent the day fishing." He glanced up at the stranger and smiled. "It might have been easier just to tell the truth in the first place."

This time the stranger was really amused. "It might have been at that," he said.

"Well, now that we've got the story straight, what was it you wanted to see me about?"

"I want to check the records on a piece of land," the man replied.

"All right," Will said, holding the door for him. "Come in."

It was not until they were inside the small office that Will noticed how tall the stranger was; three or four inches above six feet, he thought.

"Sit down," he said. "I'll hang my hat up and be right with you." He walked to a hat rack in the corner and hung up the soiled panama, then returned to the desk. The stranger had sat down in the cane-bottom chair across from him.

"Now where is the tract located?" Will asked, taking up a pad of paper.

"I don't know the exact location," the stranger replied. "I only know that it's near a river, ten or twelve miles from town." He paused. "I know that isn't much help."

"No, I'm afraid we'll have to pin it down closer than that," Will said. "There are thirty-six farms in the river bottom . . . fourteen of them in the upper basin. Do you know who's living on the place now?"

"I don't guess anybody's living on it . . . the land originally belonged to a man named Delton Walters." He stopped, waited a moment, then added, "He's dead now."

Will looked at the stranger, for a minute unable to think of a suitable reply; he had the strange feeling that he had just made a startling discovery. Finally he said, "Are you Walters' son?"

"Yes . . . I'm Chad Walters."

Again there was a pause; the ticking of the clock above the door was loud in the small office. For the moment at a loss for words, Will wrote on the pad: "Delton Walters"; then, beneath it: "Chad Walters, son."

At last he said, "Yes, I know the place. It's located in the eastern end of the valley. Just a minute, I'll get the folder." He walked across to the filing cabinet in the corner. Without looking around, he said, "As a matter of fact, there is a family living there now."

Walters made no reply; Will removed the folder, then walked back to the desk and sat down. For several minutes he pretended to study the papers it contained, but he was thinking of something else. The return of Chad Walters to the river country had created a number of problems, and whether he liked it or not, he was officially involved.

During the years following Delton Walters' departure from the basin, the river bottom had changed rapidly. At the time Chad Walters returned the entire region was settled as far south as Montine's Header and a small community called Carley's Crossing had grown up in the basin itself. The inhabitants of the area were not natives of Chekow County but were river dwellers by temperament and heritage. Most of them had come from the river region known as Daiker's Pitch, fifty miles farther down the river. Clannish by nature and largely motivated by tribal loyalties, they were notoriously bad farmers and most of them supplemented their needs by fishing, a profession more suited to their taste. They drank more than was good for them and were quick to fight, not infrequently among themselves. People in Gipson called them gumbo rats and deplored their swaggering, brawling ways; but they came to town in droves every Saturday and the merchants, whatever their personal feelings in the matter, were well aware that a good part of their revenue originated in the basin.

Will Kelly's relationship with the gumbo rats was unusual, for he was the one outsider whom they accepted more or less on equal terms. This was, of course, due in part to the fact that as Land Agent he was in a position to do them favors; but beyond this professional advantage, Will had the happy faculty of taking people as they were, of asking no more nor less of them than they were willing or capable of giving. It was an attitude the river people respected.

The only farm in the basin which was not owned by gumbo rats was the Walters place. However, legal ownership meant nothing to the river people and through the years a number of families had occupied the land at one time or another. At the time he became Land Agent Will had thought seriously about putting a stop to this practice, but in time he gave the idea up. He knew that the gumbo rats would not understand the technicalities of a restraining notice and that he would simply complicate his relationship with the basin landowners by issuing one.

Chad Walters' return to the river bottom was also untimely. A family by the name of Boone then occupied the farm, and it was with them that the problems took definite form. In many ways old man Lance Boone was the valley patriarch; gnarled, lame, tough as a hickory knot, he had lived in the basin for almost thirty years. A decisive, strong minded man, he had fought his way to a place of leadership with the river people and was often called upon now to settle disputes of one kind or another which arose between the gumbo rats; he conducted the affairs of this office with dispatch and impartiality. His Old Testament sense of justice was precisely what the gumbo rats understood best, and his word was never questioned. On more than one occasion, it was said, old Lance had ordered violators of the unwritten basin law to leave the valley; and these, too, had moved away without once questioning the authority which exiled them.

Living with Lance were his three grown sons, Mase, Lewt and Ben; and there was also a daughter, Emma. People in Gipson would have said that the Boone boys were "typical gumbo rats." Given to all the excesses of their heritage, they prided themselves on their physical strength and fanatical loyalty to the clan. Lewt was the most vicious of the three, for he was the vainest. His reputation throughout the river country as a ladies' man was clearly established, and more than one aspiring gumbo youth had learned that he would defend that reputation with fist or knife. Mase, the oldest, was somewhat quieter than the others and always stood in command when old Lance was away.

Emma was another matter. A dark, pretty girl of eighteen, she was both sister and mother to the three boys; even old Lance treated her with marked respect. Though reserved by nature, Emma, like her father, could be strong minded when occasion demanded, and it was said that if the Boone boys were afraid of anything it was Emma's temper.

In other ways, Emma was different; a product of the gumbo society who oddly seemed to live above it. Some years ago there had been a small school at Holly Grove, about halfway between Gipson and the basin, and Emma was one of the three river children who attended. Later (after the school had burned and the Gipson school board had elected to drop the project) the teacher, Mrs. Sarah Adasa, would remember "the beautiful little Boone girl with the willful ways." She had never had a brighter pupil than Emma, she would say; then, shaking her head, nor a more changeable one. After the school had burned, Mrs. Adasa had gone to the valley and talked to old Lance about sending Emma to the school in Gipson, but nothing had ever come of that. Now, largely because of the stories Mrs. Adasa had told, the people of Gipson were, in a rather impersonal way, fond of Emma. She, of all the others, seemed least like a gumbo rat.

Thinking of Emma as he sat leafing through the Walters file, Will thought that of all the river people, she alone might understand the claims of Chad Walters; at least her sense of fair play would be less restrictive and her point of view more objective.

Finally, he pushed the folder aside and looked again at the man seated across the desk. Knowing the question was a shot in the dark, he said, "Well, the papers seem to be in order . . . what are your plans, to sell the place?"

It was a moment before he answered.

"No. I came to live on it."

Will leaned back in his chair and reached for his pipe; he filled it from his tobacco pouch, tamped it carefully, then lit it. The pipe is a handy device, he thought, when you need time. And time is exactly what I need now.

One thing was clear; mincing words with Walters would be unwise; there was a directness in his manner which demanded directness in return; anything less than that would be a mistake.

"If you've got a few minutes," Will said at last, "there are some things about this situation that you should know."

24

Walters nodded. "I'm in no hurry."

"Since your pa left the basin, a lot has happened," Will began, choosing his words carefully. "The whole area is settled now and there's a community down there called Carley's Crossing. The people who live in the river bottom are not like other people. Folks here in Gipson call them gumbo rats, and they don't mean the term to be a compliment. Most of the river people came up from Daiker's Pitch, farther down the river, and they've never known anything but river life . . . they've lived outside what some people call the civilizing influences. There's a saying around here that the gumbo rats are all kinfolks . . . it's a kind of a joke, but in a way it's true. For most of them the world begins and ends at the rim of the basin. Of course, they come into town of a Saturday, but they come as strangers and people in Gipson are always glad when they go back to the river. They're sullen and suspicious, especially around strangers. There's a reason for that. To them every stranger is a potential enemy. They've spent most of their lives trying to get roots down . . . and now, at last, they own something, and they figure that sooner or later somebody is going to try to take it away from them. They live by their own customs, their own ways . . . and sometimes they're pretty hard for an outsider to understand."

Will stopped talking and sat quietly, puffing his pipe and watching Walters.

For a full minute, Walters said nothing. Finally, he said, "You're telling me to stay out of the basin."

"No. I'm not telling you to stay out," Will said. "I'm simply saying that I don't think you'll be happy there. Other men have tried it . . . and it's always the same—two or three months later they're back in town, looking for a buyer." He paused, groping for the right words; suddenly it seemed very important to make Walters understand. "Put it this way . . . the gumbo rats figure the basin is theirs . . . all of it. Right or wrong, that's the way they look at it . . . they don't want to move in with anybody else and they don't want anybody else moving in with them. They figure that's little enough to ask . . . and maybe they've got a point. Your farm is the only one left that isn't owned by one of the river men."

Walters sat very still for a moment, watching Will; then he stood up and walked across to the front window. For some time he stood there quietly, looking out at the dusty main street. The sun had gone down and the street was empty except for a lean, black hound sniffing at a candy wrapper near the front steps of the land office. Without looking around Walters said, "I don't want to cause any trouble for you . . . or anybody else. The people who are living on the farm have no right to be there. They'll have to leave . . . where they go is their problem. The land is mine. I came back to live on it, and now that I'm here, I guess I'll stay." The words were not adamant; he was simply stating a fact.

He stood a moment longer at the window, then walked back to the chair and sat down. Will waited, knowing that he had more to say, knowing that he was not by nature a man who used words easily.

After a time, talking very slowly, Walters said, "When I was nine years old my pa died. He had never mentioned the farm before, but when they told him that he was going to die, he called me to his bed and gave me the deed. He said the land was mine if I wanted it . . . he said it was a poor country, unfit for farming—a 'mean country' he called it, without promise or hope. He died there, with me watching him, talking about the river bottom, still hating it . . . but even through his hatred you could see what the land had meant to him. He talked about the river and the valley and the house he had built on a rise near the river bluff. He talked about the flood that finally ran him out. . . ."

Walters suddenly stopped talking and sat for a moment, looking down at the palms of his hands. "You know about all that. . . ."

"Yes," Will said. "They still talk about your father around here."

They sat for a time in silence, then Walters continued. "I didn't think about the farm again for a good many years. I grew up around Santa Fe and later hired out as a range rider. During the next fifteen years I worked my way from New Mexico to Montana and back again, twenty times or more. Then one day I met a fellow, fifty . . . sixty years old . . . all he'd ever wanted was a little outfit of his own, a hundred acres and ten head of stock . . . but when I knew him he was still riding for the other man . . . still hoping he'd get far enough ahead to buy his way out. After that I got to thinking about the farm my pa had left me . . . a couple of years passed and after a while it got to where I didn't think much about anything else. It seemed like I could remember the farm . . . even the smell of the river. It took me another year to make up my mind, but finally, a couple of months ago, I cashed in and started this way." He smiled. "And now I'm here . . . I mean to live on the land and work it and make the best of what's there."

For a full minute, Will sat listening to the tick of the clock above the door; then he stood up and held out his hand. "My name's Will Kelly," he said. "I'm glad you're back . . . I know what you mean about the land. And you're right, it's yours, outright and legal. I guess it isn't my place to tell you what to do with it."

Walters gripped his hand and nodded, almost a formal gesture. Then he put on his hat and turned to the door.

"If it's all right with you," Will said. "I'll ride down that way with you tomorrow. I'll be going anyhow . . . and it might be better if I break the news to the Boones myself."

"All right. I'll be glad to have you."

"Suppose we meet here at eight in the morning," Will suggested. "It's only nine miles to the basin."

"Fine. I'll be here."

The two men walked out to the front porch and Will stood watching as Walters swung up to the mare's back.

"There's a rooming house at the lower end of town," Will said. "Breeson's. You can get a good bed there."

Walters touched his hat. "Thanks," he said. "And thanks for your time." Then he reined the mare around and rode off down the street.

Watching him, Will was curiously disturbed. His first fear had been that the Boones would make trouble; that they might, in fact, force Walters to sell out. But now, after his brief visit with Chad, he knew that he had the courage and strength to make it a full scale war. He walked back inside the office and sat down. For several minutes he remained there, staring across the desk at the blank wall.

In a lifetime, he thought, you rarely meet a man like that. He is a man with beliefs, and he'll fight to defend them if he's forced to it.

He remembered a saying in the river country about such men: "He's a man to ride with. . . ."

He was sure of one thing; Walters was that kind of man.

Later that night, at Breeson's Boarding House, Chad Walters lay on his bed, staring up at the darkness. His body ached from the long day's ride; but he could not sleep. Somewhere up the hall the night-bell tinkled and a moment later Mrs. Breeson's padded footsteps passed his door; there were muffled voices, then footsteps again as Mrs. Breeson led the late roomer back down the hall; a door opened and closed, the landlady padding back to her room, then silence. Chad closed his eyes, thinking again of his talk with Will Kelly.

The land agent was a good man, a man you could trust; but he had his own problems. He expected trouble with the Boones, that much was clear; and he didn't like it. You couldn't blame him for that; no man in his right mind wanted trouble. And no man could avoid it either. Maybe he should sell out; maybe for once he should try the easy way. But what was the easy way? He had not told Kelly everything; there were things you couldn't say with words; or, if you did they wouldn't make sense to anybody but you. . . .

The long years between, the boy's years, when you roamed the earth, learning too much too fast, crying yourself to sleep and hating the tears because, at fifteen, you were already a man and knew the futility of self-pity. And then you found someone, an old man in a railroad yard, dying; lying in the rain by a pile of cross-ties dying of loneliness, talking to you, weeping and bitter, still not understanding. And you stood there and watched him die and told yourself that every man is alone and that you must begin there . . . promising yourself that you'd never be lonely because you'd learned that much.

But there was always the farm . . . not loneliness but wanting something, wanting at last a place to stop and think, something to hold to. You couldn't tell a man about that . . . or the other times when you'd learned the rule over again: watching the boy from Montana die under his horse . . . or the red-eyed negro in Tallow's Fork, stupid drunk, blinking in the sun at the angry faced mob, actually helping them adjust the rope around his neck, dying for a crime that he knew nothing about . . . or the rancher's wife in Cleaburne who went mad and shot her husband and the three children; and when you got there, running through the snow from the bunkhouse, there was nothing but the spattered blood and the crazy woman, standing in the kitchen, still holding the carbine, weeping. . . .

You couldn't tell a man any of those things because they happened to you and nobody else. And at last you came back, came back to a poor bottom farm because it was yours and that was all you wanted, to own something, a place to stop and put the pieces together . . . and you found out that maybe it wasn't yours at all, because someone said it wasn't. But now that didn't matter . . . you had to stay and fight because there was really nothing to go back to . . . and that, too, was a part of the game. . . .

Somewhere, far off, he heard again the thin tinkle of the night-bell; the click of Mrs. Breeson's door . . . then he slept.

CHAPTER 3

SHORTLY AFTER EIGHT o'clock the next morning Will and Chad Walters left Gipson, riding west toward the river. Although the distance from Gipson to the upper basin was less than five miles, it was necessary to travel almost twice that far in order to reach the Carley's Crossing community, for the only bridge across the river was located at a point seven miles due west of town. There the road turned back east and followed the bank of the river to the spiny ridges which enclosed the basin.

The day was already hot when Will and Chad left town, and the sun, three hours in the sky, beat down heavily. For some time they rode in silence, the clip-clop of the horses' hooves loud against the hard baked clay road. Will watched Walters out of the corner of his eye and wondered again (as he had wondered the day before) what he was thinking. Walters observed the countryside with interest as they rode along, but he said nothing. Somehow his impervious attitude faintly annoyed Will whose agitation continued to mount with each mile. He tried to minimize his uneasiness by remembering that he had on a number of occasions fished with the Boones and that they had always treated him genially enough. Perhaps, he told himself, the Boones would be reasonable, once they learned that the land legally belonged to Walters; perhaps he was making too much of the affair. But this line of thought afforded him scant comfort, for he knew that the Boones were unwitting men and that they would react to the appearance of Walters—and his claims on the land—with something less than charitable understanding.

Once or twice, trying to divert himself from this unpleasant state of mind, Will pointed out some landmark or commented passingly about river life. To these halfhearted attempts at conversation Walters listened with interest, but made no reply.

It was not until they had crossed the Havener's Bay bridge and had turned back up the river that Will finally spoke of the Boones.

"The family that is living on your farm," he said offhandedly. "I'm afraid they're going to take this pretty hard."

Walters glanced at him and nodded.

"Like I told you yesterday," Will went on, "the gumbo rats are funny people. Trouble is, the Boones think the farm is theirs by rights. They won't like giving it up."

"Nobody likes to give up something he's come to look on as his own," Walters said. "I guess I'd feel the same way."

After that, Will did not mention the Boones again. How could you explain to a man like Walters that the Boones would fight before they'd move off the land? How could you even *say* it? Walters had a way of putting an end to a conversation by one simple remark.

At last they topped the ridge which marked the northern rim of the basin. Below them, in a spotty grove of pinoaks, lay the settlement. Will pulled Dandy up and took off his hat.

"That's Carley's Crossing," he said, wiping his face on the sleeve of his shirt. "The big building that looks like a barn is the general store . . . across the street is the blacksmith shop. The building on down is vacant."

From the ridge, the dusty village looked desolate and abandoned. Walters sat for a moment, looking down at the valley. Then he dismounted and walked across to the edge of the road. "Yeah, I remember this," he said. "The bluff up there to the east . . . the valley . . . the way it levels out at the lower end of the basin." He turned to Will and smiled. "Anyhow, it seems like I do."

He turned back to the basin and Will waited, saying nothing, remembering that for Walters it was a homecoming.

Finally Walters walked back to the gelding and mounted. "I'm ready if you are," he said.

"All right." Will put his hat on and nudged Dandy. "No point in going through Carley's Crossing, it'll be closer around the edge of the basin."

They followed the wagon trail that skirted the rim of the

basin for three or four hundred yards, then dropped off sharply into the valley. Will's mind turned again to the Boones and his uneasiness returned. Neither of them spoke as they rode along. When they reached the first cultivated fields, Walters studied the land carefully; once he leaned down and pulled a withered head of high gear from the stalk and crumpled it in his hand.

A moment later they crossed the piney ridge that separated the main valley from the bluff; ahead of them, on the toe of a long, low rise, was the Walters place.

The house, which was better by a good margin than any other in the basin, had suffered at the hands of the Boones. The chimney was cracked, the front porch sagged and the front fence was a straggle of rusty wire hanging to rotting fence posts.

Will glanced at Chad. "That's the place," he said.

Chad nodded but said nothing.

"The Boones have let it run down some . . . but it's a good house."

Again Chad nodded.

They crossed the narrow strip of meadow land leading up to the rise. With a feeling almost of guilt, Will found himself hoping that the Boones would not be at home; but an instant later he saw old Lance and two of the boys—Lewt and Ben—working under the well shed in the front yard.

Chad and Will had reached the front gate before the Boones were aware of their presence. Old Lance straightened up, then walked to the edge of the shed, bending slightly forward, squinting against the sun. The boys too stopped working and waited, standing perfectly still, holding the trotline between them.

"Hellow Lance . . . Lewt, Ben," Will said. He was conscious of Chad beside him as they walked across the yard to where old Lance was waiting.

The old man, his bullet face hard and suspicious, nodded curtly to Will but said nothing. His eyes were fixed on Chad.

"Looks like you boys are getting ready for the first rain," Will tried again.

"Some mending had to be done," Lance said. He was still

watching Chad. For a moment they all waited. "What's on your mind, Will?"

The reception was even less cordial than Will had anticipated. The disease which had stricken Lance lame had also distorted the features of his face, pulling one side of his mouth down in an eternal grimace. Standing now in the shade of the well shed, he looked like the devil himself.

Will suddenly felt perfectly calm. He knew now what he had to do. "Lance," he said, "I want you to meet Chad Walters."

Either the statement itself, or the way Will said it, had a noticeable effect upon the Boones. Lewt and Ben let the trotline slip slowly from their hands; then they walked to the edge of the shed and stopped behind their father. Old Lance glanced sharply at Will. His eyes turned back to Chad.

Will tried to think of some tactful way to word his next remark; but there was none. "Walters is the owner of this farm," he said.

The old man stood without moving for a full minute, scowling against the sunlight. Lewt took his hands out of his pockets, and the movement carried the weight of a threat.

Slowly Lance turned to Will, his eyes narrowed. "I don't understand that, Will," he said. "What is it you're trying to tell me?"

"I mean that Walters is the legal owner of this land," Will replied. "I'm sorry, Lance, but that's the way it is. The deed is written in his father's name . . . it was willed over to Chad thirty years ago."

Old Lance looked out across the valley, shaking his head again. "Thirty years . . . that's a long time. I don't know nothing about the law . . . but thirty years is a long time, I know that." Slowly he turned back to Chad. "This here's my farm," he said evenly.

"No, Lance . . . the farm never belonged to you," Will said. "Any more than it belonged to the other families that lived here. It was something I should have stopped long ago, but somehow I never got around to it. Most likely I never would have, if Walters hadn't come back. But now he's here, asking for his land, and the law says you've got to move off."

Lance blinked slowly, but the line of his mouth tightened; almost imperceptibly the corner of his mouth twitched. He spoke to Chad, quietly, threateningly.

"You think this is your farm, mister?"

"Yes. The farm belongs to me."

Lance limped forward a few steps, stopping directly in front of Chad. Again he waited. At last he said, "Like I said, I don't know nothing about the law . . . but I know this farm. It was growed up and wasting when I moved on it two years ago . . . there wasn't nothing here but bramble patches and fennel weed. Me and my boys cleaned it up and put seeds in the ground and made something out of it. Farming ain't easy work . . . it takes a man's time and wears him down . . . but we done it because we had to have some place to live. Now a fellar I ain't never seen comes along and tells me I got to get off, says it's the law. . . ."

Lance stopped talking and waited, measuring Walters. Then he said, "You reckon I'm gonna pack and move off just cause some stranger that I ain't never seen wants the land. Is that what you figure?"

"The land is mine. I came to live on it."

"This here's my farm, mister," Lance snapped. "And there ain't nobody putting me off it . . . the law or you or nobody else. I reckon the quicker you understand that the better off you'll be."

"All right, Lance," Will Kelly said. "If that's the way you want it. No point in trying to work it out now. Tomorrow I'll have to file an eviction notice with Sheriff McKnight."

Lance swung around, looking darkly at Will. Will thought he detected a flicker of uneasiness in the old man's eyes but he wasn't sure.

"I'm sorry," he said shortly. "But you don't give me any other choice." He turned to Chad. "We'd better be getting back to town."

"You don't scare me none with that talk about McKnight!" Lance snarled. With a sudden, snakelike gesture he reached out and grasped the front of Chad's shirt. "Listen to what I say, mister. . . . I don't know who you are or where you come from . . . you ain't done nothing yet I won't forget

. . . but I'm telling you . . . don't ever come back to this basin. . . ."

"I'll be back," Chad replied quietly. "Now take your hand off my shirt."

For a long moment the two men stood motionless in a strange test of wills; then slowly old Lance's hand fell back at his side.

Lewt Boone moved forward, his lean, handsome face flushed with anger. "If I ever see you again," he said, "I'll kill you."

Chad turned his eyes from Lance and looked directly at Lewt; a faint smile crossed his face.

The old man snapped at his son. "Shut up."

Will moved toward the group, then stopped. "If you're ready, Walters," he said.

For a full minute Chad and the Boones stood face to face; no one moved. Then Chad turned and walked away.

Will followed him, a knot in his stomach. They mounted and rode side by side down the rise and across the meadow strip. It was not until they were crossing the piney ridge beyond that Will looked back. Old Lance and his sons were still standing in the front yard, as motionless as stones.

Without looking at Walters, Will said, "I was afraid of that."

Walters said nothing.

Will was working at his desk in the land office the following afternoon when Sheriff McKnight rode up to the front hitch rail and dismounted. McKnight, a huge, red-faced man, lumbered up the front steps and entered without knocking.

"The house is empty," he said. He shook his head. "I don't know what to make of it, but they're gone. I reckon Walters can move in when he's ready."

Will pursed his lips thoughtfully. At last he said, "Any trouble?"

"Nope. I took John Greenwood down with me . . . the Boones were gone when we got there. Moved out this morning, I guess. We didn't get down to the Crossing, but we ran into Ferd Hammons on the way back to town. He said the Boones moved into that empty house on the Sugsby place . . . said the whole basin was in a stir about it. I reckon the Boones were riled too . . . they wrecked the Walters house before they left."

"Wrecked it?"

"Yep. Mostly stuff that can be repaired without much trouble. They tore the doors off the hinges and broke some of the windows. Somebody had even rammed a pole through the kitchen roof." He paused, then added, "Enough to call it a case against them if you say so."

Will sat a moment thinking. "I guess we'd better leave that up to Walters," he said at last. "For the time being, forget about it."

He turned in his chair and looked out the front window. He had not expected the Boones to leave the land without a fight; but in a way, it figured. The gumbo rats had the renegade's fear of official authority. And there were other ways; the waiting game. The entire river basin would rally behind old Lance, and he knew it. Whatever his plans, one thing was certain; the affair was not ended.

Will stood up. "Well, we've done all we can for the time," he said. "They're gone, that's the main thing. Thanks for your trouble."

"No trouble," McKnight said. Then he grinned. "But I was mighty happy to find them Boones gone."

Will nodded. "I know what you mean. If you've got time, I wish you'd drop by Mrs. Breeson's boarding house and tell Walters what happened."

"Glad to," McKnight replied, turning to go. "I'll be passing by there on my way home anyhow." He walked to the door, then stopped. "I'm glad it's Walters moving to the basin instead of me," he said. "The way them gumboes are stirred up, it'll be like moving in with a nest of rattlesnakes."

After McKnight had gone, Will sat for several minutes trying to finish his work. At last he dropped his pencil on the desk, leaned back in his chair and stared up at the ceiling. Finally he stood up, locked the file, put on his hat and went home.

CHAPTER 4

THE MOST SERVICEABLE institution in the basin was "Such"
Farnsworth's general store; it not only provided the gumbo
rats with the staple needs of their lives but also served a very
real social purpose. Summer and winter the river men
gathered there, sitting on cane-bottomed chairs and upturned
nail kegs around the huge, pot-bellied stove, swapping stories
and exchanging information; generally bent on nothing more
serious than satisfying the strong communal urge which they
all shared.

Aside from these informal gatherings, the general store was
also used for numerous social events; dances, quilting bees,
pie suppers and pounding parties were held throughout the
year; and it was these affairs, to a considerable extent, that
gave focus and meaning to the lives of the river folk.

The year's big event was the catfish dance, held the second
Saturday in September. Chad Walters' first trip to Carley's
Crossing was to an almost fateful degree untimely, for it came
on a day when fifteen or twenty of the river men had gathered
at the general store to discuss the approaching dance.

As usual, Such Farnsworth was in charge of the meeting;
because he allowed the river people to use his store for all
their activities, the chairmanship of the big event was his by
tacit agreement.

Such was in many ways a paradox in the basin. A huge,
powerful man with a great sagging belly, he was not really a
gumbo rat at all, for he had originally come from somewhere
in Indiana. However, he had lived in the basin for a number
of years and the river people had come to accept him as one
of their own. His professional relationship with the gumboes

was generous and he frequently carried their accounts for a year or more. If he had ever pressed for payment of an overdue account, no one remembered it. Such was also looked upon as a man of great wit and oratorical capacity; he had, in fact, become a kind of spokesman for them in formal matters requiring contact with the outside world. He kept in the general store an official account of births and deaths in the basin, composed letters for those who could not write, and had once acted as defense counsel for a gumbo boy who had gotten himself involved in a knife fight in Gipson. Next to old Lance, he was the most influential member of the community.

On the afternoon in question, Such was carrying out the duties of his office with a flair that impressed the assembled river men. He had made out a long list of "committees" which he read off in a formal, magisterial tone; he gave a special dignity to the assembly by addressing the members present as "mister" and suggesting that they refer to him as "Mr. Chairman." The meeting dragged on for an hour or more and it was only after everything had been discussed and rediscussed a number of times that Such at last declared an adjournment. Even then, most of the men stayed on, reluctant to go home or back to work.

It was not unusual that the conversation should turn after a time to Chad Walters. Since he had taken up residence in the basin, three days before, the river folks had talked of little else. It seemed to them that his appearance in the river bottom was an insult to the entire community and they took the eviction of the Boone family as a personal affront. Of the men present in the general store that day, only Lewt Boone had actually seen Walters. Speaking of him now, Lewt's face darkened and there was an edged quality in his voice.

The others listened as he recounted again the appearance of Walters and Will Kelly at the farm. When he had finished they sat quietly, nursing their inarticulate resentment, feeling the weighted significance of the moment.

Lewt's eyes moved slowly around the group. "But I'll git

him," he said. "And he knows it. I'd have jumped him that day if Pa hadn't held me back. Next time we meet, it'll be me or him. . . ."

"What kind of a fellar is he?" one of the men asked.

Lewt shrugged. "Big . . . raw-bone . . . always got a sneer on his face. He looks like what he is, a halfbreed. They all look alike to me."

Such Farnsworth spoke, his voice mockly sinister and suggestive. "Might be we ought to pay him a little visit. Just go up there and have a talk with him. That'd be the easiest way to get rid of him." He had meant the remark to be funny, but no one laughed.

Lewt shook his head. "That'd just bring the law down on us," he said. "Besides I aim to take care of Walters myself . . . he'll step out of line sooner or later . . . and when he does, I'll jump him. . . ."

The men nodded, smiling appreciatively.

And so the discussion continued for almost an hour. At last Lewt stood up and put on his hat. "I reckon I'd better be getting up to the house," he said. Then he smiled. "If any of you boys see Walters, tell him I'm looking for him."

It was at that improbable moment that Chad Walters appeared in the door of the general store. He had tied his horse at the hitch rail below the front porch and none of the men saw him until he walked through the doorway. His appearance was so sudden and unexpected that for a moment the gumbo rats simply stared. Lewt, who was walking toward the front of the store, stopped.

Seeing the men assembled around the stove, Chad too paused for an instant; then he walked slowly toward them. As he walked past Lewt, he nodded briefly; the gesture somehow took on the tone of an insult. Lewt turned and watched him, but remained standing where he was.

Chad stopped four or five feet from where the men were sitting. "Which one of you is the proprietor?" he asked.

The men simply glared, their eyes hard and suspicious.

Such glanced at Lewt; Lewt nodded, an almost imperceptible movement.

"I'm the proprietor," he said, taking a step forward. "We're having a business meeting here . . . what's on your mind?"

Chad reached in his shirt pocket and took out a folded slip of paper. "I've got a list here," he said. "Some groceries I need. . . ."

Now Lewt Boone walked slowly back toward the group, stopping directly behind Walters.

"Maybe you didn't hear Mr. Farnsworth," he said, spacing his words evenly. "We're having a business meeting . . . a private meeting."

Chad did not move; he did not, in fact, directly acknowledge the remark at all. When he spoke again, he addressed his words to Such.

"I didn't know about the meeting," he said, "or I would have waited till another time. It won't take but a minute to fill this order." He turned and walked across to the counter, his back now turned to the men around the stove.

The river men waited, watching Lewt, acknowledging his leadership. For a full minute no one moved or spoke. Finally Walters turned.

"I'll need three pounds of salt pork," he said.

Such glowered. "I'm out of salt pork."

Chad nodded slowly, then glanced back at the list in his hand.

"A pound of beans."

"I'm out of beans, too."

"Flour?"

"No flour."

Chad stood for some time, looking down at the list; then he carefully folded the paper and put it back in his shirt pocket. Finally, he looked at Such.

"I'm out of everything," Such said. "Whatever it is you want, I ain't got it."

Chad's eyes shifted, taking in the entire group. A cat jumped up on the counter and walked slowly to where he stood, swishing its tail. Without taking his eyes from the group, Chad ran his hand along the cat's back. The cat began to purr. The gumbo rats watched him, waiting.

At last Chad smiled; but it was not quite a smile either.

"All right," he said. "I guess I'll have to pick this stuff up in town."

Such felt the moment slipping away from him. "And I won't have it the next time you come," he said. "So it might be better if you just stayed away from here. . . ."

Walters' face remained outwardly calm, but there was a nameless, indefinable change in his expression; and not one of the river men missed it.

"I'll remember," he said; then he turned to go.

"Well keep it in mind," Such said, taking a step forward. "I serve who I please. Up to now, I ain't had to deal with nobody but niggers and white men . . . the niggers know to go to the back door. . . ."

Chad, who had started to leave, stopped and turned.

"Is that all?"

"No, it ain't," Such said. "The way I see it, an Injun ain't no better than a nigger . . . maybe you'd better keep that in mind. . . ."

One of the men around the stove laughed; but the laughter hung brittle in the air, an embarrassed sound.

Slowly Chad walked back to where Such was standing. He spoke so quietly that some of the river men leaned forward to catch the words.

"Don't push your luck, mister," he said. "There's a limit to what I'll take from a man like you."

Such flushed and licked his lips nervously. "There ain't no halfbreed telling me . . ."

Walters struck so suddenly and with such viciousness that Such was unable to raise his arms against the attack. The first blow spun him half around, and as he fell another caught him full in the mouth, driving him back into the stove. The men scattered as the stove careened off its foundation, bringing down the vent pipes in a landslide of soot and guy-wires. Such rolled away from the falling pipes and rose to one knee; his eyes were glazed; he tried to get his breath through the blood that bubbled up in his mouth. Instinctively, he held his arm up to protect his face, but the gesture came too

41

late. Chad's fist slammed against his jaw with a leaden thump, spinning him backwards against the wall. Such tried again to rise, his face twisted with pain and fear. Chad's hand shot out, grasping him by the front of the shirt, lifting him bodily to his feet. Such's head lolled to one side; the gumbo rats winced, waiting for the next blow. But it never came. Chad simply stood for a moment, looking at the blubbering, bloody mass before him; then he pushed Such away, and turned slowly toward the men standing around the stove.

No one moved. Chad's glance moved across to Lewt. Lewt said nothing. Finally Chad picked up his hat where it had fallen during the fight, put it on his head, then turned and walked out the front door.

For a full minute the river men stood motionless, watching Lewt. Such moved, groaning, the sound of a wounded animal. The cat on the counter meowed softly.

Lewt glanced at the gumbo rats, the muscles in his jaw quivered; then, without speaking, he left the store.

CHAPTER 5

THE LIFE OF the river bottom woman was regulated by traditions as old and enduring as the gumbo society itself. Like her mother and grandmother before her, she dedicated her time and energy to the task of keeping the men in her family happy; and because she had never known anything else, this seemed to her a worthy and honorable goal. In return she asked only for a reasonable fidelity from her husband, and such respect from her sons and daughters as gumbo society decreed proper. In the basin a woman's success or failure was measured by three cardinal principles: her ability to bear her husband a large brood of healthy children; the forebearance to accept her lot without undue complaints; and the ability to keep her husband contented, both in bed and out. If she failed to fulfill these basic obligations, the fault was presumed to lie with her, whatever the circumstances involved. If she could not bear children, it was supposed that she had committed some hidden sin for which she was being punished; if she found her lot too hard to bear and turned to complaints or scolding, she was held to be unworthy of her calling; and if her husband was known to commit infidelities, it was assumed that his wife had not yet learned the first rule of marital bliss: that love began in bed, and that without that understanding any marriage was foredoomed.

Socially the gumbo woman knew her place and accepted it without question. On the rare occasions when she walked abroad with her husband, she remained always a discreet distance behind him, and in his presence she spoke only when spoken to; at mealtime she remained standing a respectful distance from the table, always watchful for a plate or cup that needed refilling; later, she took her food with the small children; if her husband had a guest, she served coffee or whisky, as he directed, then retired to her own part of the house and remained there unless summoned. These restrictions did not seem to her at all unreasonable. She was conditioned to one central fact: that she lived in a man's world and that all else was subordinated to his wishes and needs.

Of all the women in the river basin only Emma Boone, the dark, handsome daughter of old Lance, took liberties with the traditions of her sex. Although her "moods" were sometimes difficult for the basin women to understand, she was more characteristically cheerful and the gumbo women loved her as their own. She came and went as it pleased her, and it would not have occurred to anyone in the community to question her right to do so. Her freedom was doubtless due in part to the fact that she was old Lance's daughter, for this gave her a privilege that no other gumbo woman would have dared presume; but even without that advantage it is unlikely that Emma would have accepted the restrictions placed upon the women in her society; her mother had died when she was two and it was perhaps inevitable that the older Boone boys and old Lance would give her rather more attention than was good for a growing child. Still, she had grown into a fine young lady, people said; if at times she was perhaps a little high-handed, that was probably the fault of Lance and the boys; she had a heart bigger than the basin itself, and in times of trouble the gumbo women turned almost instinctively to her, as their men turned to her father.

Like everyone else in the river bottom, Emma had heard Chad Walters discussed and rediscussed a thousand times since his appearance in the valley. On the day that he and Will Kelly had gone to the farm, she had been visiting friends at the lower end of the basin. She had heard Lewt and her father review the incident numerous times. At first she had shared their resentment; she had loved the big, airy house on the rise, which, in comparison to the cramped, dilapidated

Sugsby place, seemed now almost palatial. Even her father's assurance that they would "move back to the Walters place before the year was out" did not make the change any easier. In fact, as the talk continued, she found herself a victim of mixed emotion. The more she thought about it, the less certain she was that they had any right to move back. It was, after all, Will Kelly who had issued the eviction order and she could not bring herself to believe that he had acted dishonestly. In truth, the facts seemed plain enough; although her father and brothers insisted that the land belonged to them, she could not see that their case rested on any stronger evidence than illegal possession. When she had mentioned this viewpoint to her father, he had smiled and patted her shoulder, saying: "You'd better leave this to us . . . it's not a woman's problem."

There were times when she felt no real resentment toward Walters at all; when, on the contrary, her sentiment seemed unaccountably to favor his side of the argument. And through it all, her woman's curiosity increased. She had heard her father speak of Walters as a "dirty injun," and another time Lewt had described him as a "big, raw-bone man with a mean face"; but she knew that these were at best prejudiced comments and they excited rather than satisfied her inquisitiveness. In her mind she associated Chad with the stories she had heard about his father, a reflection that was further colored by her romantic belief that all Indians were somewhat mythical and exotic beings from another world.

The Such Farnsworth incident struck her first of all as vastly amusing. She considered Such a pompous, boorish man; and in his presence she had always been a little uncomfortable. There was something about the way he looked at her when she went alone to the general store that left her uneasy and slightly shaken; he had never, of course, overstepped the bounds of propriety—but it was a look that no woman would mistake. Anyhow, she told herself, if Walters had thrashed Such, that at least was something in his favor.

One afternoon, about a week after the general store incident, old Lance and the boys went fishing, leaving Emma

45

alone at the house. She spent the morning sewing on the new dress she was readying for the catfish dance and was disturbed to discover that her thoughts kept turning, with a curious persistence, to Chad Walters. Her imagination drew visual pictures which turned out rather more favorably than Lewt's description. After a time she threw the dress aside and went to the kitchen; it was almost noon but she wasn't hungry; she stood for several minutes at the window, watching a dirty ruffled sparrow flit in and out of the water trough at the back gate. Finally she turned away, bored and restless. She started toward the front room; then suddenly stopped; she stood for a moment, her head tilted slightly to one side. I will not put another stitch in that dress, she thought; it is much too pretty a day to stay cooped up in this house; I'll go to the river and pick muscadines. She emphasized this decision with a shake of her head, then went to the pantry and took a bucket from the shelf. A moment later she left the house, walking westward toward the river.

But the muscadines, like everything else, had suffered from the drought; she walked as far south as Lenox Cove, but the vines along the way were already turning brown; it was mid-afternoon when she returned to the point of the river where she had begun, and her bucket was less than half full. She remained for a moment, tossing sticks into the slow, turgid waters; then, suddenly, she remembered that there were muscadine patches along the bluff at the upper end of the basin. They were, of course, on Walters farm and her father had forbade her ever to go near the place. Still, she told herself, it would be a simple matter to reach the bluff without being seen—either by Walters or anyone else. She stood for several minutes, turning the idea over in her mind; a slow smile came over her face; why not? Walters didn't own the whole valley.

Twenty minutes later she reached the first foothills that marked the beginning of Walters land. She could see now the chimney of his house across the ridges. Staying close to the bank of the river, where the trees offered some protection, she climbed upward toward the bluff. Finally she reached a clearing, from which point the Walters farm was plainly visible. Looking down at the house a quick sense of excitement came over her. The mare was standing in the barn lot, her head high to the wind; but Walters was not in sight. She stood watching for several minutes, hoping to catch a glimpse of the stranger who had so upset the even tenor of life in the basin; but he did not appear and finally she walked on to the muscadine patches higher up. The vines had been recently picked and only a handful of berries remained. However, reluctant to return home so early, she sat down on a fallen tree and took off her bonnet. A slight breeze stirred along the bluff; the pine boughs overhead were filled with the muted drone of insects. Far down the valley she could see Carley's Crossing, a dusty huddle of buildings, desolate and deserted under the glaring August sun; and on beyond, the river, a thin, yellow ribbon, twisting its way south. During the years her family had lived on the Walters farm Emma had come often to the bluff; it was here that she had lived with the dreams. She had heard Will Kelly talk of the world beyond the basin, of cities bigger than the entire river bottom. Now she sighed. It all seemed very romantic—and very far away. Someday, she told herself—someday I will see that other world; I'll wear a beautiful red dress and jewels in my hair and no one will know that I'm a gumbo rat. She leaned her head back against the tree and closed her eyes. Why, Will Kelly said. . . .

She was awakened some time later by the sharp ring of an ax. It sounded so close that she jumped up with a start, almost spilling the muscadines she had picked. She stood perfectly still, her heart pounding. A full minute elapsed before the sound came again. This time it did not seem so close. She stood for a time, listening. The sound occurred now with a regular cadence, the sharp spat of an ax blade against wood. It was Walters, of course. Certainly none of the gumbo rats would be gathering wood on his land. It was impossible to say how far away he was; at all events, it was foolish to remain in the clearing, Emma told herself. Her heart refused to behave; she was frightened but it was a fear tempered with curiosity. She remained for some time, motionless, listening. After a while she moved slowly to the edge of the clearing and hung the bucket of muscadines on the limb of a tree; then, picking her way carefully, she walked down the bluff toward the sound of the ax. The pine thickets grew dense along the ridge and she stayed under the cover of their foliage. As the ring of the ax grew louder, her heart seemed to pick up the tempo, pounding so furiously that it almost took her breath. She stopped, breathing deeply; this is a crazy thing to do, she thought: I must go back. At that moment there was a quick rustle of brush to the right of her. She whirled, pressing her hand against her mouth to stifle a scream. Frozen, unable to move, she waited. An instant later a boney, brindle cow ambled leisurely out of the thicket; seeing Emma, she stopped, fixed her for a moment with huge baleful eyes, then swung her head at the swarm of flies that hovered around her, and wandered on up the bluff. Emma did not move until the cow had disappeared from sight, then she sank down on a log; she didn't know whether to cry or laugh. But there was no time to decide; she was suddenly struck by the stillness in the glade; the sound of the ax had stopped. Slowly she turned her head, peering intently at the line of trees. Nothing moved, but she could not escape the feeling that she was being watched. Except for the sound of the retreating cow farther up the ridge, there was perfect quiet. Then, a flicker of movement—and she saw him, standing in a clump of pines not ten feet from where she sat! He was looking directly at her, his face as solemn as a rain cloud. At that moment he stepped out.

Emma was no longer afraid. She looked at him with a calm detachment, thinking how unfair Lewt had been in his description. "A big, rawbone man," indeed. He was, in fact, very handsome.

"I thought I heard my cow floundering around up here," he said. A faint smile touched the corners of his mouth. "I guess it must have been you."

Either the smile, or what he said, was an insult; she was not sure which.

48

"You were right the first time," she said, rising. "It *was* your cow . . . if you mean that stack of bones that just went up the hill."

He shook his head and smiled again, that brief change of expression that was hardly a smile at all. "She is a little underweight right now," he said gravely. "Funny thing, the man down at Gipson that I bought her from said she was the finest cow he'd ever owned." He looked directly at her, his eyes amused. "Just shows you how attached you can get to a cow when somebody wants to buy her."

In spite of herself, Emma smiled. "Well, I'm sure he's more attached to her than I am . . . she nearly scared me out of my wits."

He stood watching her, but said nothing. It occurred to her that she owed him some explanation.

"I've been picking muscadines," she said. "I left my bucket up on the bluff." That, of course, was hardly an explanation. "Then I walked down this way," she finished lamely.

Walters nodded gravely, whatever that meant. She had the uncomfortable feeling that he knew exactly why she had "walked down this way."

"I picked those patches out yesterday," he said. "Of course, I didn't know you were coming."

She tried to think of something to say, but somehow there was no way to turn the conversation; she glanced down at the palms of her hands, then rubbed them along the sides of her skirt. Still she could think of nothing to say; to walk off without saying anything would have been rude.

"I'm Emma Boone."

"Sure. You Boones all look alike."

She glanced up at him; that remark could have been an insult, but she decided that he had not meant it to be.

"People say I look like Lewt," she said, wondering why every remark she made seemed stupid.

Again Walters grinned. "You're better looking than he is."

She flushed, feeling that he had somehow got the upper hand.

"I guess you're wondering what I'm doing on your land,"

49

she said, with a faint belligerence.

"You've already told me," he said.

"I heard you working," Emma went on. For some reason she wanted him to know that she was not trying to deceive him; that she was not afraid. "I was slipping up on you. . . . I wanted to see what you look like."

Suddenly, looking at each other, they both smiled; sharing, it seemed, some private joke. Emma felt her embarrassment return; what was the joke?

"Well . . . I'd better be getting back," she said, flushing again.

He nodded. "If you don't mind, I'll walk that way with you," he said. "I don't guess my cow will wander far, without somebody helps her."

Emma was not sure that it would be proper to accept the invitation, but under the circumstances she was not sure that she had any choice. Without replying one way or the other, she turned back up the bluff and Walters fell in beside her. Together they walked up the ridge; neither of them spoke. At one point, where a log had fallen across the path, he took her arm and helped her step over the trunk. Except for a strange stir in her breast, the gesture seemed perfectly natural. A moment later they found the cow in the clearing where Emma had left her bucket. For an instant, they both stood looking at the cow; then they looked at each other and began laughing.

Chad shook his head. "Yessir, that's a fine cow," he said. "I expect that man hated to let her go."

The cow watched them for a moment, then lowered her head and lowed mournfully.

Still laughing, Emma said, "Poor thing . . . we mustn't make fun of her any more."

She walked to the tree and got the bucket of muscadines while Chad turned the cow down the ridge and shouted her away. He stood watching her, gravely concerned. "Well, if she falls, I guess she'll roll on to the bottom," he said, so seriously that Emma laughed again.

Chad turned and walked to where she was standing. "If

you don't mind," he said, "I'll walk on down the hill with you. I've been meaning to check the drainage in the lower end of my meadow anyhow."

Emma hesitated, remembering her father and brothers; they would of course be infuriated if they ever found out that she had come to the bluff. What a strange, unreal afternoon it had been.

"All right," she said smiling. "After all, it's your land."

He returned the smile. "I guess you and me are the only two people in the basin that think so," he said.

They walked down the ridge to the clearing where Emma had stopped to rest on the way up. They paused and stood for a moment, looking down at the valley. Suddenly, Emma began talking, musingly, almost speaking the words to herself, telling him the things she had never been able to tell anyone before. "I used to come up here often when we lived down on the rise. I think it's the nicest spot in the whole basin." She laughed, a short, half-embarrassed laugh. "From here I can see beyond the basin . . . in my mind."

The words sounded strange after she had said them, but the *idea,* the desire to tell Chad about her dreams, seemed a natural and comfortable thing to do.

Now she glanced at him. He was watching her, his face thoughtful but not mocking.

She laughed again and looked away. "I know it's silly," she said. "I used to make things up . . . I used to dream up whole worlds where people were singing and laughing and dancing and I was always in the middle of it . . . a million miles from here. . . ." Abruptly she stopped talking; how silly her words must sound to him, who had seen so much.

"I don't think it's silly," he said, his voice low and pleasant to hear. "Dreams are pretty important." He looked at her and smiled. "I used to dream about this land—about having something of my own. I thought about it for a good many years, about putting seed in the ground and watching it grow; about getting up in the morning and looking at what I'd done and thinking 'that's mine . . . whatever's there, I put it there.'" For a moment he said nothing; then he said,

"That's about all there is to life. Seeing something you've made where there wasn't anything before."

For some time Emma remained silent, looking out across the valley. She seemed to be in a kind of suspended enchantment, still hearing the words, still feeling the quiet sincerity that made them seem so important. Suddenly, she wanted to tell Chad that she believed in him; that she understood about the land and about watching things grow and about building things that were good because you had made them yourself.

She glanced at him and for an instant their eyes met; then she turned away. "I'm sorry about the way you've been treated," she said quietly. "I'm sorry about papa . . . and the boys . . . and everyone else . . ."

"They can't help it," he said. "I guess, in their place, I'd feel the same way. It's always hard to give up something that you've come to think of as yours. Anyhow, I should have come back sooner . . . then maybe this wouldn't have happened."

For a time they sat without speaking. There were a thousand things Emma wanted to say, but somehow she could not find the right words. She heard Chad move, his footstep behind her; sensing his nearness, she felt the rush of blood in her veins, the pounding at her temples. She wanted to turn to him but something held her motionless. At last, her voice a whisper, she said, "I must go home. Thanks for walking with me."

"Thanks for helping me find my cow."

She walked away without looking back. At the line of trees below the rise, she stopped and turned. He was still standing in the clearing, watching her. Impulsively, she waved to him, and felt a quick flutter in her stomach when he waved back. Then she turned quickly and ran across the field toward Carley's Crossing.

CHAPTER 6

IT WAS NOT until later, after she had reached home, that Emma was struck by the folly of what she had done. If she had been seen by anyone in the basin, they would take it as a matter of obligation to report the incident to old Lance. The thought was unnerving and her imagination created a thousand fearful scenes. But at last she forced herself to think of other things; she had seen no one on her trip to the bluff and she was reasonably sure that no one had seen her.

It was shortly after dark when her father and brothers returned. Hearing their voices in the front yard, she went to the kitchen and began laying the table. A moment later they tramped in and sat down, covered with mud and smelling of the river. Their luck had been bad and they were generally ill-tempered. They ate in silence, filling the room with their heavy breathing and the animal sounds of hunger. The meal seemed longer than usual, but at last Lance pushed back his plate, wiped his greasy mouth on the sleeve of his shirt; then, without a word, got up and stalked out. A moment later Lewt and Ben followed him. Mase remained at the table.

Emma poured him more coffee, then began clearing the dishes away. Suddenly, she sensed Mase's eyes watching her. She turned. He was looking directly at her, a sardonic, knowing expression on his face. The look startled her; it was unlike Mase, who was by nature pleasant and companionable. For a moment they simply waited, engaged in some kind of indefinable conflict. Then she turned back to the sink and began washing the dishes. She felt the tightness in her stomach, the slow stir of fear. At first she decided to wait him out; but she knew that he was better at that than she was; besides, he had the upper hand, and he knew it.

At last, without looking at him, she said, "I take it the fish weren't biting."

"You take it right." Even his voice was different, insinuating, almost sarcastic.

Emma continued to work. Several minutes passed. The silence between them became at last a challenge.

Finally Emma turned and looked directly at him. "Is something wrong with you?" she asked.

"Not with me," Mase replied; then, his voice faintly intimidating, he said, "How about you?"

Emma walked to the table where he sat and began wiping it briskly with a damp rag. Worst of all was the pretense. "Nothing except that you're in the way," she said shortly.

Mase leaned back until she had finished cleaning the table, then he pushed his empty coffee cup toward her. She filled it, sloshing some out on the table.

Mase grinned. "Got the shakes?"

Emma sat the pot down and turned toward him. "Look, Mase, if something's bothering you, out with it . . . what's the big secret?"

Mase took his time; too much time. He put sugar and cream in his coffee, then sat for a moment, stirring it elaborately. Finally he glanced up. "We stopped by the general store on the way back from the header," he said, lowering his voice. "Pa and the boys went inside but I stopped out front and got to talking with Nig Botts . . . he was down on the river this afternoon, fishing out the channel south of the bluff." He stopped talking and took a long swallow from the coffee cup. Emma said nothing; there was nothing she could say—it was Mase's show.

"Yeah, old Nig got to telling me a crazy story about something he seen down there." Mase weighed the words, enjoying his advantage. "Said about two-thirty this afternoon he was sitting in the crotch of a tree, half asleep, when he saw some woman walking up the river bank. East, toward the bluff." He glanced up at Emma and grinned again. "I reckon he must have been drunk . . . or dreaming. He said the woman looked like you."

54

Emma looked at him and felt the tightness in her throat; it would be foolish to deny the accusation; Mase had already made up his mind about Nig's story.

Emma said, "It was me."

Mase sat for a moment, his eyebrows arched thoughtfully; then he said, "Oh?"

"Yes. I was picking muscadines. There weren't enough at the bay to fill my bucket so I went to the bluff. Anything wrong with that?"

"No . . . I reckon not," Mase said slowly. "It all depends."

"On what?"

Mase grinned again. "Take it easy. I was just wondering if you saw Walters. . . ."

Emma sensed a trap; how much had Nig seen; how much had he told Mase?

"What did Nig say?" she snapped. "He seems to have the whole story."

"Well, as a matter of fact, he did say something about it. He said he was still sitting in the tree when the woman came back down about an hour later . . . only this time there was a man with her. Course, Nig hadn't never seen Walters, but he kinda figured that's who it was. He said the woman and this man—whoever it was—stopped in the clearing above the south ridge and stood awhile talking . . . it seemed to Nig like they was pretty chummy. . . ."

Emma weighed his words carefully; it would of course be a mistake to let Mase know how much he had upset her. She waited, trying to regain her composure.

Then she said, "It was Walters. I met him on the bluff . . . he was looking for his cow. . . ."

Mase looked away from her, running his knuckle along his chin thoughtfully. At last he said, "You mean it was accidental?"

"Of course it was accidental," she said. "You don't think I planned it do you? He was looking for his cow . . . I was picking muscadines . . . we just bumped into each other."

"Then he walked you home?"

"He came as far as the meadow. I was on his land . . . if

55

he wanted to walk with me there was nothing I could do about it."

Mase looked directly at her, his eyes doubting the story. "I reckon not," he said. "Anyhow, I'd rather take your word for it than Nig's." He stood up and turned toward the door. "But I wouldn't go back up there if I was you . . . it might stir up trouble."

The threat was unmistakable. Emma spoke evenly. "Don't tell me what I can do, Mase. I'm old enough to know what's right and wrong . . . just don't try to tell me what I can do."

Mase stopped and looked around. "I ain't telling you what to do," he said. "I'm just telling you what I'd do if I was in your place." Then he was gone.

Emma stood for a long moment, watching the door; then, trembling and shaken, she sat down at the table and thought of Chad Walters.

For several days after her talk with Mase, Emma remained close to home. This was not always easy. Sometimes when her father and brothers were away she went to the back porch and stood for several minutes, looking eastward toward the bluff. Again and again she relived the afternoon she had spent with Chad, remembering the odd sense of strength that came to her in his presence, the way he laughed, the curious expression—half-amused half-serious—that came over his face when he was thinking. Then she would smile inwardly, telling herself that she was acting like a child. Walters had probably forgotten the incident by now; he probably had a girl already, out west—or wherever it was he had come from. What would he think of her if he knew how she mooned over their meeting on the bluff. He would probably take her for what she was, a foolish, frivolous girl.

So Emma rationalized her brief meeting with Chad Walters. But the answers were less than satisfactory. Deep inside, her woman's instinct told her that Chad too remembered; that the magic of that afternoon was not alone the product of her romantic imagination.

At mealtime (meals were usually the single occasions for a family gathering) she waited for her brothers to mention Chad, to relate some incident involving her relationship with the basin people; but a week passed and they said nothing. It seemed that Chad, after his trouble with Such Farnsworth, had not returned to the general store; nor, apparently, had he been seen by anyone in Carley's Crossing. Slowly, a thought took form in Emma's mind; perhaps he had gone away! Perhaps he had simply admitted to himself that he would never belong in the basin, that he would never be accepted by the river people. . . .

But, remembering Chad, the things he had talked about, the quiet determination in his voice, Emma put the thought from her mind. He was not that kind of man, she told herself; he would not run away. But as a possibility the thought persisted and it was strangely disturbing.

On a Saturday, ten days after her meeting on the bluff with Chad, Emma accompanied her brother Ben into Gipson. Mase too had planned to go but decided at the last minute to remain at home and help his father and Lewt mend some fishing tackle. When, at the breakfast table, Mase declined to go along, he looked directly at Emma; she turned away, determined not to let him upset her. Later, when she was dressing, there was a knock at her door. She was not surprised when she opened it to see Mase standing in the hallway.

"Can I come in?" he asked, amiably enough.

"Of course," she replied, walking back to the mirror.

"Couple of things I want you to get for me in town," he said. "I'd ask Ben to pick them up but he's a mite forgetful." He walked over and sat down on the bed and took a sack of tobacco from his pocket.

Emma combed her hair and waited; since their discussion of her trip to the bluff, they had exchanged less than a dozen words. Sometimes, however, when she was cooking or setting the table, she would feel him watching her; and, glancing at him, she would see the knowing smile that she now despised. Now, a sense of restraint stood between them; Mase too was waiting.

"All right," Emma said at last, turning toward him. "What is it?"

He took a folded piece of paper from his pocket and handed it to her. "Just some fishing hooks and tobacco . . . give it to Harry McFarland at the hardware, he'll fill it out. Tell him to bill me."

She took the paper, glanced at it, then tucked it in the pocket of her dress. Mase remained on the bed. She walked back to the mirror, took the ribbon out of her hair, and began combing it again. In the mirror she could see Mase, staring down at his hands, a thin swirl of smoke curling upward from his cigarette. Determined not to let him know how uneasy she was in his presence, she finished combing her hair, retied it, then turned to the bed.

"How do I look?" she said, turning completely around.

"Fine." He stood up. "Just fine." He gave his belt a tug and turned away. "I reckon Ben's ready."

Emma smiled inwardly. For the moment she had the upper hand; whatever it was that Mase had meant to say, he was unable now to say it.

"I won't forget the fish-hooks," she said; then she whisked past him and turned up the hall.

Ben was waiting in the front yard. The mules already looked tired; the wheels of the wagon were crusted with black mud. Ben look uncomfortable in a clean shirt, his hair combed slick against his head. Lewt and Lance were standing by the front steps.

"See you don't kill the whole day up there," Lance told Ben gruffly. "They's work to be done here."

"Yessir," Ben said. He jumped down from the wagon and helped Emma up to the spring seat, then climbed up beside her. "Anything else, Pa?" he asked.

"Just don't spend the whole day up there," Lance said again, turning back to the steps.

Ben nodded, then shook the reins and spoke to the mules;

the wagon creaked away.

Emma turned to wave and noticed Mase standing in the doorway; he was looking directly at her, a scowl on his face. She turned away. Pooh on him; let him look if he didn't have anything better to do.

It was already hot when they reached the north rim of the valley; Emma dabbed at the beads of perspiration on her forehead and worried about her wilting dress. Well, it didn't matter; this was her first trip to Gipson in almost a month and she wasn't going to let anything spoil it.

Beside her, Ben complained about almost everything; the heat, the slow pace of the mules, the way Lance treated him —"like a two year old kid." Emma, only half listening, offered her sympathy from time to time. Poor Ben.

It was a few minutes after ten when they turned into the main street of Gipson. The town was already full of people. Even before they had passed the gin, Emma had seen several people she knew and some of them shouted and waved. Ben pulled and fretted at the mules and even cussed a little. Passing the Blue Goose café, Emma saw Dottie Goodman, a girl her own age from the basin. She turned to Ben. "Let me out here," she said. He sawed on the reins and gritted his teeth. When the wagon stopped, Emma jumped down.

"I'll tie up at the other end of town," Ben said. "Next to Mabry's. Pa says we got to be back pretty soon . . . so don't you get lost."

"I won't," Emma said laughing. "Don't you let those mules run away with you."

Dottie was waiting on the boardwalk. "Did you ever see such a mess of people," she said. "I'm wore out already."

"I don't mind," Emma said, laughing again. "I like people." She took Dottie's arm. "Come on, I've got to get something for Mase up at McFarland's . . . it won't take a minute."

The girls pushed their way through the crowd and Emma left the list with McFarland, promising to pick it up later. Then she and Dottie went back to main street and turned toward the upper end of town.

"Who's taking you to the catfish dance?" Dottie asked.

"Good heavens," Emma said. "I haven't even thought about the dance, and it only a week off. I guess I'll go with Goodie, he asked me back in March."

"I guess I'll go with Thomas Bridgeman," Dottie said with exaggerated unconcern. "He asked me last night . . . but I haven't decided yet."

Emma almost laughed in her face. Everyone in the basin knew that Dottie had had her feathers up for Thomas since he moved to the valley two years back.

"Well, I envy you," Emma said. "He's about the best looking man in the river bottom."

Dottie blushed happily. "Well, I don't know yet. . . ."

They walked on, talking about the dance, stopping along the way to look in the store windows, sharing the freedom of a Saturday in town.

A moment later, as they were passing Freemont's Drygood store, Emma's breath caught in her throat. Coming toward them, his black beaver hat towering half a head above everyone else, was Chad Walters! Her first impulse was to turn up the alley between Freemont's and the barbershop; and she did, in fact, take a step in that direction. Then she stopped, annoyed that she had felt the need to escape. She certainly could not be held accountable every time she met Chad Walters on the streets of Gipson.

At that instant Chad saw her. He smiled.

Emma, terrified, elated, frustrated by a thousand different emotions, simply waited.

Chad stopped beside her and touched the brim of his hat. "Hello, Emma," he said.

Emma tried to speak, but could only nod. She glanced behind her, then at Dottie, who was waiting just ahead of them, a puzzled expression on her face.

"Are you with someone?" Chad asked, glancing around.

"No . . . yes." She tried to smile; whatever she had felt about Chad before, he was a complete stranger at that moment. "I'm with Dottie Goodman," she said. "A girl from the basin."

"Well then, I won't keep you," Chad said. "Maybe I'll see you at the dance." He touched his hat again, and was gone.

For a long moment, Emma remained perfectly still. She had the crazy feeling that she was going to faint. Then someone jostled her and she saw Dottie waiting. She walked on and Dottie fell in beside her. Neither of them spoke for some time; then Dottie said, "Didn't that man speak to you?"

"Yes. He did." Emma was already framing an answer to the next question.

Dottie gave her time to volunteer further information, then she said, "I don't think I've ever seen him before."

"His name is Chad Walters," Emma replied. "He's the man who moved onto our farm. That is, the one we were living on."

She could almost hear Dottie's inward gasp. "Chad Walters!"

"Yes. I met him one day on the bluff. When I was looking for muscadines."

"But . . ."

"Dottie, he simply said hello. There's no need to have a heart attack."

"But Chad Walters," Dottie said. "I mean . . ."

Suddenly, it was all very funny; Dottie's gaping mouth, the almost moral indignation that Chad's name aroused. Emma laughed. "Come on," she said. "We'll stop at Mabry's and get a soda . . . that's just what we both need."

A moment later, Emma stopped dead still. She remembered for the first time something Chad had said: *maybe I'll see you at the dance.* The dance! He couldn't have meant the catfish dance—oh, good Lord, he couldn't have meant that!

"Emma, is anything wrong?" Dottie asked.

Emma managed a smile. "No," she said, taking Dottie's arm. "It's just the heat, I guess. I'm all right now."

As they walked on, she thought: he did mean the catfish dance; it would be just like him.

CHAPTER 7

WILL KELLY SAT at his desk in the land office and watched the people through the front window. It seemed unusually hot for September and the flies, which should have retired for the year, buzzed persistently against the screen door. From time to time Will rose from his chair with a mighty effort, walked to the rear of the office and got a battered fly spray, then returned to the front door and pumped half-heartedly at the insects.

After a time he turned his attention to some title claims lying on his desk, but his mind kept wandering to other things. At last he pushed the papers aside, leaned back in his chair, and turned again to the window. The shopping crowd was small for a Saturday, but that was due of course to the fact that the basin folks were holding their annual catfish dance, an affair that began early in the morning and lasted far into the night. It was this thought that had been hovering around in the back of Will's mind all morning. He had not missed a catfish dance during the ten years he had held the job as land agent; but at the moment, he was considering the wisdom of driving to the basin that day. Actually he had always taken a certain pride in the fact that he had a standing invitation to the event, but since his recent involvement in the Walters affair, he thought he had detected a marked coolness on the part of the river people. It was not something you could put your finger on, and of course he could be wrong; but the feeling persisted and it posed a tricky problem. He had not seen old Lance since the day he had accompanied Walters to the farm. And old Lance held the answer. If he chose to make an issue of Will's interference in the affair, the gumbo rats would take his attitude as a personal and official order. In time this would make Will's duties as land agent both unpleasant and difficult. If, on the other hand, Lance decided to forget the entire affair. . . .

Ironically, as Will sat musing over his problem, he saw the tall, spare figure of Chad Walters ride past outside. Although he had seen Walters only once since he moved to the basin, he had heard about his fight with Such Farnsworth; and, if the truth were told, he had derived a personal satisfaction from the account. For his own part, he had never cared for Such, a bullish, boasting man who—like most people—talked too much. But his natural sympathy with Walters, a nameless thing, was based upon more than his dislike for Such. There was something about Chad—his manner, his quiet way of speaking, even his remoteness—that Will liked. On his trips to the basin he had not, of course, spoken in Walters behalf. He had enough trouble as matters stood. But the feeling remained and he was happy to see Chad rein the mare through the wagons passing along the street and pull up at the land office hitch rail. He watched him dismount and tie up, then walk up the front steps.

"Come in," Will called. "I was just thinking about you."

Walters appeared in the doorway, ducking under the sill. "You busy?"

"Haven't hit a lick all day," Will said. "Drag up that chair and sit awhile."

Walters sat down, took off his hat, wiped his face on the sleeve of his shirt, then crossed his legs and looked laconically out the front window.

A minute passed; neither of the men spoke. Will grinned inwardly; Walters was the most unaccountable fellow.

Finally Will said, "Any thing I can do for you?"

"Nope," Walters replied. "I just dropped by to say hello."

Will nodded, thinking: it'll probably take him half a day to say it.

"Fine," he said. "Always glad to have company."

Another minute passed. Will tried again.

"How are things in the basin?"

"I'm staying busy."

"Well, I'm glad things worked out as well as they did," Will replied. "The gumbo rats are stubborn people. Revengeful too, when they want to be. I was afraid they might make trouble for you."

Chad grinned. "They haven't invited me over for dinner yet," he said. "But we're getting along as well as could be expected."

"Just kind of agreed to leave each other alone, huh?"

"I guess that's about it."

They sat for several minutes, sharing the silence. Then Will said, "I hear you had a little run-in with Farnsworth."

It was an instant before Chad replied; then he said, "Yep, that was the first mistake I made. Such talks a lot; he'll make it a point not to let them forget that."

"Well, there are times when a man's self-respect is worth more to him than staying out of trouble," Will said. "The way I heard it you did what you had to do."

Chad shook his head. "No, I didn't have to fight him. And it wasn't my self-respect I was worried about. I just got mad."

"That happens to all of us."

"Yep. No need for it though."

Will reached for his pipe; there seemed to be nothing else to say; he filled the pipe and lit it, then got up and walked to the back of the office, returning with the fly spray. He gave the flies around the door three squirts.

"Late for flies," he said.

"Yep."

A few minutes later Chad stood up and put on his hat. "I better be getting back," he said. "I've got some sprouting to do in the meadow."

"Glad you dropped by," Will replied. "Always glad to visit with you." Suddenly, he remembered the catfish dance. It occurred to him that he had no real choice about attending; to stay away would be an unmistakable gesture. Besides, he'd have to find out sooner or later where old Lance stood. He followed Chad outside and waited until he had mounted the mare. Then he said, "What time are you going back to the basin?"

"About thirty minutes, I guess," Walters replied. "I've got to pick up some horseshoes and a few groceries. You riding that way?"

"Thought I might," Will said. "Drop back by if you're

riding alone. I'll get my mare saddled."

"All right, I'll be ready in half an hour."

Will watched him rein the mare around and ride off down the street; then he grinned and went back into the land office. I don't believe he ever did say hello, he thought.

Chad and Will reached the rim of the basin shortly before noon. Chad had been rather more talkative on the ride out, telling Will about his plan to terrace the ridge below the farm and about his hopes of getting another five acres cleared before spring planting time. But even these remarks were made briefly and Will, as usual, had carried the conversation.

At the crossroads above Carley's Crossing, Chad said, "I guess I'll leave you here. As a rule, I try to stay clear of the community."

"Sure," Will answered. "I can see the point in that. Come see me when you're in town."

"I'll do that," Chad replied, and rode off.

Will watched him for a moment, wondering if he were a lonely man. Probably not, he decided. Loneliness was a social problem. He tapped his heels against Dandy's flank and rode into the valley.

The catfish dance officially began at noon when the basin men (who had spent the morning in the general store, working up the festive spirit with moonshine made in their own stills) repaired to a clearing just above the Diehole header for dinner. The women, of course, had gone to the clearing shortly after daybreak and spent the entire morning gossiping, watching the children and preparing the endless stringers of catfish that had been brought up the night before. By the time the men appeared, flushed and a little drunk, the affair was in full swing.

When Will Kelly reached the turn at the north end of Carley's Crossing, he saw the horses tied in front of the general store and knew that the men had not yet gone to the clearing. This state of affairs was, he thought, unfortunate, for he had hoped to make his appearance at dinner where the presence of the entire community would lend collective support to his case. But it didn't really matter, he told himself; everybody would be watching old Lance anyhow, and Lance would scarcely be influenced by the women and children.

Will could hear the men inside the general store long before he reached the hitchrail out front, and he gathered from the sound that the moonshine had rather got the best of it.

He dismounted below the store and tied Dandy at the lower end of the hitchrail. The shouts and laughter inside brought a tightness to his stomach; it was possible that the gumbo rats had drunk too much. A few drinks made them expansive; beyond that, they got mean. He pressed his lips together and walked up the front steps; as he entered the door, the mingled smells of whisky and leather struck his nostrils.

The men were gathered at the rear of the store, some seated on the stacks of feed, others on the long counter. There must have been a hundred or more present and it seemed to Will that they were all talking at the same time. He spotted old Lance sitting in a cane bottom chair near the stove, cold sober, the perpetual scowl on his twisted face. At the same moment, some of the men looked toward the door; slowly the laughter subsided.

Will walked toward the group, keeping his eyes on Lance.

"Sounds like you boys got an early start," he said, smiling.

Old Lance glanced up, leaning slightly forward in his chair; the others watched him, waiting. For an instant the scowl on his face deepened; then he smiled.

"Been here since daybreak," he said. "You got a lot of catching up to do." He turned to Lewt, standing behind him. "Give Will some of that whisky," he said. "We'll see what kind of man he is."

Lewt went to the table in the rear and the gumbo rats, taking the cue from Lance, clapped Will on the back and shouted their welcome. The crisis was over. Will took the cup of whisky from Lewt and someone at the back shouted, "That'll put hair on your chest, Will." Everyone laughed; and Will, breathing an inward sigh of relief, took a sip of the strong, rank brew.

CHAPTER 8

SINCE HER MEETING with Chad Walters on the streets of Gipson, Emma had not slept at all well. To make matters worse, she could not escape a slight sense of guilt about the whole affair; she tried perhaps too hard to keep this feeling hid from her family and in the end felt that she had overplayed the part. Mase, she thought, was watching her with a new interest, and even Ben seemed at times oddly knowing. Try as she would, she could not forget Chad's remarks about the dance. It was foolish to worry about it, she told herself. It was absurd to think that he meant the catfish dance. But somehow these thoughts were not altogether reassuring. Perhaps he didn't really know how intensely the basin people hated him, or how deeply they could hate. There were times when she considered slipping away at night and going to the Walters farm, but the idea never went beyond a vague possibility. In the first place, she had not once been left alone all week; and even if she had been, she was not sure that she would have had the courage to carry out the plan.

Now, standing with several of the gumbo women at the cleaning tubs in the clearing, she tried to dismiss the thought from her mind. The clearing was filled with the gamey smell of fish and the shrill shouts of the children, who insisted on remaining underfoot. It was a moment so curiously exclusive, so often experienced, that she could not imagine interference from an outsider.

Beside her, Mary Driscoll said, "Well, they'll be here in a minute. And chances are my man'll be drunk as a coot." She was looking across the rise where the tin roof of the general store glistened in the sun.

Emma laughed. "Chances are they'll all be a little light headed," she said.

She pulled another catfish from the stringer and laid it on the table. Expertly she cut skin-deep around the gills and along the backbone and belly, then threw it across to Mrs. Felder, one of the skinners.

"I'd like to see one catfish dance come and go," Mary was saying, "without Thomas making a fool of hisself. The more he drinks, the worse he gets . . . and he won't stop drinking till the river runs dry." She glanced at Emma and shrugged philosophically. "Time we get home in the morning he'll be mean as a bluetick hound."

"Maybe not," Emma replied. "Maybe this time he'll go to bed."

Mary shook her head. "Not 'fore he beats the daylights out of me he won't. He figgers the party's not over till we've had it around."

For a moment, Emma watched Mary's face, beaded with perspiration, her lips pressed tightly together as she ran the knife swiftly along the body of the fish. Again she marveled at the staying power of the gumbo women. Not only did Mary expect Thomas Driscoll to "beat the daylights" out of her before he sobered up, but she didn't really mind. Perhaps she would be disappointed if he didn't. Emma shook her head and reached for another fish.

A moment later, Mrs. Felder, a huge, red-faced woman, said, "There they come, girls . . . mean as a pack of dogs."

Emma looked toward the general store, shading her eyes against the bright sunlight. Some of the men had already started walking toward the clearing, others were mounting their horses in front of the general store. All of the women in the clearing were watching, work momentarily at a standstill. Whatever abuses they would suffer later in the day, this was the moment they had waited for; the moment they had anticipated for weeks and even months.

Riding, walking, carrying their jugs, the younger boys walking in a group, the men straggled into the clearing like a routed army. The children ran from the cleaning tables to meet them and were rewarded with a tossle of the hair, or put in their proper place by a stern look. At the head of the group was old Lance, dragging his lame leg, glowering fiercely against the sun—the patriarch leading his people to higher ground.

Suddenly, Emma saw Will Kelly, riding beside Lewt. The sight of the wrinkled, wiry little man sent a rush of warmth through her; it seemed at that moment that she realized for the first time how genuinely fond of him she was.

The men on horseback dismounted and tied up in a grove of trees at the edge of the clearing, the others, oddly ill at ease, joined their women around the cleaning tables. Emma put down the fish she was cleaning and walked across the clearing to meet Will.

"I was afraid you weren't coming," she said, holding out her hands.

Will took them and smiled. "Why? I've never missed a catfish dance yet."

Emma realized that her remark was a little indiscreet under the circumstances. "I don't know," she said. "I didn't mean it the way it sounded."

"I know what you mean," Will said, lowering his voice. "I guess your pa decided to let me off this time."

"I'm glad," Emma said, squeezing his hands. "It wouldn't have been a catfish dance without you."

One of the men shouted, "Come on, Will. You can gab with the women folks later."

The men were now gathered around the heaping platters of fried catfish and greasy potatoes, eating like ravenous animals. The women scurried about, cleaning and frying more fish, refilling the platters on the tables as they were emptied. The children too waited, seated cross-legged in a group nearby, watching their fathers and brothers like so many big-eyed puppies.

"You go along," Emma told Will. "I'll see you after dinner." Then, impulsively, she added, "There's something I want to talk to you about."

Will raised his eyebrows questioningly.

"It's not really important, I guess," Emma assured him. "Probably just my imagination. I'll tell you later."

The men remained in the clearing for an hour, by which time the ground was littered with fish bones and scraps of bread. At last old Lance stood up and wiped his mouth on the sleeve of his shirt. Taking this as a signal, the others too got up and stretched.

"All right," Lance called out. "Let's get over to the hogshead and separate the men from the boys." The men laughed and began moving away. Lance remained a moment longer. He glanced briefly at the women around the tables. "Good vittles," he grunted, paying a rare compliment to their morning's work. The women beamed, wiping their hands on their aprons.

The hogshead was another smaller clearing forty or fifty yards down the river. It was here the men went to spend the afternoon at games, most of them as old as the river itself, all of them designed to test the courage and physical strength of the participants.

Will followed the others to the clearing and sat down in the shade of a huge wateroak. The gumbo rats, drinking freely from the endless brown jugs, formed two lines along either side of the clearing and waited. After a moment, old Lance limped out into the glaring sunlight, a crooked grin on his face. He held up his hands and waited until the clearing grew perfectly still.

"All right, boys," he said, "we've got a couple of grudge matches to work off first thing. Tooley Hammons and Tom Driscoll been at it all summer 'bout that mare Tooley sold Tom last spring." A wave of laughter swept along the lines; Lance held up his hands again. "All right, you boys step out here."

The two men moved out, from opposite sides of the clearing, and walked to where old Lance waited. Hammons, a gaunt, lean-flanked boy of twenty or so, shuffled along self-consciously, his eyes fixed on the ground; Driscoll, a barrel-chested bull of a man with a ragged beard, grinned expansively, removing his shirt as he came.

Lance took a stick and drew a circle on the ground six or seven feet across; then, through the center of the circle he drew a straight line, dividing it exactly in half. "You boys know how to play hound dog," he said, speaking to the spectators rather than the participants. "First one that turns loose ain't got sand in his craw."

The spectators roared their approval and some of them applauded. Hammons and Driscoll stood a moment, rubbing their sweaty palms against their trousers; then they stepped into the circle, facing each other across the center line. Hammons eyed the older man apprehensively; Driscoll grinned broadly, relishing the moment.

Lance watched the men, giving them time to get their feet firmly planted; then he shouted, *"HOUND DOG!"*

The rules of the game were simple. The two men in the circle simply began swinging with their free hands, trying by sheer brute force to knock each other out of the prescribed fighting area. The spectators closed in, forming a ring, shouting "hound dog" over and over in a kind of rhythmic chant. The dust billowed up around the battlers, the dull thud of fist against bone and muscle punctuated the shouts that filled the clearing.

Watching the fighters Will wondered, as he had wondered a thousand times before, what curious sense of honor compelled men to test themselves in such a manner. Perhaps, he thought, it is because they do not honor any of the formal institutions that normally give meaning to men's lives; perhaps it is because they have no lasting ambition, no hope of achieving something over a period of years or even a lifetime; their satisfactions rise or fall in a moment like this, they are like children, preserving the one test they understand—the test of physical superiority.

As he watched the men fight, an odd sense of depression came over him; he thought of Emma and wondered what she had wanted to tell him; of all the gumbo rats, Emma could still be helped.

His thoughts were interrupted by a quickened shout from the spectators. Through a narrow opening in the crowd he could see the two men struggling. The Hammons boy, his face raw and bleeding, was down; Driscoll stood over him, striking at his head and back, grunting with every blow. At last old Lance stepped forward, pushing Driscoll away.

"All right, that's it," he said with official impartiality. "Driscoll tops Hammons."

A cheer went up from the crowd; some of the men helped the boy to his feet, others congratulated Driscoll. Then, according to custom, the boy staggered across to his opponent and offered his hand, an abject gesture of defeat. Driscoll clasped the outstretched hand, and together the two men walked away from the fighting ring.

Old Lance held up his hands for silence. "Now we got another grudge fight," he began. "Dick Helms and Nolan Harris . . ."

And so the afternoon wore on. The games continued without a break; hound dog, Indian wrestling and bare-fisted boxing. The jugs of whisky were emptied and the younger boys sent to stills nearby to refill them. The sun slid across the western sky, casting streaks of light through the swirls of dust that hung like a cloud over the clearing.

After a time the women joined the men in the clearing, standing together under the trees, more subdued than their husbands and sons but hardly less enthusiastic. Will looked for Emma in the group but did not see her; he got up and walked slowly around the edge of the clearing and back through the trees to the picnic grounds. Emma was sitting alone under a tree, looking across the basin toward the bluff. Watching her, Will thought: she is really a beautiful woman. It was a beauty neither perfect nor striking; you saw it only after you had come to know her.

Will walked to where she sat; she looked up and smiled.

"I looked for you at the clearing," he said.

She shook her head. "Somehow, today, I just can't take it," she said. "I used to go. I used to think it was very exciting. Then that summer—when was it, five years ago—I stood there and watched Ben fight John Sedgewick. Suddenly, for the first time, I saw them for what they are, animals with nothing better to do than beat each other senseless. I remember Ben on his knees, holding his arms up against the blows and nobody wanted to stop the fight. That's when I ran out and tried to stop it." She glanced up at Will and smiled. "You remember . . . that's when Papa slapped me, right there before everybody, telling me it wasn't a woman's game. It was the only time he ever touched me."

"Yes," Will said. "I remember." At the time he had scarcely known her; a child, different only because she was Lance Boone's daughter.

"He was right," Emma said. "I had no business butting in. But I learned a lesson. Now I just don't go any more."

Will took off his hat and sat down on the ground beside her. For some time they said nothing; then Will asked, "Do you still have something to tell me?"

Emma glanced at him, and then away. "Yes." She paused a moment, searching for the right words. Then she said, "Will, how do you feel about Chad Walters?"

Will looked at her carefully, trying to read the thought behind the question.

"I think he's a good man," he said. "I've only seen him once or twice, but I like him."

"Why?"

He leaned back, looking up at the sky. "I don't know exactly," he said. "Maybe it's because I believe in him." Emma watched him, curiously intent. "He's bigger than most men I've known," Will went on. "Maybe that's it. I like him because I think he's bigger than his problems. I think he always will be. Walters has learned one simple trick of living: that you can't run away from your problems. You've got to learn to live with them." He smiled. "That's a trick some of us never learn."

After a moment Emma said, "I believe in him too. And I know what you mean about him being bigger than other men. I've felt that."

Strangely, Emma's remark was not surprising.

"Have you met him?" Will asked.

"Yes. One day on the bluff. I was picking muscadines. . . ."

Will reached for his pipe. You never know, he thought; in some illogical way it all makes sense. Emma Boone and Chad Walters; for all the distance between them, they are in many ways alike.

"Of course, no one else knows," Emma said. "If papa found out, I think he'd try to kill Chad."

Will could not help noticing the "Chad."

"Have you seen him since?"

"Yes . . . in Gipson last Saturday. I met him on the street." She turned, looking directly at Will. "That's what I want to talk to you about . . . I think he's coming to the dance tonight."

This remark brought Will up; if it's true, he thought, Heaven help us. It was just the kind of a thing Walters might do, not as a gesture of defiance, but as an attempt to break down the barrier that stood between him and the river people.

"Did he tell you that?" he asked.

"Not exactly," she replied. "It was something he said when I met him in Gipson. Maybe I'm wrong . . . I was afraid someone would see us talking . . . but as he walked away, he said something about the dance. I thought he said 'I'll see you at the dance.' " She sat a moment, thinking. "Yes, I'm sure that's what he said. He must have been talking about the dance tonight. He couldn't have meant anything else." She put her hand on Will's arm, disturbed now as she had not been before, convinced by her own words that she had taken the whole matter too lightly. "Will, what can we do?"

With less assurance then he felt, Will said, "I expect you misunderstood him. We rode out together from Gipson this morning. He didn't mention the dance then, which would be unusual if he planned to attend." He smiled. "But if it will make you feel any better, I'll ride up that way and talk to him."

"I wish you would," Emma replied, obviously relieved. "You know what will happen if he comes to the dance."

"I've got an idea," Will said; he stood up. "I'd better leave now, while the men are still at the hogshead." Together they walked across to the grove of trees where Will had left Dandy. He mounted and pulled the mare around.

"Don't worry," he said. "If it's necessary, I'll just tell him not to come."

"All right," Emma said. "Tell him I . . . don't want him to come." Will nodded. "And, Will . . . tell him why."

"Sure," Will said, and rode away.

When he reached the Walters farm the house was empty and the sorrel mare was gone. The sun now was low against the western rim of the basin and a hushed quiet hung over the valley. Will tied Dandy to the front gate, then went to the steps and sat down. He filled his pipe, lit it, and waited.

The afternoon passed away and dusk came suddenly. Will remained until the first night sounds rose in scattered cries along the river; but Chad did not return.

At last he stood up and put his pipe away. The more he thought about it, the less likely Emma's story sounded. She had admitted that the circumstances were vague; she had been frightened, and even startled, by the meeting on the streets of Gipson. And, Will decided with an inward smile, she acted very much like a young lady about to fall in love.

He walked to the front gate and mounted Dandy. He sat for a moment watching the first twinkling stars brighten against the shadow of the sky; then he rode down the hill toward Carley's Crossing.

The catfish dance was already in full swing when he reached the general store. He tied up at the hitch rail and went inside. The scene that met his eyes was wildly festive. The counters and show-cases had been taken to the rear of the store to make room for the dancers; the dancing area itself was packed, which, considering the style of dancing fashionable in the basin, created a perilous situation. The dance was called the Devil's Stomp, which was, Will thought, an appropriate title. As nearly as he could judge, the steps were performed by no set pattern; it was necessary only that the men stomp the floor as frequently as possible; the harder the better. It seemed that those who were considered the best dancers were the ones who stomped the hardest. To add to the confusion, the dancers kept up a constant stream of shouting and laughter, so shrill at times that it literally drowned out the music.

The music was furnished by a two-piece string band from Daiker's Pitch, the same one that had been performing at the catfish dance since before Will's time. Old Lazuras Bates, a gaunt, bearded fiddler, sat in a cane-bottom chair near the stove, his ear pressed close to the strings of his instrument, his eyes closed; he was playing "Green Corn," a basin favorite. Beside him sat the "tinner," a thin, sallow-faced man with an enormous Adam's apple which actually seemed to jump in time to the music; between his second and third finger he held a long, thin strip of metal which he tapped rhythmically against the fiddle strings behind the bridge; from time to time he would shout shrill above the din, a kind of long, drawn out catcall, presumably moved by the music he was helping create.

A row of chairs and benches had been placed along the left wall for the "old folks." After a moment, in a dull, smoky lamplight, Will saw old Lance. The chair beside him was empty. Will made his way around the seething swirl of dancers and walked to where Lance sat; Lance looked up and nodded. Leaning forward, he cupped one hand around his mouth. "Thought you'd went back to town . . . have a chair."

Will thought of Chad Walters as he sat down. To Lance he said, "Lazuras is in good form tonight. . . ."

"Never better," Lance said, tapping his foot in time to the music.

Watching him Will thought how strangely alike men were; underneath the man was the child, happy only when he could forget for a moment what he really was; even old Lance, the ruler, the ancient king, happiest when he could put aside his crown.

The dance ended and the building rocked with applause. Someone shouted "Lost Sheep" at Lazuras; someone else called out "Millie was a Lady." Oblivious to it all, Lazuras picked up a tin cup, spat a stream of tobacco juice into it, again tucked his fiddle under his chin and began playing "Thunder Mountain." Everyone laughed and again the floor swayed under the ferocity of the Devil's Stomp.

Will grinned; maybe I'm too high and mighty, he thought; maybe this is the answer after all. He looked for Emma and saw her dancing with Al Goodman, one of the young basin eligibles. He tried to catch her eye but she moved away. Someone touched his shoulder; he turned and saw Such Farnsworth holding out a cup of whisky.

"Thanks," Will shouted, taking the cup.

"Good dance, ain't it?" Such grinned drunkenly.

"Fine."

A moment later Emma danced by; seeing Will, she spoke to her partner and together they walked to where Will and Lance were sitting. "Hi, papa," she said, dabbing at the perspiration on her face with a lace handkerchief. "This is the best dance we've ever had."

The old man beamed at his handsome daughter, but said nothing. Will stood up, offering her his chair.

"I haven't time to sit down," she said. "I just wanted to warn you that we're having the next dance together."

Will laughed. "You'd better stick with Al, he's young enough to keep up with you."

Young Goodman flushed and tried to find something to do with his hands.

"No excuses," Emma said. "You just be ready, that's all." She turned back to Al and they danced away.

Will glanced at old Lance. "Emma's mighty pretty tonight."

Lance scowled, trying to hide his pride; he nodded and muttered something that Will did not understand.

When the dance ended a moment later, Emma came back to where they sat. Will stood up and held out his arm to her. Dancers on the floor were calling out their favorite numbers to Lazuras, who, still impervious to it all, was saying something to the tinner. An instant later he struck up a lively hoedown.

Will shook his head. "I'm afraid that one's a little too fast for an old man."

"We don't have to dance the stomp," Emma said, leading him out to the floor. "We'll just dance."

When they had moved a safe distance from Lance, she said, "Did you see him?"

"It's all right," he said. "He wasn't there. I waited until after dark, he must have gone back to Gipson."

After a pause, Emma said, "All right. I feel better now. I haven't been able to think of anything else since this afternoon." She smiled. "Thanks for going up there."

Will tried to avoid the center of the dance floor where the most inspired stompers seemed to congregate; and in spite of the jostling, he discovered after the first few halting steps that he was enjoying himself. As they danced by the musicians' stand the thin-faced tinner let out a shrill, soul-stirring shriek and they both laughed.

Suddenly, Emma stopped dancing, her body perfectly rigid; he heard the sharp intake of her breath. "Oh, no," she whispered. "Oh, please . . . no. . . ."

When Will glanced at her, she was looking directly past him, toward the front of the building, a look almost of panic on her face. At the same moment he was conscious of the silence that had fallen over the entire room; the scrape of feet subsided, the shouts from the dancers stopped abruptly; only the shrill screech of Lazuras' fiddle whined on, an almost hysterical sound in the sudden stillness. Then someone spoke to Lazuras in an undertone and the music too ceased. Everyone in the room stood perfectly still, looking toward the door. Will turned and saw Chad Walters standing under the smoky lamp that hung suspended above the doorway, his dark face a shadow in the dim light. He was dressed in a black cord suit, a white shirt and a black string tie, which gave an oddly ministerial air to his appearance. For the space of an instant no one moved; then Chad bowed slightly to a group of ladies sitting near the front, and walked slowly toward the dance floor.

78

Will glanced at Emma; her face was strained and white; she gripped his hand so intensely that he could feel the sharp point of her nails biting into his palm. Walters was coming directly toward them! Then he was standing there, smiling, the even line of his teeth incredibly white against his dark features. He nodded to Will, then spoke to Emma.

"May I have the next dance?" He spoke quietly, but the effect could not have been more startling if he had shouted the words.

For what seemed like an eternity, Emma said nothing; then, in an an almost inaudible voice, she replied, "The next dance is taken."

The expression on his face did not change. "And the dance after that?"

"It's taken too . . . all of them are taken." There was another moment of silence. When Emma spoke again her voice was clearly audible across the room. "You must understand . . . you are not wanted here."

"I didn't know that," Chad said. "If I had I wouldn't have come." Still he did not go. "Do you speak for yourself?"

There was a sudden movement near the center of the dance floor and Lewt Boone pressed through the crowd. He stopped beside Chad, his handsome face flushed with whisky and anger.

"She's speaking for all of us," he said. "You'd better go."

Chad glanced at him, then looked again at Emma. It was a look of dismissal, too obvious to ignore; Lewt grabbed Chad by the arm, spinning him around. "I said get out!" He stood in a half crouch, fist clenched, his arms held away from his body.

For a long moment Chad looked at him, his face reflecting absolutely nothing. Then he said, "All right. I guess I'd better." He turned to go, then, almost as an afterthought, he stopped and looked again at Lewt. "One other thing," he said. "Don't ever put your hand on me unless you mean it."

The gumbo rats remained perfectly motionless as Chad walked around the edge of the room. At the door, he bowed again to the ladies seated there, then walked out into the darkness.

It appeared to Will that the gumbo rats did not know exactly how to react to the incident they had just witnessed. There was a strained, uncertain silence for a full minute, broken only when old Lance rapped his cane against the floor and called out, "All right, let's get on with the dance."

Lazuras tucked his fiddle under his chin and began playing, but somehow even the music seemed less spirited than before. One by one the dancers moved, hesitantly, as if they were not sure that it was the right thing to do.

Lewt Boone had not moved. He stood beside Will and Emma, his lips pressed together in a hard line, still looking toward the front door; the veins stood out on his forehead, the muscled knot of his jaw tightened. At last he turned and looked at Will. "This time he went too far," he said, his voice tight with anger. "And before I'm through, he'll know it." Then he turned and walked off the floor.

Will looked at Emma. "Maybe we'd better sit down," he said.

She shook her head. "No, let's finish the dance."

When the music stopped, Will led her back to where Lance was seated. He scowled up at her, his eyes questioning. Around them the gumbo rats were trying, without any real success, to regain their former gaiety.

"You all right?" Lance asked.

"Fine, papa," Emma said, smiling down at him.

At that moment Mase walked up. Will could not help noticing the look he gave Emma, something between embarrassment and admiration; he was a little drunk.

"I reckon you told him off," he said to Emma. "You put him straight all right."

Lazuras' fiddle bow rasped jerkily across the strings and the tinner piper shrilly.

"You haven't danced with me yet," Emma said.

Mase flushed and took her arm. As they danced away, old Lance watched them; then his eyes dropped and he sat for a long while without moving, staring fiercely into his cup of whisky.

The dance continued for almost an hour, by which time the steady flow of whisky had reduced the immediate importance of Chad's earlier appearance; tomorrow, of course, the matter would be discussed and rediscussed a hundred times, but the gumbo rats were determined now, it seemed, not to let him spoil their evening.

Will sat beside Lance, trying to keep his eyes open. I could have passed up that last cup of moonshine, he thought; maybe I should have passed up the whole affair—then someone would have *told* me about the Walters incident, which would have been a lot less painful than watching it. What could Walters have been thinking? Didn't he know that the river people would never accept him? What did Emma have to do with it? Perhaps Emma had not told him everything that afternoon. . . .

At that moment he heard her voice, speaking to Lance.

"Papa, I've got a headache. If it's all right with you, I'd like to go home." She looked tired, her face strained and drawn.

Lance glanced up at her sharply and it was a long moment before he replied. Then he said, "All right. I'll send Mase with you." He stood up until he caught Mase's eye, then called him over with a nod of his head.

"Take Emma home," he said. "She's tired."

"You ain't sick, are you?" Mase asked with genuine concern.

"No. Just tired."

Young Goodman had joined the group. "If you're ready to go home," he said, "I'll be happy to walk with you."

"Mase'll take her," old Lance said gruffly; and young Goodman stood crestfallen as Mase and Emma walked away.

When they reached the Boone farm, Emma turned to Mase. "I'll be all right now," she said.

Mase had said nothing during the walk home, but he had

stumbled more than once along the road and Emma was sure that he had had several drinks too many. Now he stood looking at her, waving slightly in the moonlight.

"All right," he said. "I reckon I had it wrong about you and Walters."

"I've forgotten that," she replied. "Thanks for bringing me home." She turned and walked up the steps and into the house. She lit a lamp, then went back to the front window and pulled the curtain aside. Mase was walking away, a shadow moving shakily along the road. She watched until he had disappeared in the darkness. For several minutes she stood by the window, watching the road. Then, moving quickly, she went to the closet by the fireplace and took down a shawl which she threw across her shoulders; a moment later she slipped out the back door and walked hurriedly across the field toward the bluff.

The moon hung pale and opalescent against thin, scattered clouds that raced across the sky like the ghosts of birds. Behind her, far off, she could hear the muted wail of Lazuras' fiddle and the muffled shouts of the dancers. Then the music and shouts grew dimmer and at last she heard them no more.

Her heart beat a wild rhythm as she moved through the damp fields. Then she saw the dark outline of the Walters house; suddenly, unaccountably, her mind cleared and the beat of her heart subsided. She walked across the meadow and up the rise. There was no light in the house. She opened the front gate, conscious of the creaking hinges in the stillness; turning, she saw the glow of a cigarette, the shadowed outline on the front steps. She walked across the yard and stopped beside him.

"You shouldn't have come up here," he said. Again, hearing his voice, she felt the strange sense of peace, the physical presence of him, the sense of detachment that lifted her out of the world she lived in.

For a moment she could think of nothing to say. Finally she said, "I'm sorry about tonight. I didn't mean what I said. . . ."

"I know."

"You shouldn't have come."

He looked away from her, across the valley, bathed in moonlight. "I know that too," he said quietly. "But I didn't know it then. It seems funny now that I wouldn't have known how it would turn out. I thought all day about the dance. I'd made up my mind not to go. Then tonight, after I came back from Gipson, I was sitting here on the front porch and somehow it seemed different. So, without thinking, I got up and went down there. I knew when I walked in that it was the wrong thing to do. But then it was too late."

Emma sat down on the steps beside him and put her hand on his arm. "Does it really matter, whether they accept you or not?"

"It didn't until I met you."

There were so many things she wanted to ask him, so much she wanted to know.

"Are you lonely?" she said.

He sat a moment, thinking.

"No, it isn't loneliness. It's just that I don't like living against men . . . and having them live against me. It's more like I've failed at living, failed to measure up to something that's important to me." He took her hand and for a time said nothing. Then he said, "And you're mixed up in it too. You're a part of whatever it is I want. As long as I'm fighting your people, in some way I'll be fighting you too."

"I don't care about them now," she said softly. "I care only about you . . . about us . . ."

He stood up, pulling her up beside him; she closed her eyes, shutting out the world of her father and the gumbo rats and the hatred and the fear. She felt his arms around her, his lips against hers. Only that mattered.

He held her away from him. "I'll take you home."

She saw his face in the moonlight and pressed her head against his chest.

"I love you," she said. "And I always will."

CHAPTER 9

THE FOLLOWING DAY dawned grey and dismal. Emma, after returning from the Walters farm the night before, had slept fitfully. Lance and the boys had come home sometime after two. Lewt and Ben, both obviously drunk, had been arguing about something; finally their words became so heated that Lance had sent them both to bed. Emma had lain awake, listening; then, after the house had grown quiet, she had heard the footsteps approaching her door. There was a long silence, then the door creaked slowly open.

"Emma?" It was Mase.

"I'm awake, Mase. What do you want?"

Mase walked across to the foot of her bed. "How come you're not asleep?" he asked, the infuriating note of suspicion in his voice. "I thought you was tired."

"I was asleep," Emma said. "Ben and Lewt woke me up."

For a long moment Mase said nothing, then in a tone oddly ingratiating he asked, "How do you feel?"

She watched the shadow, weaving in the darkness, smelled the sour whisky breath. "I feel fine," she said. "Go to bed."

"All right. I just wanted to make sure you wasn't sick."

You just wanted to make sure I wasn't *out,* she thought; somehow Mase was no longer a real threat. Now he only seemed a little foolish.

"No. I'm not sick."

Mase remained a moment in the darkness, as if he had something else to say. Then he turned and walked out; his knee hit the door-facing and he cursed. The door closed behind him and Emma listened to his unsteady footsteps retreating up the hallway.

Now, with the first light of day, she got out of bed and

84

dressed, then went to the kitchen and put on a pot of coffee. While it was boiling, she walked out to the back porch. The air was heavy and humid; the sky dark with the threat of rain. Her eyes turned toward the upper rim of the basin; the line of trees that marked the beginning of the Walters farm were bleak spires against the leaden sky. Thinking of Chad, her mind refused to draw clear lines. The memory of last night was a memory without substance, timeless and unreal; the words they had spoken were hollow, wooden sounds, spoken out of a dream. Perhaps it was a dream, all of it: the dance, Chad Walters, her fears. Perhaps she would awaken soon and her life would be just as it had always been.

She looked up at the sky and seemed to feel the weight of it pressing down upon her. It is not a dream, she told herself; he is up there, alone, in the house on the rise; and I love him, knowing that it is a love that can only mean unhappiness for both of us.

She walked back into the kitchen. Her father was seated at the table, his dark, twisted face turned toward her.

"Hello, Papa," she said.

He made no reply. She took a cup from the shelf and poured his coffee. He did not reach for the cup nor turn away. She poured coffee for herself and sat down. She did not look at him; neither of them spoke for some time.

When he spoke at last, she was not surprised at his words.

"I sent Ben to look after you last night." There was an eternal pause. "He said you wasn't here."

She felt the tightness in her throat, the slow creep of fear, the sudden panic. She smiled, framing the lie.

"I went out for some air. . . . I walked down to the barn."

He sat watching her, saying nothing, his eyes like stones.

"I was in bed by midnight."

"I know," he said. "Ben waited till you got back."

She could not bring herself to look at him. How much had Ben seen? She waited for her father to continue; but he too waited.

At last she said, "Then he must have seen me come up from the barn lot."

After a long pause, Lance said, "Yes. He saw you."

Mase entered the kitchen. Relieved by any interruption, Emma got up and poured his coffee. A moment later Lewt and Ben appeared. Lance was drinking his coffee, apparently satisfied with her story. The four men sat at the table, silent, red eyed, their breath still strong with the smell of whisky. To Emma the room seemed suddenly unbearable, her father and brother strangers. She took the water bucket and went to the well porch outside. The sky now had grown darker; thin, jagged flashes of lightning streaked the skyline above the basin rim. Try as she might Emma could not shake off the deep sense of depression that had settled over her; the lowering clouds, the talk with her father, the close, sour smell of the kitchen all added to the uneasy feeling that something ominous was in the wind. Somehow Chad too was a part of her depression, although she could not clearly say how. She was only aware, in some vague and indefinable way, that she needed him, needed the comfort of his presence, the sound of his voice.

When she returned to the kitchen only Ben was still sitting at the table. She breathed an inward sigh; whatever Ben thought, he was still a boy; she could handle him.

"I came looking for you last night," he said, a faint, small-boy arrogance in his voice.

Suddenly she was furious. Ben too! Did everybody know?

"I know," she said shortly. "Papa told me."

"You wasn't here. . . ."

"I was down at the barn. Papa and I have been through all that . . . now please shut up about it."

Ben watched her for a moment, then shrugged and took a sip of coffee.

Suddenly it was Lance, calling from the front of the house.

"Ben! Get out here . . . quick!" It was more than a summons; it was a command, sharp and urgent, charged with meaning.

Ben jumped up and ran out the door. For a moment unable to move, Emma remained at the table; she heard the pounding of her heart, and thought: I must be calm. What-

86

ever it is, I must be calm. Then she put down the cup she was holding and went to the living room. The others were standing on the front porch, looking east toward Carley's Crossing, their faces strained and intense. She crossed hurriedly to the door; her breath caught in her throat; somehow she had known that it was Chad Walters, but now, seeing him, she was so shaken that she held to the door-facing for support. He was riding directly up the road toward the house, dressed in the black suit that he had worn to the dance. He rode slowly, calmly looking up at the sky, as if contemplating the unseasonableness of the weather.

Emma looked at her father; there was in his face a curious sense of uncertainty that she had never seen before. After a time he said, "Ain't that Walters?"

"That's him all right," Lewt replied, speaking in a whisper.

Chad was less than a hundred yards away. The men on the porch waited, not speaking or moving.

Chad stopped at the front gate and for the first time looked toward the porch.

"Morning," he said cordially, nodding.

He dismounted and walked across the yard. His manner was that of an old family friend who had dropped by for a casual visit.

"Looks like we're going to get a rain," he said, glancing again at the sky.

"Stop where you're at!" Lance spat out the words. "What is it you want?"

Chad stopped; the pretense was over and he seemed to know it. When he spoke his voice was quiet and determined.

"I want to talk to you."

"About what?"

"Two or three things," Chad said. "First, I want to say I'm sorry about the dance. I shouldn't have come without an invitation."

"That's done with and forgot about," Lance said.

For the first time, Chad looked at Emma; she met his glance and could not turn away.

"Is that all?" Lance growled.

Chad was still looking at Emma. With the fear and panic inside her, the terror that clutched at her heart, she smiled, answering the question his eyes were asking.

Slowly Chad turned back to Lance.

"No. There is something else. I came to ask your leave to call on Emma."

For what seemed an eternity old Lance simply stared at the man before him, his face an unreadable mask. Then in a husky, strained whisper he said, "Ben . . . get my gun."

Suddenly Emma opened the door and walked out on the porch; the panic, the fear, the terror were gone now.

"No, papa. He's come asking your permission to call on me . . . you can't expect more of him than that."

"The gun, Ben! Get the gun!"

Ben brushed past her and went into the house; she walked across to where Lance was standing.

"All right, papa. If you kill him, you'll have to kill me too."

The old man turned slowly, his face unbelieving. For the first time in her life she saw hurt in his eyes; a pathetic, bewildered look that touched her heart.

"Papa . . ."

Then the face twisted and only hatred remained. "Shut up!" he shouted. "And get in the house!"

Her voice now was perfectly calm. "No, papa, I won't go. Please try to understand . . . I love him. What has he ever done to you? What reason have you got to hate him? Please, papa, try to understand . . . more than anything else I want you to say it's all right."

"It ain't all right!" he screamed, his voice rising to a shrill pitch. "It ain't all right, do you hear me! You've brought disgrace on me and your dead mammy . . . Mase knew what was going on, he told me and I wouldn't believe it . . . my own daughter! Well, you ain't no daughter of mine . . . hear what I say, you ain't no daughter of mine!"

Emma looked at him, and understood, and suddenly loved him as she had never loved him before.

"Papa, I love him. I couldn't stop loving him even if I wanted to. Don't you understand . . ."

88

"Hussy! That's what you are . . . a dirty little hussy!"

"I'm sorry, papa," she said. "I'm really very sorry." She turned and looked at Chad. "If you want me, I'll go with you now," she said.

She walked down the steps and put her hand in his; together they walked across the yard and up the road toward Carley's Crossing, Chad leading the mare behind them.

Emma looked back once. Her father and brothers were still standing on the front porch, Ben holding the rifle in the crook of his arm; she began to cry.

Beside her Chad said softly, "Do you want to go back?"

"No," she said. "I'm crying for papa. I came because I want to be with you . . . nothing will ever change that." For a moment they walked in silence; then she said, "I know it was a shameless thing I did. Of course, you don't have to marry me . . . I just didn't know what else to do."

He stopped and took her by the shoulders, turning her toward him. "I want to marry you, Emma . . . now, today. You're the only woman I've ever loved . . . you're the only woman I ever will."

As they walked on, the first scattered drops of rain began to fall.

Will Kelly sat at his desk in the land office and looked out on the rain-washed street. The water still gurgled in muddy rivulets along the drain ditches, but the dark clouds were breaking above the mountain ranges to the north and the sky overhead was lifting. As he watched, the refracted rays of the sun broke through, casting a pale, apple-yellow hue over the wet earth.

Will turned back to the papers that littered his desk, oddly at peace with the moment. The work should have been done earlier, but with the first drops of rain he had turned aside and sat for almost an hour, watching the steady fall, smelling the sharp, pungent odor of the rain on dry fields and dusty roads.

The sun had gone down and the first long shadows of dusk were falling over the town when he replaced the papers in their folders and stood up. He was filing the deeds away in the metal cabinet behind the stove when he heard footsteps on the porch; when he turned, an instant later, Chad and Emma were standing beside the desk; Chad was, as usual, grave and somber, but Emma's expression was almost elfish, something between a smile and a secret.

"Well . . ." Will said, wholly at a loss for words. "How are things in the basin? . . ."

Emma smiled and glanced up at Chad. "Fine," she said. "Things in the basin are just fine."

Will closed the file and walked back to the desk; something was in the wind, that was plain. Still, it was not his business to ask. . . .

"Have a chair," he said. "I take it this is a social call. . . ."

Emma laughed. "I guess you could call it that."

Will noticed that Chad held her chair while she sat down; then he remained standing beside her. Will was not sure but he thought there was a curious possessiveness in Chad's manner.

For several seconds no one spoke; then Emma said, "Will, we've come to get married."

Remembering the moment later, it seemed odd to Will that he should have been so completely floored by the remark. The night before, riding back from the dance, he had thought about them, had told himself that they were already in love. Now he could only blink, his mind refusing to believe the words.

Chad smiled. "Aren't you going to congratulate us?"

Emma Boone and Chad Walters; marriage . . . the heartache, the pain, the bloodshed—did they know about that? Of course they did, but those things didn't matter, not now. Will smiled at them, feeling a sudden warmth inside him.

"Congratulations," he said. "I think it's wonderful . . . it just took me a minute to get used to the idea." He was still thinking of old Lance, of all the gumbo rats. "When will the big event come off?" he asked, trying to sound jovial.

"Now," Emma said. "That's why we're here. We don't even know a preacher."

"Well, I'm a Baptist," Will replied. "Brother Hemstead

is the preacher down there . . . I'm sure he'll be glad to perform the ceremony. . . ."

Emma glanced up at Chad.

"We'd like for you to be best man," he said.

"I'd be honored."

Emma said, "We want you to know that papa didn't give his permission. If you'd rather not go with us, we'll understand."

"Does he know?" Will asked.

"Yes, he knows," Emma said. "Chad came to the house this morning . . . there was a scene. I left with Chad . . . we waited at his house until the rain let up. After what happened, I can never go home again."

"No," Will said. "Lance won't forget . . . or forgive you. That's one idea you'll have to get used to." He stood up. "But that's your problem, and you'll have to meet it your own way. For my part, I'm glad you're getting married. Whatever happens in the basin, I think you're doing the right thing." He went to the rack in the corner and got his hat; who can say what's right? he thought; but that's what I feel. It seems right to me. "I'm ready if you are," he said.

Outside Chad helped Emma up to the seat of the wagon; Will went to the shed behind the land office and returned a moment later riding Dandy. "It's only four blocks," he said. "The Reverend's at home . . . I saw him an hour ago."

It was almost dark when they reached the front gate of the parsonage, a small frame building almost buried in a grove of trees; the pale yellow glow of a lamp shone through the window.

Will waited while Chad helped Emma down, then together they walked up the path to the front door. In answer to Will's knock, a thin, wizened little lady appeared.

"Yes?" she said, squinting against the gloom.

"It's Will Kelly, Mrs. Hemstead . . . is the Reverend here?"

"Oh, Will . . . yes, he's here. Come in."

Will held the door for Emma and Chad, then followed them into the living room.

"Mrs. Hemstead, this is Miss Emma Boone and Mr. Chad Walters . . . they want to get married."

A thin, timorous smile came over Mrs. Hemstead's features, giving a curious warmth to her face; she looked at Chad and Emma. "The marriage ceremony never grows old for me," she said softly. "Every time it's new and different. I'll get Reverend Hemstead. . . ."

She disappeared down a darkened hallway and reappeared a moment later with her husband, a tall, gaunt man with deepset, inquiring eyes.

"Good evening, Will," he said, nodding; then he turned to Chad and Emma. "Chad Walters and Emma Boone . . . and you want to get married." He smiled. "I've married hundreds of young people," he said. "I think it is the function of my office that I enjoy most. I don't know you, do I?"

"No sir," Emma said. "We're from the river bottom."

"Are you members of a church?"

"No sir."

"Well, I don't think that's as important as some of us try to make it sound," Reverend Hemstead said. "The church isn't God . . . God is in the hearts of men." He turned to his wife. "Will you get me the Bible, dear?"

Mrs. Hemstead went to a table in the corner and brought him the huge family Bible; he took it from her and stood for a moment looking down at it, his fingers moving across the worn leather binding. "May this book sanctify this marriage," he said.

He looked at Chad and Emma. "You may take her hand," he said, smiling.

And in the thin, yellow glow of the flickering lamp the ceremony began. . . .

"Dearly Beloved, we are gathered here . . ."

Emma looked at Chad and thought: *who is this dark, strange man that I love so much, that I give myself to now so utterly and completely, leaving behind me all that I know and am . . .*

"Do you take this woman . . ."

"I do."

What is he really like, will I ever know; but now I must walk by his side and feel with his heart and see with his eyes; will he always love me as he loves me now . . .

"Do you take this man . . ."

"I do."

I know only that I am where I belong, now and forever; I know only that for me there is no other way.

"I now pronounce you man and wife. . . ."

Chad turned toward her and she lifted up her face, felt his lips warm against her own.

"I hope you'll be very happy," Reverend Hemstead said. Mrs. Hemstead took her hands and smiled and said, "Be happy, my dear"; and Will Kelly kissed her on the cheek and said nothing.

When Chad tried to pay Reverend Hemstead for performing the ceremony, he shook his head. "I never charge for the wedding service," he said. "It is a special privilege for me."

Reverend Hemstead and his wife accompanied them to the front gate and waited while Chad helped Emma up to the seat.

"Thank you . . . all of you," Chad said; then he pulled the mules around and drove off up the dark street.

"I like those people," Reverend Hemstead said.

"Yes," Will replied. "I like them too."

"He's Delton Walters' son."

"Yes."

"Then it will be hard for them, living in the basin."

"I'm afraid so. I hope they're strong enough to face it."

Reverend Hemstead smiled. "I have a feeling they are," he said.

The sky had cleared and the moon bathed the basin in a pure silvery light as Chad and Emma crossed the meadow land below the house. The crickets croaked wildly in the damp grass along the way; the wheels creaked noisily.

The ride from Gipson had seemed long and after a time both Chad and Emma had given up the pretense of light conversation. Now Emma thought of her father and brothers;

she no longer really cared what they thought about her marriage to Chad, nor was she saddened by the thought that she would never again be welcome in her father's house. Her only thought now was the fearful realization that they were men capable of a lasting vengeance; perhaps in time they could have learned to live with the idea that the basin was not theirs alone, but they would never forget that Chad had married Lance Boone's daughter.

She looked at Chad and he turned to her and smiled; she put her arm through his and leaned against him, thinking, his smile can settle so many things.

A moment later he stopped the wagon in front of the house. He stepped down and held up his hands to her, swinging her to the ground. Together they walked up the pathway to the front porch; she waited while he went inside and lit a lamp, then she followed him into the living room. He stood perfectly still, watching her. She wanted to say something but could think of nothing to say. A long moment of silence passed.

At last he said, "I'll unhitch the mules."

"All right."

Still he didn't go.

"I won't be long."

"All right."

He smiled, then nodded almost formally and walked out.

Emma remained for several minutes, standing alone in the flickering lamplight. Her mind raced back, grasping for some perspective; nothing made much sense. It had all happened too suddenly; Chad's appearance that morning, the terrible words of her father, the long ride to Gipson, the warm pleasant room and the soft voice of the preacher. And now, alone in this house with a perfect stranger. Perhaps they should have waited . . . perhaps . . .

She walked across to the table by the window and sat down. Suddenly a shocking thought occurred to her. She had left all of her clothes at home! She had nothing to sleep in . . . on her wedding night! It was too much! I mustn't cry, she thought; I'm a grown married woman now, I mustn't be

94

silly. Then she thought of her own bed, the privacy of her room; she buried her face in her hands and wept.

Moments later she heard Chad's footsteps on the front porch; she wiped her eyes, turning her head away. He entered and stood for a long moment, watching her.

"Have you been crying?" he asked.

"No," she said. "I wasn't really crying . . . it's just that I haven't got anything to wear."

There was a long pause, then he said, "Oh."

She got up and walked to where he stood. Suddenly she wanted to laugh; he was like a small boy who had stumbled upon a forbidden subject. She put her arms around his waist; now he was not a stranger at all.

"I can get them for you," he said.

"I'll get them tomorrow . . . when papa and the boys are gone."

"Well . . . all right."

She put her head against his chest and could hear the beat of his heart.

"Sometimes I sleep . . . like that anyhow," she whispered.

She felt his arms move around her, drawing her close, felt the trembling in the pit of her stomach.

She stepped back, smoothing her dress with her hands. For a time neither of them spoke; then, without looking at him, she said, "It's late . . . I suppose we'd better go to bed."

He nodded. "Well . . . you go on," he said. "I want to straighten this room up . . . I'll be there in a minute."

She turned and walked up the hallway to the dark bedroom; she entered and closed the door behind her. She was no longer afraid or lonely; her heart beat wildly, the blood raced through her veins and pounded against the walls of her being. She undressed in the darkness and climbed into the four-postered bed; the moonlight through the window splashed palely across the covers. She listened to the footsteps in the living room . . . and waited.

After what seemed an eternity the footsteps moved down the hallway; outside the door they stopped and for a long moment there was only silence; then, muted and far away, the shrill cricket cry. The door opened and closed. She felt his presence in the room, heard above the pounding of her heart the scrape of a chair, his steps approaching the bed, his breathing.

She waited, trembling in the darkness, for the touch of his hand. Out of the shuddering, quivering silence, his voice was tender.

"Are you still afraid?"

"No."

She turned toward him, pressing her body against his, feeling the gaunt line of his body trembling too. His hand touched her thigh, drew back, returned. She whispered in the darkness, felt the weight of him, the bursting of her heart in total surrender, the shudder of the earth beneath her.

Later she lay quietly in his arms, spent and fulfilled; somewhere across the valley a night bird piped thinly.

She touched his face, tracing the line of his nose with her finger. "The preacher was a nice man," she said. "We must ask him out to dinner."

PART II

THE RIVER

As long as skies are blue, and fields
    are green,
Evening must usher night, night urge
    the morrow,
Month follow month with woe, and
    year wake year to sorrow.

—Percy Bysshe Shelley

CHAPTER 10

WINTER CAME EARLY that year. Through most of November the wind blew out of the north, shrieking across the valley in gusty blasts; then, early in December the first snow fell.

Emma saw it through the front window where she had seated herself in the light to mend a dress. It was Saturday; Chad was at the barn lot, saddling the mare for the weekly trip to town. Emma watched excitedly as the first slow flakes drifted down, then impulsively she tossed the dress aside and ran through the kitchen and out the back door.

Chad had finished saddling the mare and was leading her up the path toward the house. Seeing Emma racing down the lane toward him, he stopped.

"It's snowing!" she shouted, laughing as she ran.

He smiled and turned his face up to the falling flakes. Suddenly, seeing him there, Emma felt again the nameless barrier that stood between them; the frightening realization (which seemed always to come over her at such queer, unrelated moments) that she did not really know or understand him at all. She rushed on, feeling the wind against her face.

He caught her to him, falling back a step; then he laughed and pressed her head against his chest.

"If it gets any worse," he said, "I'll have to lock you up."

He put his hand under her chin and tried to lift her face toward him, but she pushed his hand away and held her face close against his shoulder. Then, crazily, she was crying.

Gently he held her away from him.

"Emma, what's wrong . . . what is it?"

She turned her head away; there was no explanation, that was the worst of it; she didn't *know* what was wrong.

"Nothing," she said. "You'll just have to get used to a

woman's ways." She tried to smile. "Maybe it's because I'm not going into Gipson with you. You mustn't pay any attention to me . . . it's silly. . . ."

"But I asked you to go with me," he said. "You were the one who decided to stay at home." He took a bandana from his pocket and wiped her face. "You run back to the house and get ready," he said, "I'll go back and hitch up the mules."

"No . . . I'm all right now. I'll have to stay by myself sometime . . . and I've got a thousand things to do here. I'm being an awful baby. You go on . . . and don't worry about me."

She looked at him and knew that he was not convinced. She was furious with herself; somehow she had failed to measure up again. Now, standing beside him, her tears seemed so unreasonable.

"But it is snowing," she said. And then they both laughed.

She walked with him to the front gate and waited while he mounted.

"Sure you're all right?" he asked.

"Never better. Don't forget to go by Will Kelly's. Tell him we're expecting him for dinner next week."

"I'll remember." Still he sat, looking down at her.

"I'm fine," she said. "And thoroughly ashamed of myself. Now have a good time . . . and don't worry."

"All right," he replied, turning up his coat collar. "I'll be back by noon."

"Don't worry . . . visit awhile with Will."

She watched him swing the mare around and ride off down the rise. Crossing the meadow strip, he turned back and waved.

Emma returned to the house and sat down in the chair by the window; she picked up the dress she had been mending, sat for a moment looking at it, then dropped it on the floor. She turned to the window; the flakes were falling faster now and a thin layer of snow covered the ground.

Again the strange sense of melancholy came over her, the persistent nameless sense of being utterly alone. Since her marriage to Chad she had never stayed alone for more than two or three hours at a time. When the weather was nice she even went with him to the fields, sitting nearby while he cleared land or mended a fence. Her gumbo upbringing told her that this was childish, if not downright improper. Except on special occasions, gumbo women were expected to remain at home, doing the work that befitted their station. She remembered something Mrs. Griffeth used to say: "A man's got to run on a long leash, same as a dog; try to take away his freedom and he's sure to wander." And Mrs. Griffeth meant more than the freedom to fish along the river or gab at the general store.

But Chad was not a gumbo rat; nor was she. He seemed genuinely pleased to have her with him; and for her that was enough.

In spite of herself, Emma often thought of her family; at time the desire to see them was so strong that she could think of nothing else. Since Chad still bought supplies in Gipson, there was no occasion for them to go near Carley's Crossing; since her marriage she had not so much as seen any of her people. As a rule, she was perfectly willing to accept this fact, for she had known that the gumbo rats would not forgive her until her father did; and she had known her father too well to expect a change of heart. But, the fact remained that she missed them more than she had thought possible; and there were times when Chad was not enough.

She did not know how long she had been sitting at the window when she saw a horseman dimly outlined through the falling snow. The ground now was covered and the wind had risen, whipping the flakes into drifts along the fence row. She leaned closer to the window, rubbing away the frost; the rider now was approaching the rise, leaning forward against the thrust of the wind, his hat pulled low across his face. Emma went to the front door and opened it. The rider topped the rise and stopped at the gate. It was not until he was dismounting that she recognized him—it was Mase! Her heart missed a beat; something was wrong or he wouldn't have come. Mase ran across the yard and up the front steps; then he saw her and stopped.

For a moment neither of them spoke; then Emma said, "Mase . . . is anything wrong?"

"No . . . I just dropped by to see how you're getting along."

Suddenly, relieved, Emma held out her hands to him; an affection for Mase she had never known before welled up inside her.

"You'll never know how glad I am to see you," she said. "Come in out of the weather . . . I was afraid something had happened to papa."

He took her hands and she led him into the living room. Awkwardly he took off his hat and stood holding it behind him; even that gesture touched Emma.

"Here, let me have your hat. . . ."

"I'll just hold it," he said. "I can't stay long." He paused a moment, then said again, "I just dropped by to see how you're getting along."

"I'm getting along fine, Mase," Emma said. "Chad's gone into Gipson . . . this is the first time I've stayed alone. You couldn't have come at a better time. I guess I was feeling a little sorry for myself."

"I passed him on the road . . . your husband, I mean . . . I went to town early, trying to beat the weather. . . ."

For a full minute they said nothing. Mase stared into the flames leaping up from the fireplace; Emma watched him, wanting him to talk, to tell her everything.

Finally she said, "How's papa . . . and Ben and Lewt . . . and you?"

"Papa's fine," he said, looking down at his hat. "Ben and Lewt, too. Lewt got in a fight with Ray Hill last week, got cut up a little, but he ain't hurt." Suddenly he glanced up and smiled. "I guess I didn't tell you," he said. "I'm getting married next month . . . me and Lucy."

She walked to where he stood and put her hand on his arm.

"You and Lucy? Married? Mase, that's wonderful . . . and high time too."

Mase looked away, flushing slightly. "That's what Lucy said."

Finally Mase sat down and, as the awkwardness passed away, began to talk. He told her about the death of the Brendon baby and about the plans they were making for the New Year's dance and about the marriages and births and love affairs in the basin. Emma listened eagerly, waiting for him to speak of their father; but he didn't.

After a time another silence fell between them; then Emma said quietly, "Mase, how does papa feel now . . . about me?"

For a long while Mase stared down at the palms of his hands, his face hard. Finally he said, "He ain't forgive you . . . and he won't. He just don't talk about it one way or another. Once, at the table, Ben slipped and mentioned your name. Papa didn't rant . . . he just got up and walked off."

"And Lewt . . . Ben?"

"Them too. Lewt worst of all."

For a moment they sat silently; the crackle of the fire filled the room; the wind outside shook the windows and whined away across the valley.

"And you, Mase . . . do you still hate me too?"

He rubbed the palms of his hands together and said nothing; she was sorry she had asked; it was unfair to him.

"I shouldn't have asked that," she said. "You came to see me, that's enough."

"I don't hate you," Mase said, the words hard for him. "I still don't know how come you to do it . . . but now it's done and over with. I don't see where they's anything to be gained by making trouble." He glanced up at her, then away. "Anyhow, I don't hate you."

She blinked back the tears; it was hard enough for him without her crying. "I'm glad you don't hate me," she said. "I miss all of you very much."

Mase turned and looked directly at her. "You happy?" he asked.

"Yes, Mase . . . I'm happy. Chad is good to me; I think he's the kindest man I've ever known. Sometimes, even now, he's like a stranger, but that's because I don't understand him yet. It's like nothing ever touches him; maybe I want him to need me more than he does." She saw that her words were embarrassing Mase, that he did not understand; then she realized that she was trying to say something that she did not really understand herself. "But I am happy," she said. "And I'm never lonely when he's with me. . . ."

"Well, I reckon you know what you want," Mase said, getting up. "I'd better get on back to the house . . . papa'll be wondering what come of me."

Emma did not ask him to stay longer; it was enough that he had come, enough that one of her family had forgiven her; or almost.

She walked with him to the door. "You'll come again, won't you?"

"Sure . . . I'll be back." He stopped on the porch and turned to face her. "You take care of yourself," he said.

"I will . . . and I'm awfully happy about you and Lucy. I wish I could come to the wedding."

"Well . . ."

"I know," Emma said. "Anyhow I'll be thinking of you."

"That'll be fine. . . ."

Emma started to speak, but the words caught in her throat. Over Mase's shoulder, through the gusty swirls of snow, she saw Chad, not fifty yards from the front gate. She put her hand on Mase's arm.

"Mase," she said quietly. "There's Chad . . . please don't make a scene."

For an instant Mase stood perfectly still, tense and expectant; then, slowly, he turned. Chad stopped at the gate; seeing Mase and Emma, he leaned forward in the saddle, holding his hand up against the falling snow. Then he swung down, took the bag of groceries from behind the saddle and walked across the yard toward them.

Neither Mase nor Emma moved.

Chad smiled, holding out his hand. "Hello, Mase. Glad to see you." His manner was relaxed; the manner of an old friend.

Mase took a step forward; his hand moved up, then fell

back to his side. Chad waited. Mase's hand moved up again, slowly, taking Chad's.

"I just came by to say hello to Emma," he said.

"I'm glad you did," Chad replied. "She misses her family." He put his hand on Mase's shoulder. "Come in and tell me all the Carley's Crossing news. . . ."

"I'd better get on back. . . ."

"We're always glad to see you . . . you know that. Why don't you come up soon and take a meal with us."

Mase nodded. "Well . . . all right. . . . Thanks." He stood a moment longer, nodding; then he turned and walked down the steps.

They waited on the porch until he had mounted and ridden off down the rise. Then Chad leaned down and kissed Emma on the forehead. "It was good of Mase to come," he said. "Is everything all right in the basin?"

She smiled up at him. "Yes. Everything's fine. How was your trip?"

"About the same. I'll tell you about it later." He put his arm around her. "Come on inside, I brought you some dress material."

Chad unpacked the groceries, then took the mare to the barn and unsaddled her. When he returned to the house Emma was cooking dinner, so he sat at the table and told her about his trip to Gipson; he had seen Mr. Shepard and they were "pretty close together" on a cow he'd been trying to buy; Will Kelly was well and had promised to ride down early next week and have supper with them; he had seen Ben at a distance but "didn't get close enough to say hello." Emma laughed at his story about the cow and could not help smiling when he spoke so casually of Ben.

Neither of them mentioned Mase's visit again until they were sitting at the table; they ate in silence for a time, then Chad glanced up.

"Did Mase say anything about your father?"

"Yes. He's fine," Emma replied, keeping her eyes on her plate.

Chad watched her.

"Maybe you should pay him a visit."

"No . . . I can't do that."

She knew that he was watching her but she could not meet his eyes.

"Well, I guess you know what's best," he said.

She put down her fork and looked up. "Mase says he just doesn't talk about us. I know papa . . . he's put me out of his mind. Even if the anger's gone, the hurt's still there. He'll never forgive us . . . that's the way papa is."

For some time Chad sat looking at her, running his finger thoughtfully along his cheek. "I know how you feel about your family," he said. "I know how much they meant to you . . . how much they still mean. Maybe if you went to see them . . . men can't hold a grudge forever. . . ."

"Papa can," Emma said. "If he wants to see me, he can let me know."

The fire in the cookstove popped in the stillness; Emma got up and poured more coffee.

When she glanced at Chad, there was, she thought, a strange sadness in his face. She put the coffee pot back on the stove and walked to him. He looked up at her; she leaned down and kissed him hard on the mouth.

"It doesn't matter about papa or the boys or anybody else," she said. "I'm where I want to be."

He pulled her down on his lap and she felt his arms around her and heard the howling wind.

CHAPTER 11

EMMA KNEW BY the middle of January that she was pregnant. Her first reaction was one of complete happiness; like all the gumbo women, the maternal instinct was a powerful and dominating force in her life; it was above all else the fulfillment of womanhood and the mark of a good wife. Her first impulse was to tell Chad; but this, she discovered, was not an easy thing to do. In the first place, women in the gumbo society had a curious sense of decency about such matters, and while pregnancy seemed to them a healthy and consummate function of womankind, they looked upon any discussion of that condition as unnecessary and even indelicate. This was particularly true where the husbands were concerned; not only did the gumbo women feel that it was a breach of decency to inform their husbands that they were approaching motherhood, but they actually took pains to keep it a secret as long as possible. It remained for the husband to detect by visible signs the condition of his wife, and although this discovery always led to a good deal of boasting and banter at the general store, it seldom led to an open discussion between the parents to be.

Emma had always felt that this tacit understanding was prudish and a little ridiculous; but now she found herself unable to go beyond it. She tried on several occasions to tell Chad about her condition, but somehow she could never bring herself to do so.

After two dreary months of sleet and snow, the weather cleared; by the end of February, the days were bright and lovely. One cold, clear morning, while they were eating breakfast, Chad said, "I've got to go into Carley's Crossing this morning . . . would you like to come with me?"

This startling announcement left Emma for a moment speechless. Since their marriage Chad had not left the house, except for the weekly trips to Gipson for supplies; now his casual statement that he was going to the basin village was to say the least surprising; perhaps she had misunderstood him.

"Carley's Crossing?"

He nodded. "The mare's lame. I'm going down to see if Jim Wilks will put shoes on her."

"But . . . can't you take her to Gipson?" Emma asked.

"I guess I could," he replied calmly, still refusing to make an issue of it. "But the trip would be hard on her. There's no point in going into Gipson if I can get it done here."

For a moment Emma said nothing; then she said, "I think you'd better go to Gipson . . . why look for trouble?"

He looked at her, as if he expected her to say more; but she could think of nothing else to say.

"I don't want trouble with the people down at Carley's Crossing," he said. "And if there is trouble, they'll start it. But I can't run off to Gipson everytime I need something." He paused a moment, then added, "It's got to come sooner or later . . . it might as well be now."

"What if Jim refuses to do it . . . what then?"

He smiled. "Then I'll take her to Gipson." He picked up his fork and began to eat. "I think maybe Wilks will do it," he said. "I've seen him two or three times in town . . . once we talked awhile. Anyhow, I'll ask him."

Emma sat very still, her lips pressed tightly together. She was both frightened and angry. A sense of helplessness came over her; there was in Chad's manner a faint sense of authority that she had not seen before.

At last she said evenly, "I don't want you to go to Carley's Crossing."

He glanced up, his face pleasant and unruffled. "I guess I'll have to decide about that," he said, and continued eating.

Emma did not move or eat another bite throughout the meal.

Finally Chad pushed back his plate. "I'll be back in a little while," he said, rising.

"All right," she forced herself to say as calmly as possible. "Be careful."

"I will . . . don't worry." And he was gone.

She sat at the table until he had left the house, then she went to the living room and waited until he came across the hill, leading the lame mare behind him. She watched as he disappeared down the rise, fighting the impulse to run after him; for a grown man he could be an awful fool; and he still didn't know the gumbo rats. Perhaps she should have told him about the baby then; perhaps that would have stopped him.

She went back to the kitchen and washed the dishes, then returned to the front window; she sat down, folded her hands in her lap, and waited.

Four men were sitting on the bench at the general store that morning; one of them was Lewt Boone, and it was Lewt who first saw Chad leading the lame mare into Carley's Crossing. Because he had waited for that moment, because he had known it would come and had planned his actions, he was perfectly calm.

Beside him Such Farnsworth said, in a half whisper, "Well, I'll be. . . !"

One of the other men said something, but Lewt was not listening; he was watching Chad, his eyes hard. He had thought about this day a thousand times; it was important to do exactly the right thing. Suddenly he stood up and spoke to Such. The two men went inside the general store. The men seated on the bench glanced at each other but said nothing. A moment later Lewt and Such returned. Such sat back down on the bench; Lewt remained standing.

Chad was now less than fifty yards below the general store. He walked directly in the middle of the street, looking neither to the right nor the left. None of the men on the porch of the general store moved. Chad walked past them, then turned across the street toward the blacksmith shop. Jim Wilks, a huge, barrel-chested man, was shoeing the rear foot of a mule. Chad spoke to him; he looked up and listened for a moment, then let the hoof of the mule slip from his hands and stood up. For a time the two men spoke together. Finally Wilks nodded his head and Chad tied the mare to a corner post of the outer shed. Wilks turned back to his work, slapped the mule on the leg with his rasp, then lifted the hoof, sliding it cautiously across his knee. He spoke again to Chad; Chad sat down on an upturned nail keg nearby and took a sack of tobacco from his shirt pocket. Then, for the first time, he glanced at the men on the porch of the general store. His eyes watched them for a long moment; he turned away, rolled a cigarette, lit it; he said something to Wilks who nodded.

On the porch of the general store Lewt Boone spoke to Such. "Give me two or three minutes," he said; then he walked slowly down the front steps. Behind him the three men watched, their faces tense and expectant. At the bottom of the steps Lewt paused for an instant; he rubbed the palms of his hands along his trouser legs; then he hooked his thumbs in his belt and walked slowly across the street toward the blacksmith shop.

Chad saw him coming and waited.

Lewt stopped beside Wilks. Wilks looked up, glanced across the street toward the general store, then nodded and went back to work. Lewt watched him carefully. He had not once glanced at Chad. The mule moved suddenly, yanking at his rear foot; Wilks held the hoof tightly and cursed the animal. The mule grew quiet and Wilks continued smoothing the hoof surface, moving the rasp back and forth with heavy even motions.

"Bad 'un?" Lewt asked.

"Just contrary," Wilks answered without looking up. "Just mule. You never know what they'll do next."

Suddenly, almost casually, Lewt turned toward Chad. The two men measured each other in the long moment that followed. Lewt smiled, a mean, humorless expression. He turned away and walked slowly over to where the mare was tied. He walked around her, eyeing her speculatively like a livestock judge. Without looking around, he said, "Whose horse is this, Jim?"

Wilks glanced at Chad, then bent over his work again. "That fellar's," he said.

Lewt turned, a look of mock surprise on his face; he looked directly at Chad. "You the fellar he's talking about?"

"That's right."

"Funny thing," Lewt said. "This looks a lot like a mare that was stoled from me a month ago." His words were evenly spaced, his tone unmistakable.

Chad smiled but it was a movement of his features rather than the expression of an attitude.

"I hope you find her," he said.

Lewt's glance moved across to Wilks, then back again. "Might be I've found her already," he said. "Might be this is her."

Wilks let the mule's hoof drop to the ground and stood up, watching the two men. The smile now seemed a permanent feature of Chad's face; he watched Lewt.

"Are you telling me . . . or asking me?"

"I'm just saying this looks like my horse," Lewt replied. "What do you think, Such?"

Neither Chad nor Wilks had seen Such Farnsworth approach; he stood now ten or twelve feet away.

"I'd say that's your horse all right," he said. "I'd say there ain't no doubt about it."

Chad glanced around at Such; for an instant the smile on his face changed and he seemed to be genuinely amused. "Hello, Farnsworth," he said. Then he turned back to Lewt. "You're a funny man, Lewt," he said. "It looks to me like you're always trying too hard. If you're looking for trouble why don't you say so. What is it you're after?"

"I don't want nothing . . . except what's mine," Lewt replied; he was no longer smiling; he glanced at Such. "I reckon I'll just take this mare with me when I go."

Chad dropped his cigarette; stepped on it; stood up.

"Lewt, let's get one thing straight. You won't take anything that's mine . . . now or any other time. I've seen a hundred men like you in my life, and they're all the same . . . gutless."

111

A deep flush came over Lewt's features; he licked his lips; his hands clinched and unclinched spasmodically. For a long moment he stood without moving. Then he lunged.

Chad's fist moved less than six inches but it caught Lewt full in the stomach. Lewt groaned and his hands went instinctively to his belly; he saw the next blow coming and ducked away, but the chopping left hand caught him on the side of the head, spinning him half around; he breathed deeply for air that would not come, falling away, his hand groping along the ground for a singletree he had seen there before the fight began. Chad too saw the movement and dived; the weight of him carried Lewt backward and the two men fell, kicking up a cloud of dust. Chad grabbed for the singletree in Lewt's hand; at that moment the heavy fist of Such Farnsworth struck him in the back of the head; dazed, he felt his fingers clutch the singletree; he jerked it free of Lewt's grip and instinctively ducked away as Such swung again; Chad scrambled to his feet, seeing the two men through a blur; he shook his head to clear it and saw them move forward; the singletree moved in a blinding arc, catching Such across the face; he fell backwards, blood spouting from his nose and mouth, and lay still in the dust. Still clutching the piece of wood, Chad felt Lewt's fist against his mouth; he fell back across a water tank, throwing his hands up against Lewt's charge. Lewt fought savagely now; Chad felt the rain of blows against his face; somewhere in the fighting he lost the singletree; his hand shot out, striking against Lewt's jaw; he lowered it, feeling Lewt's neck in his grasp; with what strength he had left, he clamped down, hearing as if from a great distance Lewt's sudden gasp for breath; the blows against his face stopped; he squeezed harder; Lewt's hand clawed at his wrist; he swung with his free hand and felt the weight of his fist against Lewt's jaw; Lewt made a choking, gutteral sound; Chad struck again, releasing his hold on Lewt's neck; the blow spun Lewt to one side; he fell back, gasping and holding his neck, then he pitched forward, face down, in the dust.

Chad straightened up, swaying like a drunken man, breathing heavily. Lewt lay at his feet, coughing, staining the dust with blood; he tried to rise and fell again. Chad closed his eyes tightly; he shook his head and felt the salty taste of his own blood; he turned and saw Such still lying in the road, his leg twisted beneath him; beyond, Jim Wilks stood perfectly motionless, still clutching the rasp in his hand. For a moment the two men looked at each other.

"I'm sorry, Jim," Chad said. "I'm sorry it had to happen at your shop."

Wilks said nothing.

Chad walked across to the mare and untied her, he glanced back at the two men on the ground; Lewt had risen to one knee and was trying to stand; Such lay motionless where he had fallen.

Chad looked again at Wilks; then he walked away from the blacksmith shop and up the street, leading the lame mare behind him.

Emma saw him coming, saw the still lame mare, saw Chad's halting step. For a full minute she could not move; she felt the constriction in her throat and thought of the child; then, aloud, she said, "God help us . . ." and ran out the door and down the hill to meet him.

Chad saw her and stopped. Now she could see the bruises on his face, the clotted blood on his shirt, his torn trousers. She tried to speak but the words hung somewhere inside her.

"You were right," he said quietly. "They were waiting."

"What happened? . . ."

"I had a fight . . . with Lewt."

"Oh, Chad . . . why did you go? Why . . ."

"It would have happened sooner or later anyhow," he said. "I'm glad it's out in the open. Lewt isn't hurt . . . and neither am I." He looked away from her, toward the bluff. "He was after me, Emma . . . it was fight or run."

Now that it was over, now that he had talked about it, Emma was calm. A weariness came over her; it was an effort even to talk.

"All right," she said. "It wasn't your fault. Let's go home."

CHAPTER 12

THE DAYS FOLLOWING Chad's fight with Lewt were for Emma a nightmare of waiting. She had known Lewt—as a child, and later as a man—to nurse a grudge for months; his patience at such times was infinite, for he had no capacity to forgive or forget. His fight with Chad was more than a personal conflict; it somehow involved his prestige in the community, his reputation, tacitly acknowledged, as the toughest gumbo rat in the basin; the reputation meant much to him and he had been known to go to considerable lengths to preserve it.

Now Emma waited for him to act, and as each day passed uneventfully, the waiting became an agonizing and constant ordeal. Chad's manner during this time was both annoying and senseless. He had not again mentioned the fight, nor did he seem in the least concerned about its future consequences.

At the breakfast table one morning, after three days of anxiety and frustration, Emma could stand it no longer. She sat watching Chad eat, his face calm and placid. Finally he glanced up; she said nothing.

He smiled. "Anything wrong?"

"Yes. I've been thinking about Lewt," she said. "I'm worried . . . I can't even sleep any more."

"Oh, I wouldn't worry about it," he said in the kindly tone of an adult mildly admonishing a child.

She was furious. "Of course you wouldn't worry about it . . . you don't know Lewt," she snapped. "I do. He won't forget this. He's the laughing stock of Carley's Crossing. Lewt can't stand being laughed at. He'll get even, don't you understand that? One way or another, he'll get even. . . ."

"All right, maybe he will," Chad replied. "But worrying won't help any."

"Chad, don't be a fool," she said, desperate now. "I know how Lewt's mind works . . . he's mean. That's a terrible thing to say about your own brother, but it's true. Everytime you leave the house, I wait here, terrified, not knowing whether you'll be back. I can't stand much more of it. . . ."

Chad nodded. "I know what kind of a man Lewt is, Emma. I've known other men like him. And I know that he'll come looking for me . . . tomorrow, next week, sometime, he'll come. There's nothing I can do but wait . . . and try to be ready when he does."

Emma was filled with a sense of helplessness; talking to Chad was impossible; it wasn't *what* he said so much as the way he said it, that quiet, self-assured tone that always made any further discussion seem beside the point. Unable to eat, she sat staring down at her plate.

After a moment he looked at her again. "Emma, what do you want me to do?" he asked patiently.

"Nothing . . . I don't know." This too was a characteristic of her serious discussions with Chad; the inability to express the simplest idea. Finally she said, "I just want you to be careful."

"I will be."

And that was that. A moment later he got up, walked to where she sat and kissed her on the forehead; then he left the room. Walking out, he said, "Don't worry about it"; and she had to bite her lip to keep from screaming at him.

Emma washed the breakfast dishes and set the house in order, then went to the washbench in the back yard and began washing some clothes that she had put to soak the night before. The day was clear and fresh and unusually warm for February. Somewhere up the ridge she could hear the steady ring of Chad's ax and the sound was reassuring.

She had almost finished the washing and was hanging the last garments on the line when a voice behind her said, "Hello, Emma."

She spun around, pressing her hand against her mouth to

stifle the scream. Standing at the corner of the house was Will Kelly, his wrinkled brown face wreathed in a smile. Emma sat down weakly on the washbench and began to laugh.

"Will, I could shoot you," she said. "You scared me out of a year's growth."

Will walked across the yard to where she sat. "I believe it scared me worse than it did you," he said.

"Here, sit down," Emma said, making a place for him on the bench. "Don't pay any attention to me. I haven't been myself for two or three days." She watched Will closely, wondering if he had heard about Chad's fight with Lewt. He turned away, looking toward the bluff.

"That Chad working up there?"

"Yes. He's clearing land. I can call him."

"That's not necessary," Will said. "He'll be down for dinner before long. I'm in no hurry."

She said, "You know about his fight with Lewt?"

He nodded. "Yes. I've heard about it."

"That's why I'm so jumpy," she said. "For three days I've been waiting for something to happen. It isn't over, I know that . . . Lewt won't rest until he's settled it, one way or the other." She shook her head. "Chad doesn't help any. If I could share my feelings with him, if we could just talk about it, it wouldn't be so bad. . . ."

Will was looking at her questioningly.

"Emma, don't you know that Lewt has left the basin?"

"Left the basin?"

"Yes. He and Ben left Sunday night . . . for California."

Emma sat for a long while, thinking; she was relieved to learn that Lewt was no longer an immediate threat, but she was strangely saddened too.

At last she said, "Did they go to stay?"

"I don't think so," Will replied. "Lewt told Harry McFarland that they'd be back after the fruit harvest."

Emma sat looking at her hands, her face suddenly weary and empty; Will put his hand on her arm. "Lewt's been talking about California for a long time," he said quietly.

"He stopped by the land office Saturday night. I encouraged him to go. Time can make a lot of difference in the way a man thinks . . . maybe Lewt will see things differently when he comes back."

Suddenly Emma was talking to him, telling him the things that she could not tell Chad.

"It's my family, Will . . . their breaking up. Mase getting married, now Lewt and Ben leaving. I was the first to leave . . . and soon there won't be any of them left." She looked toward the bluff and heard the ring of Chad's ax. "I'm going to have a baby, Will . . . and none of them will be here to see it. When I was a little girl I used to think about the time when I'd have a baby . . . in those days they had parties to celebrate the birth of a child . . . sometimes they'd last three or four days . . . I remember people laughed and sang and made it seem like the most important thing in the world. Thinking about all that makes me a little sad."

"I'm glad you're going to have a baby," Will said. "You need children. But I think you've missed one very important point. It wasn't the singing and laughing that made having children such a big thing . . . it was something else, something you can't say with words." He took her hands and smiled. "You can't expect things to stay the way they were. Sometimes that's hardest of all . . . some people never learn that something changes every day. That evening you and Chad came to my office and told me you were planning to get married, I thought it was a fine idea. I still do, but later, when I'd had time to think about it, I saw a side of it that I hadn't seen at first. You and Chad are different kinds of people, you come from different backgrounds, different ways of thinking. Those things are important in a marriage. All your life you've had people to go to when you were worried or in trouble. The river folks are a sharing people and what's good or bad for one of them is good or bad for all. Chad grew up alone, living his life apart from the kind of family love that you'd had . . . whatever he knew of pain or happiness, he knew it alone. So he grew up with himself, learning to live without sharing. That's hard for most of us to understand . . . but it's the thing that makes him different from other men . . . and it's the thing that makes him strong."

For a long while Emma sat looking out across the valley. "I know," she said slowly. "I know you're right. But thanks for telling me . . . sometimes I forget."

He nodded and patted her hand.

"How does Chad feel about the baby?"

"I haven't told him," she said almost sheepishly. "You know how the river women are." She smiled. "I've been trying to catch him by the fireplace with his shoes off . . . seems like he's easier to talk to when he hasn't got his shoes on."

Will laughed. "Most men are," he said. "But I think you should tell him. I think it'll mean something to both of you."

"Yes . . . I think so too. I'll tell him tonight."

They were still seated on the washbench when Chad came down an hour later. He walked with long easy steps, the ax slung across his shoulder; seeing Will and Emma, he waved; and they waved back.

A moment later he came through the back gate, his dark face streaked with sweat. "Hello, Will," he said, holding out his hand. "We've been wondering where you were." He turned to Emma and kissed her lightly on the mouth; the gesture was for him perfectly natural, and as usual he performed it with a certain graciousness. Emma could not help thinking how really unlike the gumbo rats he was. She glanced at Will, caught his eye, and blushed.

"I haven't put a thing on to cook," she told Chad apologetically. "I've sat here talking to Will and let the time slip up on me."

"There's no hurry about dinner," he replied. "If you want to, you go on and I'll finish hanging these things out." This too, she thought, was the kind of patience and understanding that was wholly alien to the men she had known; the basin men would have thought it absurd; she briefly considered

118

kissing him again, but could not bring herself to do so in front of Will.

"All right," she said. "I'll hurry."

After she had gone, Chad walked to the clothes basket and took out a wet shirt, hanging it carefully on the line. Will watched him, smiling.

Without turning, Chad said, "Emma's lonely, isn't she?"

"Some . . . it's only natural."

"I suppose so."

"You grow up close to people, you're bound to miss them when they're gone."

"That's right."

For a time neither of them spoke; then Chad said, "Did she talk about it?"

"She mentioned it. I was telling her about Lewt . . . he left for California Sunday."

Chad turned and glanced at him, then he reached again into the clothes basket.

"I'm glad you told her," he said. "She's been worrying about it."

"Well, you can't blame her for that."

"Nope."

Chad hung out the last garment, then walked back to the washbench and sat down. He took a sack of Bull Durham from his pocket and rolled a cigarette; he lit it and sat for awhile looking across the valley.

"I've been thinking," he said at last. "It might be better if Emma and I left the basin."

Will pulled a weed from its husk and put it in the corner of his mouth; he wondered if Chad was asking for advice.

"Have you talked to Emma about it yet?"

"Not yet."

"Do you want my opinion?"

"Sure. That's why I mentioned it."

"It's my guess she'll be against it."

"It's Emma I'm thinking about."

"I know. But maybe you're not thinking straight."

"Maybe not."

For a moment Will sat silently, chewing the stem of grass. Then he said, "Emma's young . . . ten, twelve years younger than you are. Some ways she's like any other woman . . . other ways she's not. She's never been a gumbo woman, you know that. Emma's still got some growing up to do . . . but she's got enough sense to make it . . . and enough courage to. She wouldn't want to leave the basin unless she thought it was what you wanted." He glanced at Chad. "Is it?"

"No. I was thinking of her."

"Then I'd forget it," Will said. "Emma'll be all right . . . give her time."

There seemed to be nothing else to say; the two men sat quietly, sharing an understanding without words. They were still sitting under the tree when Emma called them to dinner.

As they walked toward the house, Chad said, "I guess you're right"; and Will could not help smiling.

That night Emma told Chad about the baby. She made the first attempt at the supper table. They had been eating for several minutes, during which time she had tried to find the right words—and enough courage—to make the announcement. At last, flushing slightly, she said, "Chad, I have something to tell you . . . something important."

He glanced up; then, as if detecting the serious note in her voice, he placed his fork carefully beside his plate and waited.

She couldn't go on; why did he always adopt that solemn-as-a-judge air?; why did he insist on making a formal hearing out of it?

At last she said, "Lewt's gone to California."

"Yes. Will told me."

"I'm glad he went. I think that's best . . . for everyone."

"I think so." He picked up his fork.

"I guess they'll be out there until after the fruit harvest," Emma said.

He nodded.

"Well, I feel better about it anyway." Then, to hide her confusion, she got up and poured more coffee.

She tried again later, when he was seated by the fireplace with his shoes off, but somehow it just didn't seem to be the right moment.

Finally, shortly after eight, she got up and took one of the lamps from the mantle.

"I'm going to bed," she said. "Are you coming?"

He nodded. "I'll be there in a minute," he replied, looking up at her; she smiled and turned away; somehow, even now, the moment of retiring imposed a curious restraint upon them.

She went down the hall to the bedroom; she blew out the lamp and undressed in the darkness, then climbed into bed. A few minutes later she heard his footsteps; the door opened and closed. He undressed and walked across to the bed; the springs squeaked beneath his weight.

She lay with her back to him, facing the wall; he moved once, then lay still.

"Chad?"

"Yes."

"I'm going to have a baby."

There was a long silence; she trembled, waiting for him to speak, wondering if she should have told him later.

At last he said, "Do you want a baby?"

"Of course I do."

He turned toward her; she felt his arms move around her, his face against her hair.

"Did you think I wouldn't want it?" she asked.

"I didn't know."

She smiled in the darkness.

"Bearing children is a part of the river woman's life," she said. "Papa used to say I was born a mother. Once when I was a little girl, six or seven years old, I heard someone say that you found babies in blackberry patches. The next morning, before daylight, I went down in the field looking for one. Papa found me later, a mile from the house, lost and brokenhearted because I hadn't found a baby. The next day he went to Gipson and brought me back a doll, almost as big as I was. I named her Millie and always brought her to the table and made Papa and the boys treat her like a member of the family. Then one day I left her on the front porch and the dogs tore her up; I gathered up all the pieces and took them to my room and cried over them for a week." She turned to Chad and pressed her face against his. "I'll be a good mother," she said. "I promise."

"I know you will."

There was another moment of silence.

"Chad . . . do you want the baby?"

He kissed her. "Yes, Emma, I want the baby. I knew a man one time, out west, who left his wife because she had a child. It was his child . . . he just didn't want it. I could never understand that . . . other ways he was a decent man. It's always seemed to me that children are the one thing that make sense in this world . . . the one thing a man leaves behind that he knows is right."

"This one is right," she said. "Because I love you . . . and because I want him so much."

He laughed. "Him?"

"Sure. The first five will be boys . . . just like their papa. Then maybe I'll have a girl or two . . . to keep me company in my old age."

He kissed her again. "All right," he said. "But if this one's a girl, I'll take her."

CHAPTER 13

EMMA SAT IN the shade of a sweetgum tree on the crest of a hill, watching Chad work in the newly cleared field below her. He moved back and forth across the rise in long easy strides, his arm moving tirelessly and rhythmically to the bag tied around his neck, then away in a sweeping motion as he cast the seed. He had meant to plant the newground in corn; but later, thinking about the mules and the extra cow he had recently bought, he decided to sow it in bluegrass and turn it to pasture.

Watching him, Emma felt a peace and contentment that she had not known since their marriage. Already big with child, having lived with the mystery of pregnancy and the magical stir of life within her, she moved through the days now with a kind of knowing serenity, at peace with the world and herself. She closed her eyes, hearing the thin murmur of insects and the faint rustle of leaves overhead; feeling the soft breeze against her face; smelling the opening earth and the greenness. These were good days; after a trying winter, longer and more severe than usual, spring had come suddenly, bursting over the land with new smells and forgotten sounds. Chad too, it seemed, had been waiting. He worked now from sunup until dark, sowing, planting and clearing more land. He is a good farmer, Emma thought; just as he is good at anything he turns his mind to. The gumbo rats would really look upon him as a freak now; he would make more on his hundred acres than they would make on the rest of the basin.

If Emma continued to think of her family, she thought of them with less bitterness and hopeless frustration. Mase had come to see her three or four times (always when Chad was away) and the news he brought was good news; they had heard from Lewt: he and Ben were working on a ranch in northern California and thought they might stay a year or so; her father was well: Mase and Lucy were living with him now and although he had never spoken of Emma, Mase thought that he was "getting soft," that he might forgive her if he could think of some way to do it without "backing down." In the dreamlike bliss of approaching motherhood, Emma was sure that in time things would work out.

Suddenly, startled, she opened her eyes. Chad was standing in front of her, the empty seed bag in his hand. He was smiling and she wondered how long he had been there.

"Hello," he said.

"You scared me," she replied, smiling back. "I was day-dreaming again."

He dropped the bag on the ground and sat down beside her. For a while neither of them spoke; Emma had learned to live with the silence, the unspoken thoughts. Will had been right, it was somehow a part of Chad's strength, the thing that set him off from other men.

"How do you feel?" Chad asked, without looking at her. It was his way of inquiring about her condition; she shook her head, at times he was so like a little boy.

"I never felt better in my life," she said. "I feel like the whole world belongs to me . . . and everybody in it must do as I say." She laughed. "I'm a princess and the basin is my kingdom."

Chad listened gravely, nodding his head when she had finished. He took a clod of dirt and crumbled it in his hand. "That's a pretty good way to feel," he said.

Emma watched him, laughing again.

"What can I make of you?" she said. She sat a moment, her head tilted to one side. "I know. As one of my subjects, I order you to talk without stopping for twenty days."

He glanced at her and smiled.

"Twenty days. All right," he said, standing up. "You wait

right here and I'll think of something to say while I'm sowing the rest of the field."

He refilled the seed bag and turned to go.

"Chad?"

"Yes."

"Are you happy . . . the way I am . . . about us . . . the baby . . . everything?"

He dropped the bag and walked back to where she sat. He knelt beside her and took her hands.

"When you're happy, I am," he said. "That's what happiness is to me."

She pressed her hands to his lips and thought: now I'm going to cry again.

Mase came again late that afternoon. Emma was in the kitchen getting supper; Chad had returned to the bluff to work. Emma saw Mase coming across the meadow strip and went to meet him, drying her hands on her apron. Later she remembered, or *thought* she remembered, that at that instant a strange sense of misgiving had come over her; although there was no reason for it, she had a feeling that Mase was not paying a social call. She waited for him on the front porch.

Mase closed the gate carefully behind him, then walked slowly across the yard.

"How's everybody?" he said, trying—a little too hard Emma thought—to be matter of fact.

"We're fine. Come in."

He followed her into the living room and sat down; she waited for him to speak, feeling sure now that there was a special reason for his visit.

Finally he said, "Chad working?"

"Yes. He's clearing land on the bluff." Mase sat looking down at the palms of his hands, scarcely listening. "He sowed bluegrass on the newground strip this morning," Emma went on, feeling somehow compelled to carry a conversation. "He wants to make a pasture for the cow and mules. . . ."

Mase nodded. "That's a good idea," he said, still looking down at his hands. "Folks around here don't plant pasture . . . should though . . . it's a good idea."

"How's everybody in Carley's Crossing?" Emma asked.

"Fine." He looked up and smiled. "I reckon it'll be a better place when I'm gone," he said.

"Gone? Where?"

"Me and Lucy . . . we're going to Tennessee."

Tennessee. It sounded like the other end of the earth. Lewt and Ben . . . now Mase. . . .

"But why, Mase? The basin is your home . . . it's where you belong."

"Well, we've been thinking about it a month or more," he said. "It started when I met this fellar in Gipson one Saturday . . . back in January, I reckon it was. He was just passing through on his way to a job in Tennessee. Working for the railroad out there. The way he told it, they pay mighty big wages . . . better'n a hundred dollars a month counting extra time. One thing led to another and finally he asked me if I would like to work for the same company he's with . . . said he'd drop me a card soon as he got there, if he could get me on. I never thought much about it at the time, but about a week ago I got this card from him, saying it was all set, come on out."

"And you've decided to go, is that it?" Emma asked, her tone faintly accusing.

"Well . . ." He glanced up at her, then down again at his hands. "That's a lot of money . . . more'n I'll make in the basin working the rest of my life. Lucy likes the idea. . . ."

"Lucy, huh?"

"It ain't only her. It's both of us . . . course, we haven't decided definitely yet, one way or another."

Emma knew that she was being unfair; considering her own betrayal, her treatment of Mase was tyrannical. Still, there *was* a difference; he was a man, the last one left at home; he was needed.

"And what about papa?"

Mase, she thought, had expected the question. "He'll be all right, Emma. Papa ain't old . . . he'll get along."

She tried hard to contain herself; hardest of all was her own sense of loss, her family at last disrupted, her hopes for a reconciliation gone. Unreasonably, she blamed Mase for all of it.

"All right," she said evenly. "If you're going, you're going. Nothing I can say will change your mind . . . I can see that."

"No. I don't think it will."

They sat a moment longer, wordless and miserable. Mase stood up.

"I'd better be getting back," he said; she did not move or look at him. "It ain't as bad as you make it sound," he said. "Papa says it's a good thing . . . it was him that told me to go. He'll be all right."

Emma nodded but said nothing.

At last he turned and walked out. She sat perfectly still, fighting back the tears. Stirred by strangely conflicting emotions, she wanted to run after Mase, to tell him that it was all right, that she understood; but somehow she could not bring herself to do it.

Finally she began to weep, softly, soundlessly. "Poor papa," she said, "poor papa. . . ."

She was sitting on the washbench in the back yard when Chad came home about sundown. He glanced at her, then went to the porch and hung up the ax; a moment later he returned.

She looked away from him.

"Is anything wrong?" he asked.

"No."

He sat down and began rolling a cigarette.

"Something is."

"Mase is leaving."

He put the cigarette in his mouth and lit it.

"Oh? Where's he going?"

"To Tennessee . . . he's going to stay. He won't be back."

Chad said nothing for a time, and his silence was somehow intimidating.

At last he said, "Is that so bad?"

"Of course it's bad," she replied, feeling a stir of annoyance. "Papa is alone now . . . there's no one left to take care of him."

"Well, you can't put that off on Mase. He's got a life of his own to live." He looked down at the palms of his hands. "Anyhow, your papa doesn't have to live alone. He can always come here if he wants to."

Slowly she turned and looked at him, a kind of wonder in her face.

"You mean that, don't you?"

He nodded. "He's welcome any time."

"After all they've done to you . . ."

"Emma, they haven't done anything to me. I always try to put myself in the other man's place . . . maybe in your papa's place, I'd have done the same thing. I guess he did what he had to do."

She put her arm through his and looked away from him, across the valley. "Chad, you're a strange man," she said. "It's not that you try to see things the right way . . . you just do. It's just the way you are."

She leaned her head against his shoulder and they sat silently for several minutes, sharing something beyond words.

"Maybe later," she said, "after Mase has gone . . . after papa's had time to think it out . . . maybe then he'll come and live with us." She looked up at him. "I hope so."

He smiled and nodded; then he stood up.

"Well, I'd better get the ax sharpened," he said. "Else I'll never get that land cleared."

CHAPTER 14

MASE AND LUCY left the basin the following week and their departure, it seemed, set off a chain of circumstances in the lives of Chad and Emma that ended with their first real tragedy. Even the weather played a conspiratorial role in their unhappiness. After the first spate of showers early that spring, the sky cleared and what became ultimately the worst drought the basin had ever witnessed began. By late June the crops were dying in the field and the earth, cracked and parched, was a wasteland, over-run with grasshoppers and insects. The river fell lower and lower and became at last a dismal trickle, giving off the odor of wood rot and dead fish.

For Emma, these elemental failures were simply fragmentary symbols in a larger pattern. She thought almost continually of her father, now living alone, and the thought persisted to a point of obsession. She told herself again and again that she should go to Carley's Crossing and talk with him; but this was a difficult step to take. She had seen him only once (on the street in Gipson not long after Mase had moved away), but when she tried to speak to him, he turned away and brushed passed her, leaving her deeply hurt and humiliated.

Now, heavy with child, which by her own calculations would arrive the last week in July, she was physically uncomfortable and temperamentally edgy. Without quite realizing it, she began to complain; of the heat, of the crop failure, of her discomfort. She commiserated about her condition and was sure that the child was "carried too low." Chad, his face hard and unyielding as he watched his corn blister and die, was as usual patient and understanding; but to Emma he seemed more a stranger than ever. Then, with a kind of sudden realization, she would see that he too was suffering, that his long hours of toil were dying under the sun, and she would find a strange comfort in the thought. For a time, the complaints would cease.

These were days of waiting, and at last the worst of it passed. Except for the heaviness inside her, she no longer suffered physically at all. And the child became in her mind an answer to the problem of her father. The baby will set everything right, she told herself; when the baby is born, papa will come and live with us here on the rise. She told Chad and he agreed; no man, he said, could resist a grandson.

And then, suddenly, the world fell apart. One Saturday early in July Chad went into Gipson to buy supplies. Emma tried for a time to work, but the heat was unbearable and the thought of being alone was depressing. At last she gave up and went to the front window and sat down. The glare of the sun hurt her eyes; her head began to ache; she went to the well porch and washed her face in cool water, which gave her temporary relief. Finally she decided to walk up the bluff; in the pine thicket along the ridge it was even hotter than it had been at the house; her head began to pound, her eyes ached from the glare; she stopped on a rocky ledge near the bluff and looked back. The house looked miles away; suddenly, she began to breathe heavily, gasping for air. She realized that she had walked too far; she thought of the child and a sense of panic came over her. She could not have been wrong about her time; but what if the child came early. She clutched at her throat, trying to breathe, stifling the impulse to scream. The sense of being utterly alone was terrifying. I'm going mad, she thought; here, alone, with no one to help me, I'm going mad. Curiously, the thought quietened her. She walked on a few feet and sat down beneath the shade of a tree. She breathed deeply; the child kicked in her belly, but there was no pain. I must be calm, she told herself, for the child's sake I must get a grip on myself. She rested for several minutes, then stood up.

There was a wave of dizziness, but it passed. Her head still ached, but less intensely. Slowly, she made her way down the ridge toward the house.

By the time she had reached home, her breathing was normal, her headache almost gone. The house seemed cool after the sunlight. She washed her face again, then went to the back room and stretched out on the bed. She closed her eyes and a strange detachment came over her. Between consciousness and sleep, she floated in a kind of dream world, distant and oddly peaceful; she was playing with Lewt on a sandy shoal along the river. He had made a dam in the sand and they were floating chips of wood in the puddle of water that had formed behind the dam. Then the raucous screech of a bird was coming from somewhere in the tree-tops and Lewt was not with her any more. She was standing alone in a tall forest and it was dark and the screech of the bird was not frightening but reassuring. She listened to the bird and began to cry; but she still was not frightened. She was crying for some other reason, but she did not know why. Then her father was holding her hand and they were walking along a dusty road, and when she looked up it was not her father but someone else she had never seen before . . . and then she was frightened. . . .

The dream-images shifted and changed, and at last they were gone and she slept deeply.

The sun was low against the western sky when Emma awoke. She awoke suddenly, with a start, and sat up in bed. She listened for some sound, but heard nothing; Chad should be back; she climbed out of bed and hurried to the kitchen; it was just as she left it. She ran to the front porch, her breath catching in her throat. She saw Chad, a speck across the valley, riding toward home. Relieved, she sat down on the steps to wait for him.

Watching him as he drew nearer she was struck by the sense of weariness that had come over him lately. He is awfully tired, she thought, and I haven't helped; if anything I've been a burden. I must try harder; I must be what he wants me to be.

131

A moment later Chad stopped at the front gate and dismounted. He tied the mare and walked to where she sat.

"I thought you'd got lost," she said, trying to make her voice cheerful.

She stood up and walked to meet him; then, for the first time, she noticed the grave, almost pained expression on his face. It was a look so strange that she stopped, waiting for him to speak.

For a moment he looked at her, saying nothing. Then he said, "Emma, your father's sick."

The words sounded jumbled and unrelated. When the sense of them came to her, she could think of nothing to say.

Chad went on. "It's the summer sickness . . . Will told me about it. He's been sick for a week or more. Will says his own people are afraid to go near him. . . ."

Emma opened her mouth to speak, but still no words came. She felt a tightness in her throat.

Chad walked to her and put his hand on her shoulder. "I'm going down there," he said. "I think it will be better if you don't go . . . because of the baby."

Unreasonably, the suggestion infuriated her. "Of course I'll go," she said. "He's my father."

"All right . . . I'll hook the mules to the wagon." He went back to the gate and led the mare to the barn.

Emma waited, her mind churning with foreboding possibilities. The summer sickness was a common ailment among the river people and its acute contagion invested it with an almost superstitious fear. Even the midwives refused to minister to those afflicted with the disease. It remained for the immediate members of the family to care for their own sick, although this obligation was more moral than scientific for there was no known treatment for summer sickness. A buckeye worn on a string around the neck or a mudpack mixed with the urine of a dog it was thought would curtail the contagious effects; but as for a cure, the midwives would simply shake their heads sadly, their eyes looking far-off and unknowing. The disease was always accompanied by high fever, its most pronounced symptom, and had the effect of wasting away the patient; in the end came delirium, and then, more often than not, death.

Thinking of these things, Emma's imagination condemned her a thousand times; her fears for her father and her own sense of guilt were a single emotion now, persisting against all reason.

When Chad returned in the wagon, she was leaning against the gate post, trembling as if she had been stricken with a chill.

Chad jumped down and put his arm around her. "I'll take you in the house," he said quietly. "I'll stay with you until you're better, then I'll go see about your father. . . ."

She pushed his hand away roughly. "I'm all right," she said. "Papa needs me . . . he's dying. . . ." Suddenly she stared up at him. "And I killed him!"

Chad said nothing for a long moment; then he said, "All right, we'll go together."

He helped her into the wagon and climbed up beside her. They drove down the rise toward Carley's Crossing.

It was almost dark when they reached her father's house. The house was pitch black when they creaked to a stop at the front gate. A hound dog ran from beneath the porch, baying ferociously. Chad spoke to the dog, who retreated into the shadows, still barking. Then he helped Emma down from the wagon. She clung to his hand as they walked up to the porch. He stopped at the steps. "You wait here," he said, softly, "I'll go on in."

"No," she said, clutching his hand. "We'll go together."

He led her up the steps and opened the front door. The rusty hinges squeaked loudly in the stillness. They went inside and she waited in the darkness while he reached for matches. The smell of sickness was strong in the air. He struck a match along his hip; it flared and went out. He struck another, holding it above his head; there was a candle on the mantle above the fireplace; he lit it, and it cast a pale, yellow glow over the room.

Emma stood where he had left her, her face strained and white in the thin light, her hands clenched at her sides.

133

He took up the candle. "Where's the bedroom?"

"Down there." She motioned with a slight nod of her head toward the hallway, her voice scarcely audible.

He walked down the hallway and she followed. The door at the end of the hall was slightly ajar, the smell was stronger as they approached it. Chad pushed the door open with his foot, then holding the candle before him, entered the room.

Emma gasped and turned away. Old Lance was lying on the bed fully dressed. The stench of the room was almost unbearable; he had apparently lain there for days without moving. Chad walked to the edge of the bed and was surprised to find that Lance was still alive; the eyes, black and sunken in the withered, wasted face, stared up at him; it was scarcely a face at all, the twisted corner of his mouth had hung down, giving him the bizarre, distorted look of a halloween mask. Only the eyes lived, and they had already taken on the glazed expression of night.

Emma stood at the doorway, her face in her hands; it was only with a great effort that she could keep from being sick. Behind her Chad said, "Go out back and draw a bucket of water . . . hurry!" She heard the words but did not understand them.

"Emma!" He spoke softly, but there was a sharpness in his voice that penetrated her numbed senses.

Moving with no conscious realization, she went automatically to the back porch, feeling her way across the darkened kitchen. She found the well bucket and drew water, which she poured into another bucket on the wash shelf. Then she went back through the kitchen to the hallway.

Chad met her at the door of the bedroom and took the water. "Get some clean linen," he said. His voice, sharp and commanding, startled her. The door closed in her face. She turned and went back up the hall to the closet where the sheets were kept.

When she returned Chad again opened the door and took the sheets. "I'll be through in a minute," he said. "Then you can come in." The door closed.

Emma leaned against the wall, weak and shaking. The

134

weight in her belly pressed down heavily and sharp pains tugged at her heart. Inside the room she could hear movements, a chair being scraped across the floor, the squeak of bedsprings, a window being raised. After what seemed an eternity Chad opened the door. "All right . . . you can come in now."

The wasted figure of her father lay now on a clean sheet; his clothing had been removed and the lower part of his body covered with the extra linen; the candle on the bedtable flickered in the breeze that blew through the open window. Emma stood transfixed, staring at the skeleton that had been her father. She suffered no conscious emotion at all, she simply stood and looked at him, shocked and motionless.

Chad brought her a chair, then taking her by the arm, forced her to sit down. He walked back to the bedtable and dipped a piece of clean sheet into the water bucket and placed the cool rag across her father's brow. Without looking at Emma he said, "There's nothing we can do for him now. . . ."

Emma spoke, the words coming not from her but from somewhere inside her. "Will he die?"

"I don't know."

Chad stood by the bedside, dipping the rag into the water from time to time, his gaunt figure casting a shadow on the wall. How long she sat in the chair watching him, Emma never knew. At no time did her father make a sound.

The minutes, the hours, slipped by. Emma lived through them in a state of grief so engulfing that it was not grief at all. Her emotions changed; she wept at one moment and there were no tears in her the next. There were long periods when her mind seemed to leave her body and she was dreaming again. Then, with a start, she would awaken and weep softly in the mysterious shadow of her grief.

Sometime later, through her drugged sensibilities, she heard Chad's voice. "Emma . . . Emma. . . ."

She opened her eyes; he was standing beside her. She glanced past him to the bed. Her father was gone. No! He was there, but the sheet that covered his body had been

135

drawn up over his face. She glanced at Chad, her eyes wild.

"He's dead," Chad said quietly.

Emma sat perfectly still, staring at the crumpled sheet on the bed. For an instant her mind cleared, grasping the events of the night in one terrible flash; then she began to scream, and through the dark recesses of her mind the thought came to her again that she was mad.

Chad held her; and unknown to her, shared her grief.

For several days after the death of her father, Emma was seriously ill. She remained in bed for almost a week, listless and apathetic, seemingly oblivious to all that went on around her. Later she remembered almost nothing that had happened during this time. Chad was there, of course, bathing her face, changing the bed linen, urging her in a soft, soothing voice to eat; but he was a presence rather than a human being, a sound, a movement, a sense of not being alone. There was someone else, too (it was Will Kelly she learned later), but for the most part they were days of darkness, of a gnawing sense of guilt that revolved around the death of her father; and of interminable dreams.

Sometime during the week Chad went back to the farm and buried old Lance, placing the grave in a grove of pawpaw trees near the river. It was not until several months later that Emma visited the spot. She went alone to the thicket and found the small stone that Chad had used to mark the grave; standing alone in the quiet grove, she thought not of her father but of Chad, remembering out of the dim stir of pain and torment, the tall, solemn figure standing by the bedside, casting a shadow against the wall.

Slowly Emma grew stronger; by the end of the week she was sitting up in bed. She was courteous to Chad, grateful in some compulsive, impersonal way, but she spoke to him as a stranger, as someone who was caring for her in this troubled time. Strangest of all, she scarcely thought of the child she would bear. As her time drew near, she lapsed into a state of melancholy, frequently accompanied by weeping; but the child, the bigness of her belly, seemed remote and improbable. She would gaze with something like curiosity at herself, rubbing her hands across her stomach wonderingly; then she would weep, for herself, for the guilt of her father.

Finally, one afternoon just before sundown, Chad entered the room. "Emma, there's someone here to see you," he said.

She turned toward him, her face placid and childlike. Then, behind him, she saw the stranger, a thin, slightly stooped little man with a shiny bald head. He was carrying a black case. . . .

"This is Dr. Matthews," Chad said. "He's come to help you."

Emma looked at the stranger, a curious, wondering look. At last she said, "All right, won't you sit down."

The doctor turned to Chad. "I'll have to examine her," he said, "perhaps it would be better if you wait outside."

Chad nodded, then smiled at Emma and left. After he had gone, Dr. Matthews moved a chair over near the bed and sat down. He glanced at Emma and smiled.

"Well, you don't look sick," he said, opening his black bag. "Your husband tells me that you're not eating well."

"There's nothing wrong with me," Emma said quietly. "I don't know why my husband went for you. I'm going to have a baby, but there's nothing wrong with me."

Dr. Matthews hooked the stethoscope in his ears. "Fine," he said. "But since I'm here, we might as well give you a complete examination. You'll feel better when you know that everything's all right." He leaned forward.

Emma did not move.

He unhooked the instrument and let it hang around his neck. "Have you been seeing a doctor?" he asked.

"No."

He nodded, and smiled again. The old story, he thought; a delicacy born of fear and superstition. In fifteen years of practice he had never been called to the basin on an obstetrics case.

"Doctors are always hard to get used to at first," he said. "But it isn't really so bad." He paused, watching her. "We should complete an examination . . . for the baby's sake."

"It isn't the baby . . . it's me," she said. She looked away from him, staring through the window. "My father died recently. We were very close."

For a moment Dr. Matthews said nothing; the girl was not being altogether truthful, of course; he had heard the story of her "elopement" with Walters, it had been rather less than an idyllic affair.

"Do you want to tell me about that?" he said.

"There's nothing to tell. He died . . . in the house . . . alone . . . that's all there is to tell. . . ."

"Do you blame yourself for that . . . because he died alone?"

"No."

Dr. Matthews sat for a long while, drumming his fingers against his knees; the girl needed to talk, to tell someone about her guilt; but where could you begin?

At last he said, "Are you sure you feel all right?"

"Yes. I'm fine."

He coiled up the stethoscope and put it back in the bag. "All right. Send your husband if you need me."

She did not move or look at him until he was leaving; then she said, "Doctor?"

He turned. "Yes."

"Thank you for coming."

He smiled. "That's my business," he said. "You must remember to eat the right things . . . and enough of them. It's especially important now."

"I will," she said.

Chad was waiting on the front steps; he stood up when the doctor came out.

"I think your wife is all right," Dr. Matthews said. "She wouldn't let me examine her, but that isn't unusual. She's young, and the river women are accustomed to midwives. If she hasn't had any organic difficulties, there's no cause for concern on that score. But there is something else . . . involving the death of her father. She hasn't recovered well from that. . . . I get the impression that she somehow blames

138

herself. This close to the arrival of her baby it can be dangerous. Having children is both a mental and a physical experience."

Chad nodded. "Is there something I can do?"

"I think you might talk to her . . . she needs to talk it out."

"All right. I'll try."

Dr. Matthews put on his hat. "Let me know if you need me again."

"I will. Thanks for coming."

After he had gone, Chad stood for several minutes on the front porch, looking across the basin toward the foothills beyond. At last he went back into the house and down the hall to Emma's bedroom. The door was open and he went in. Emma was looking toward the window.

"Emma?"

"Yes."

"I want to talk to you."

"All right."

He walked across and sat down on the edge of the bed. "We must talk about your father. . . ."

"I know it."

"You can't blame yourself for what happened."

"I know. I've been thinking about it."

There was a moment of silence.

"Do you blame me?"

Slowly she turned and looked at him, seeing the weary lines of his face, realizing, for the first time, how much he had suffered.

"I'm sorry," she said. "I'm really sorry, Chad. I've never blamed you. I don't know what it was. I just kept remembering that night we went down to the house . . . the night papa died. Even now I can't quite believe it. He died alone . . . that's what I keep remembering . . . he died down there alone. . . ." She began to cry.

He stood up and walked around the bed; kneeling beside her, he held her while she wept. At last she grew quiet, her head resting on his shoulder.

"It must be terrible to die like that," she said. "Without even your family there."

"Emma, every man dies alone," Chad said quietly. "Sometimes that's hard to admit, but it's true. Dying wouldn't have been any different for your father if everyone in the basin had been there. He'd still have died alone . . . because that's what death is."

She raised her head and looked directly at him.

"Do you ever think about death . . . about dying?"

"I guess every man does."

"Does it scare you?"

"No, Emma, it doesn't."

She smiled. "It does me. Sometimes I dream about it." Again she put her head on his shoulder. "Have you seen a lot of people die?"

"A few."

"Is that why you're not afraid?"

"I don't know."

For a moment she made no reply; then she said, "You must teach me not to be afraid. You must teach me to be as strong as you are."

"Don't worry," he said. "In time you'll teach yourself."

CHAPTER 15

THE NEXT DAY it rained. Too late to save the crops, or to mitigate the hardships of another winter without feed for the stock or enough money to buy supplies, the rain poured down for two days on the dry, cracked earth, filling the gullies with frothy torrents of muddy water. By the end of the second day the river had risen to the top of her banks, and the basin people—who in the beginning had read a promise in the grey skies—now watched the lowering clouds uneasily, knowing that there was more to fear in too much rain than in none at all.

On the third day Chad woke about daylight. He lay for a moment looking at Emma. She slept peacefully, breathing deeply, the contour of her stomach rising and falling rhythmically. In the flush of sleep, her dark hair framing her face, she was very beautiful. I must try to understand her, he thought; I must understand that she is suffering as only a woman can suffer; that a woman's ways are not always for a man to know.

He sat up and swung his feet to the floor, moving carefully against the squeak of the bed springs. It had stopped raining but through the open bedroom window he could see the sky, a grey, leaden mass that seemed to hang just above the tree-tops. The window curtains fluttered in the rising wind.

He crossed to a chair in the corner and dressed quietly, glancing from time to time at Emma on the bed. When her time comes, he thought, I must get the doctor; but a doctor could be too late; if she would go, I would take her into Gipson and get her a room and let the doctor care for her as he should; perhaps today, if she is reasonable, I will talk to her about that; if she insists, I will stay with her in town until the baby comes.

Emma stirred on the bed, turned heavily to one side, frowning against the discomfort of turning, then lay quiet again.

Chad went to the kitchen and took a milk bucket from a nail above the sink. He walked down the rocky lane to the barn lot, watching the sky. The mare saw him and neighed softly, holding her head high in the rising wind. The mules were standing at the back gate; the cow (Emma had named her Mehitabel, but he could never bring himself to call her that) was waiting at the stall door, her bag so full that some of the milk leaked out when she moved.

He put some cottonseed hulls out for the cow and sprinkled them with meal; lightly, for man and beast alike were affected by a drought year and both suffered equally.

He had just begun to milk when he heard Emma's scream, a shriek so pentup and terrifying that even the livestock stood looking toward the house with startled expressions.

Leaving the bucket on the ground beneath the cow, Chad ran out of the stall and up the hill; the scream, he thought, had come from the rear of the house. An instant later he burst through the back door and saw Emma. She was lying on the kitchen floor where she had fallen, her body twisted to one side, as if she had tried to rise and had been unable to do so. Her hair hung down, hiding her face; as he entered, she tried again to push herself up. Chad knelt beside her, putting his arms around her shoulders.

"Emma . . . it's all right . . . don't try to get up, I'll take you back to bed. . . ."

She flung her head to one side, brushing the hair away from her face, staring at him as if he were someone she had never seen before.

"Emma . . . it's me . . . Chad. . . ."

She reached for him and he held her close, feeling her body tremble.

"It's the baby," she gasped. "The pains started. . . ." Suddenly she broke off; for an instant she closed her eyes tightly, waiting; she clamped her teeth together until the muscles in her jaw stood out; her fingers bit into Chad's arm; she pressed her head against his shoulder . . . then she screamed again and again as the pain racked her body.

He held her until the moment had passed; afterwards, he picked her up and carried her to the bedroom down the hall. She breathed heavily, her eyes closed. He placed her gently on the bed and stood looking down at her; she turned away from him, her face toward the wall.

Finally, he said, "I've got to get Dr. Matthews . . . will you be all right?"

She said nothing. Outside a clap of thunder rattled across the sky; the rain began to fall.

"Emma?"

After a time, without looking at him, she said, "Yes, you get the doctor. I'll be all right."

There was another rumble of thunder, deep in the sky now; the wind rattled the window in its frame; there was a roar, far off and then closer, as the rain came down in torrents, shaking the earth where it fell.

"Emma . . ."

"I'll be all right."

"Are you sure?"

"Yes. You'd better get the doctor."

Still he did not move, unable to leave her, knowing that he must. Then, haltingly, he reached out and touched her shoulder. "You take care of yourself," he said. "I won't be long." He crossed to the window; the rain was blowing through and the curtains were soaked; he lowered it carefully then left the room.

He stopped in the kitchen and put on his hat and slicker. The blast of rain struck him as he walked out the back door; the wind, which was rising too fast, blew the rain across the land in heavy, grey sheets. Ducking his head against the blast, he ran down the lane to the barn. The raincoat was ripped in the back and he was soaked to the skin when he reached the open shed adjoining the main stall. He went through the feed room to the mare's stable. The animal neighed softly when he crawled through the feed opening, carrying a bridle. She did not want to take the cold bit, but Chad gripped her nose tight in his hand and pressed the bit between her teeth. When he opened the back door and tried to lead her outside, she held back. Chad spoke gently and after a moment she followed, turning her head against the wind and rain. Chad took her to the open shed and saddled her, then led her up the path to the house. He tied her to the well porch and went back inside. Emma was still lying with her face to the window; he went to the end of the bed and watched her; the pain had gone out of her face and she seemed to be resting. He stood for a moment, uncertainly. Finally, he said, "I'm leaving now . . . don't worry." She did not move. He waited a moment longer, then turned back to the hall.

Outside he mounted the mare and rode down the hill. He kept her in a steady trot until he had reached the meadow strip at the foot of the rise, then he shook the reins and kicked his heels against her sides. She bowed her head in protest but slipped into a long easy lope. Chad settled in the saddle, letting her pick her way. She moved along with her head close to the ground, watching the road. The gullies along the way were filled with rushing water, reddened by the topsoil that had washed down from higher ground, beaten frothy against the rocks. The road was slick and the mare had trouble holding her footing. At the rise beyond the meadow her rear feet gave way and she slithered to her haunches in the heavy mud. Chad did not urge her but gave her full rein until she had scrambled back to her feet; then he shook the reins and kicked her again into a lope.

Riding through the rain, Chad thought of Emma. Perhaps this will be too much for her, he told himself; perhaps our marriage was a mistake, perhaps she will never be happy away from her own people. He remembered the pain in her face when he had held her in the kitchen. He tried to think of other things but the image of Emma lying on the floor persisted; the sound of her screams rang in his head above the rumble from the dark sky overhead.

When he reached the river road cutoff, he pulled the mare up. He had not thought of it before but it occurred to him now that he would save four or five miles if he turned off the main road and followed the wagon trail through the pine flats and forded the river above the bend. The river would be up and the crossing rough, but the mare was a good swimmer. Chad reined her off the road, jabbing his heels into her flank; she slipped in the mud, flung her head up, then plunged into the trees.

The log trail was a quagmire; in places the mare bogged down above her fetlocks. The road was even worse in the pine flats along the river. Where it was possible Chad reined the mare off the trail and rode in the open woods, but as they neared the river the brush became thicker and more tangled. At last it was impossible to move beyond a walk. Chad thought again of Emma and cursed himself for taking the short cut.

It was almost an hour after he had left the main road before he reached the river. He had not counted on the water being so high. The river was out of her banks and even at the narrows above the bend it was sixty or seventy yards across. The water rushed at a furious pace; logs, driftwood and trees bobbed on the surface like chips. Chad stopped on the bank above the narrows and dismounted. He checked the cinch under the mare's belly and stood for a moment, watching the raging current. Suddenly he was overcome with a sense of helplessness. The river would be a problem, even for the strength of the mare. He thought of Emma; there was no time to go back. He waited a moment longer, then mounted again, urging the mare down the hill toward the river. She moved slowly, sliding on the clayey bank. At the water's edge she stopped, frightened at the deafening roar of the water; Chad could feel her tremble. He shook the reins, pressed his heels against her flank, spoke softly. She refused to move. At last she thrust one foot out, then abruptly drew it back and tried to turn up the ridge. Chad swung her completely around, steadied her, then held his feet away from her sides and brought them down sharply. She bowed her neck, snorted once, then plunged into the racing water, pawing at the air.

Chad felt the current catch her almost at once, and he knew that she was no match for it. He slid out of the saddle and held to the pommel, swimming beside the struggling animal. Feeling the weight off her back, the mare tried to turn toward the bank, but Chad slapped her across the nose and shouted; she turned again toward the mainstream. They were carried by the current for a moment, then, suddenly, the mare seemed to make some headway. They were thirty or forty feet from the bank of the river when Chad saw the log hurtling toward them. He twisted the reins around his hand and tried by sheer force to pull the mare's head clear, but she was fighting the current and had taken the bit between her teeth. The log struck the animal high on the head with a sickening thud, spinning her around. She squealed with pain and began pawing the water, as if trying to lift herself above the surface; then she sank back and her head dipped out of sight. Chad released the reins and saddle pommel, knowing that the animal would have a better chance without his weight. Again the mare pawed her way to the surface, then, suddenly, she stopped struggling and her head sank down again. She was swept away; Chad saw her try once more, farther down, to fight against the current, then she stopped swimming and only the saddle was visible above the yellow froth.

For an instant Chad allowed himself to be carried along by the stream. He watched the bobbing saddle until it was no more than a black speck on the surface. The mare was dead, he was sure of that. Then, crazily, floating downstream on the maddened current, he thought of Emma back at the house alone. Churning with his hands and feet to stay above the choppy water, he tried to find the spot on the bank where he had entered the stream. It was no longer in sight; he was being swept along now at a breathtaking speed; it was impossible to think clearly; the roar of the river was deafening. He searched the far bank for some landmark that would tell him how far he had drifted, but he saw only a thin, dark line of trees far away against a grey sky.

Suddenly, he remembered the bend in the river; he was sure that he had not drifted that far. If he could hold his own against the current, the thrust of the shore might be within his reach where the river swung back south. He reached beneath the water and untied his shoes and felt the current tug at them as they slipped free. Then he began swimming for the north shore, holding his head high above the surface to avoid the litter that floated past. It was impossible to tell as he swam whether or not he was making headway, but when he stopped to catch his breath he could see that the shoreline behind him was almost invisible through the falling rain. He judged that he was already past midstream and the thought gave him new hope. Desperately he struck out again; his arms now were leaden weights pulling him down; he could feel the undertow of the river grasping at his legs. Then, ahead of him, he saw the north shore, clear and distinct.

It seemed that he had been swimming for hours when he saw the spur of land that told him he was nearing the bend. A moment later the river began to swing south; directly ahead of him he could see the trees along the bank, their lower limbs dragging in the water. He lashed out furiously, trying to reach the quieter channel before the current swept him again into the mainstream. The trees were not more than ten feet away. Suddenly the cross-current yanked at his body, the force of it swinging him half around in the water. By the time he had righted himself the spur of land was just ahead; then, he felt the river bed beneath his feet; the water eddied around him in small muddy circles. With a great effort he pulled his feet through the water; his chest ached and the air burned his lungs. He dragged himself to the bank of the river and sat down, gasping for air. He sat without moving for a long while, his head resting on his arms. There was a sickness in his stomach and his mind was incapable of thinking about anything. Then, with a startling suddenness, the image of Emma returned. He shook his head and stood

147

up; he felt the cold rain on his back. He began walking. He crossed a muddy field; then a wooded section. At last he reached a road, which, after a moment he recognized. He was less than a mile from Gipson.

Dr. Matthews sat in the parlor of his home, reading a report on typhoid fever in the current issue of *American Doctor*. From time to time, he glanced with some impatience toward the kitchen door; at last his wife appeared with a cup of coffee. She placed the coffee on the table beside his chair and returned to the kitchen. Dr. Matthews picked up the cup, sipped it tentatively, then pursed his lips and put it back in the saucer. He tried to resume the article he was reading but his mind wandered. At length he let the magazine fall on his lap and sat looking through the window at the steady drizzle of rain falling from the eaves. Dr. Matthews, whatever else could be said of him, was an extremely conscientious man; he was thinking now of the Walters woman. The ignorance, the superstition, of the basin women was amazing; of course, he could have refused to accompany Walters to the river bottom at all, thus saving himself the agitation of having somehow failed to measure up to his medical creed. But he had not refused—and he was agitated. The woman obviously needed attention and he could not help blaming himself for having given up too quickly. Dr. Matthews was perfectly aware that the psychology of medicine was one of his weaker points and that his ability to instill confidence in the patient was always in doubt. If the woman dies giving birth to a child, he told himself, a part of the blame will rest with me. He picked up the magazine he had been reading and tried again; but it was no use. There is no point in getting worked up, he rationalized; not one basin woman in a hundred has the benefit of a doctor in childbirth. But perhaps that's why the birthrate in the river country is so appallingly low. . . .

Mrs. Matthews appeared in the doorway. "Breakfast is ready, doctor," she told him; she always addressed him as "doctor," a foolish conceit.

148

Dr. Matthews stood up and laid the *American Doctor* on the table. He stopped, listening. Above the sound of the rain he was sure he had heard footsteps on the front porch. He waited for a knock which did not come. He glanced at his wife questioningly; her blank stare told him that she had heard nothing. Again he turned toward the kitchen. The knock came then, faintly. He crossed the room and opened the door. It was a startled instant before he recognized the man outside. It was Walters; his shoes were missing and one leg of his trousers was torn to the knee; his face was bleeding from a scratch on the cheek. Idiotically, Dr. Matthews stood for a moment simply staring at him.

In a voice perfectly contained, Chad said, "You'll have to come . . . it's my wife. . . ."

The Walters woman. "Of course . . . come in, I'll get my bag."

"I'll wait here . . . I had to swim the river. . . ."

"Never mind that." Dr. Matthews spoke with incongruous authority. He opened the door and took Chad's arm. "Come in out of the weather . . . I won't be a minute."

Chad followed him into the living room and stopped just inside the door, the water dripping on the faded red carpet.

Dr. Matthews left the room and returned an instant later carrying his bag and dressed in a raincoat which was too long. "We'll have to go by the livery stable and get my buggy," he said. To Mrs. Matthews he said, "I don't know when I'll get back . . . don't worry about me."

The two men left the house and walked through the rain up the muddy road to the livery stable. They waited in the outer office while a negro boy hooked the doctor's team to his buckboard.

Dr. Matthews watched Chad, wanting to say something but unable to think of a sensible question. Finally he asked, "Is your wife in labor?"

"I think so."

"Had the pains just started when you left?"

"The bad ones had . . . she might have had some before I heard her."

"Perhaps we'll get there in time," the doctor said, trying to be reassuring. "It is not unusual for a woman to labor for several hours . . . particularly with the first child."

"She's alone out there," Chad said.

Dr. Matthews nodded. Walters was right, of course; the woman was alone, that was the worst of it. He stood up and walked to the front window.

"The rain's letting up some. . . ."

Walters said nothing. He is a strange one, Dr. Matthews thought; Will Kelly was right about that. A man to ride with, Will had said, quoting an old river saying; you could see what he meant. A man who expected life to be hard, that always made it easier to be strong when you had to be, knowing that life was no soft touch.

The negro boy came through the breezeway, leading Dr. Matthews' big-footed buggy mare.

Dr. Matthews picked up his bag. "If you're ready . . ."

On the ride to the river basin, Dr. Matthews kept the mare in a brisk trot. Once or twice he made an attempt to strike up a conversation but Chad said almost nothing in response to his comments; finally they rode in silence.

By the time they had turned back up the river road beyond the bridge, the rain had stopped and a streak of lighter sky shone through the grey along the eastern horizon.

As they crossed the meadow strip below the house, Dr. Matthews felt a curious tension mounting within him; the sensation annoyed him because he felt that it was a violation of his professional confidence. He glanced at Chad, who was looking toward the house, his hard, lean face drawn by the ordeal he had lived through; and also, Dr. Matthews decided, by an intense concern for his wife.

"She's in the back bedroom, I suppose," Dr. Matthews said.

"Yes . . . that's where I left her."

They pulled up at the front gate and jumped down. Dr. Matthews grabbed his bag and followed Chad up the walk and into the house. Together they went down the hallway to the back room. Dr. Matthews touched Chad's arm. "I think it will be better . . . considering your wife's state of mind . . . if you let me go in alone."

It was a moment before Chad replied. "All right," he said. "I'll be in the kitchen if you need me." He glanced toward the bedroom door; inside it was perfectly quiet.

Dr. Matthews entered the room; then, an instant later, the door closed.

Chad returned to the kitchen and sat down. He felt a tightness in his belly. Something is wrong, he thought, something is wrong or the doctor wouldn't have closed the door; it was too quiet when we came in.

He stood up and walked to the back porch. The rain was over. The clouds were rising and the streak of light along the horizon had become patches of blue sky. Chad sat down on the steps and watched the clouds break. He listened for some sound from the bedroom, but heard none. By some habit of living, he forced himself to prepare for the worst; whatever happens in there, he thought, life will go on, and I must go with it; man is made to live and work until his time is out; the trick of living is to know that life takes away whatever it gives, that what gives happiness one moment brings sadness the next; that whoever made the world made it that way, and that's the way it is.

A moment later he heard the doctor's footsteps in the hallway. He stood up and went into the kitchen; Dr. Matthews was there; he had a bundle in his arms, wrapped in a quilt. Chad stopped, waiting for him to speak.

"The child was born dead . . . it was a boy."

Chad did not move. For a long moment neither of them spoke.

At last Chad said, "Before we came?"

"Yes . . . about an hour ago."

"My wife . . ."

"She's very weak, but I think she'll pull through. She's sleeping now, I've given her a sedative."

"Can you stay until I bury the child? . . ."

"Yes . . . I'll wait."

Chad walked to him and he placed the bundle in his arms. He watched Chad's face, saw the deep hurt in his eyes, and beneath the hurt, the somehow frightening strength. God help us! he thought, the suffering one has to share; the suffering that never becomes any easier.

"I'm sorry. . . ."

Chad turned and left the room, holding the dead child close to him. He stopped at the well porch and got a shovel, then walked up the ridge toward the bluff. He stopped in a grove of pine trees at the top of the rise and gently laid the bundle on the ground; then he picked up the shovel and began to dig. He worked without pause for almost an hour; at last he stopped and leaned the shovel against a tree. He stood a moment, breathing deeply, looking up through the trees at the clearing sky. Finally, he walked back to the bundle on the ground and knelt beside it. Slowly he pulled away the corners of the quilt; for a long while he knelt there, motionless, looking at the body of his dead son. Then he covered the child again; carefully he picked up the bundle and placed it in the grave. He took the shovel and began scraping in the loose dirt.

As he worked, the clouds lifted and the first thin rays of sunlight shone through the wet pines.

CHAPTER 16

FOLLOWING THE DEATH of her child, Emma remained in bed for almost a month. There was nothing to be done for her since she refused to do anything for herself. Dr. Matthews, who in some curious way had become emotionally involved, made regular calls three times weekly; and, much to his annoyance, thought about the case almost constantly. At last, he realized that Emma's trouble was psychological rather than organic; she simply refused to participate in her recovery and remained in bed long after her physical responses were normal. There were times when she severely tested his patience, for he held the will to live as a basic and natural force in the pattern of human existence; when people no longer wanted to live, he was both annoyed and disturbed.

For almost two weeks Emma lay on the bed, pale and wasting, oblivious to her surroundings. She ate almost nothing and steadily lost weight; alarmed, Dr. Matthews cajoled and pleaded, and at last considered feeding her through a tube inserted through her nose. Uncertain and agitated (at himself and Emma) he tried, as a final resort, to talk to her about her state of mind. She listened to his words, which he deliberately made rather brusque in an effort to shock her into understanding; when he had finished, she made no comment, nor did she take food. The following day, Dr. Matthews reached a decision. He went to the kitchen and prepared a plate of food himself; then he took the plate to her room and placed it on the table beside the bed. "Here is your food, Mrs. Walters," he said evenly. "If you expect to live, you'll have to eat. That is a decision you'll have to make for yourself." Then he left the room. When he returned later the plate was empty; she continued to eat regularly and from that time on gained strength; but her general state of mind was little improved.

Dr. Matthews realized that his interest in the "Walters case" went beyond the professional obligation of medicine. His feelings about Emma invariably included her husband, who was, he thought, the most complex personality he had ever known. Walters was solicitous of his wife's needs and quietly concerned about her welfare; but his naturally remote and stoical manner was a distinct barrier to her recovery. In fact, Dr. Matthews decided, her indifference to her own well-being was in some way a negation of her husband. Often, when Walters accompanied him to the bedroom, he would see in Emma's face a faint flicker of expression; and the look was unpleasant to watch. It was not quite a look of hatred, but rather of distrust, as if her husband were a stranger in whose presence she was uneasy. What had happened between them before the child's death? Walters did not mistreat his wife, did not physically abuse her as so many of the river men did, he was sure of that. It was something else; a clash of personality, a lack of understanding and sympathy. The girl was young and the stillbirth had been a shock; perhaps, as Will Kelly had suggested, the marriage had been a mistake; the gumbo women were generally emotional, quick to laugh or weep; the girl must certainly have had some difficulty adjusting to her husband. Walters might supply the tears, Dr. Matthews thought dourly, but Emma would have to find her laughter elsewhere.

Still, he liked the man. Not personally, as men are sometimes deeply attached by common interests or great understanding; but objectively, as men are drawn, almost instinctively, to courage and strength in other men. He wanted to know Chad better, but found this somehow a difficult business. There was something in Walters' manner, in the dark, unchanging face, that discouraged intimacy. I must talk to him about his wife, Dr. Matthews thought a thousand times; I must tell him that she needs his love, that he must do his part too. But somehow he could never bring himself to discuss these things with Chad.

In the end, Chad spoke of them himself. Dr. Matthews had made a regular call, which by now had become largely perfunctory; when he came from Emma's room, Chad was waiting on the front porch, mending a bridle. Dr. Matthews watched him work for a moment and could not help smiling inwardly; he had never seen the man really idle. Chad glanced up and nodded briefly, then returned to his work. Dr. Matthews placed his bag on a chair by the door and sat down on the steps beside him. The sun had set behind the ridge at the lower end of the basin and the first faint night breezes stirred across the valley. The world can be very peaceful, when it wants to be, Dr. Matthews thought. Misery is a human thing.

Without looking at him, Chad said, "How is she?"

Dr. Matthews did not immediately answer. He watched Chad, his face faintly curious. It was not a question; Walters had simply *said* the words with no thought of what they meant. At that moment he learned something else about Chad. A part of Walters strength lay in the fact of acceptance; unlike most men, he did not worry about what he could not change. He had decided that he could not help Emma, and he had accepted, totally and without reservations, the circumstances of that decision. Perhaps I should tell him now, Dr. Matthews thought; perhaps this is the time to say the things I've wanted to say, to tell him that no man can decide for himself what he can or cannot do for others.

Instead he said, "About the same. . . ."

Chad continued to work and for a time neither of them spoke. Finally Chad laid the bridle aside; he sat for a long while, looking across the valley, as motionless as a tree.

"Part of it's me," he said quietly. "I know that."

Dr. Matthews waited for him to continue, trying to anticipate his remarks before he made them; trying to frame his own answers. The conversation was off balance; now that the moment had come, now that Walters himself had opened the way, Dr. Matthews felt strangely intimidated.

"She doesn't trust me," Chad said. "I can feel that."

"Yes . . . I've sensed that too. I expect your wife finds it hard to live away from her own people . . . the river folks are clannish . . . almost tribal in their family relationships."

"Yes. I know."

There was no point in mincing words; for the girl's sake,

Walters had to understand.

"Your wife has had a very hard time of it," Dr. Matthews said. "First there was the death of her father . . . and then the child. She's quite young, just a girl really. Childbirth is always a mysterious business; a stillborn child is invariably a severe shock, psychologically and otherwise; naturally the shock is greater when the mother is a woman of sensitive feelings. Going through that alone, here in the house, was a pretty horrible experience. That your wife would suffer a period of depression, even irrationality, afterward is not unusual. In fact, I think she has done remarkably well." He looked directly at Chad, gauging his reactions. "I can't help feeling," he went on, "that she needs more sympathy and understanding than you've . . . been able to give her. She needs to know that you've been a part of her suffering . . . that she hasn't been . . . and isn't . . . alone. . . ." He broke off, wanting to say more, annoyed because he could not find the right words.

Chad sat for a long while, looking down at the palms of his hands, nodding slowly; but he made no reply.

"Have you talked to her at all . . . about the child?" Dr. Matthews asked.

"No."

"I think she needs that now . . . more than medicine or anything else."

There was another moment of silence; then Chad said, "Sometimes it's hard to say the right thing."

"Yes, I know," Dr. Matthews replied, feeling that the answer was meaningless; somehow with Walters it was impossible to say exactly what you wanted to say.

After a time, Chad said, "I'll try. I know I've let her down . . . I'll try."

They sat a moment longer in the gathering darkness; then Dr. Matthews stood up and walked back to the chair where he had left his bag. He had the feeling that the matter was not satisfactorily settled, that he had somehow failed again. He spoke abruptly.

"I'll be back Saturday." He walked down the steps and across the yard to his buggy.

At the foot of the rise, he glanced back. Chad was still sitting on the porch; the faint glow of his cigarette shone through the night.

Dr. Matthews turned away. It isn't my fault, he told himself; to help a man you must understand him; you must know what it is he needs. And you must be stronger than he is.

The following morning, on the twenty-seventh day of her convalescence, Emma left her bed. Voluntarily, without urging, she simply got up, carefully cleaned her room and went to the kitchen. When Chad returned from the barn lot, shortly after seven, he found her there, preparing breakfast. She stood at the kitchen table, her back to him, making biscuits; she did not turn or speak when he came in. For a moment he stood watching her, then he walked across to the cabinet and strained the milk into a pan. When he turned, she was placing the biscuits in the oven.

"It's good to see you up," he said. "You're feeling better?"

"I'm fine." She spoke in a low, strained voice, obviously dreading the presence of words between them.

"Well, that's good," he said. He waited for her reply, but she said nothing; sensing that words now were important, he said, "Dr. Matthews will be back Saturday."

"I don't need Dr. Matthews any more," she said in a quiet, almost formal, tone. "You'd better ride into Gipson this afternoon and tell him that I'm up and well now."

He nodded. "All right. I guess you're the best judge of that." He stood a moment, looking down at the floor. "Maybe you'd like to ride in with me," he said.

"No. I'll stay here."

"All right," he said. "I wouldn't try to do too much the first day or two." Unable to think of anything further to say, he simply watched her; she took up the meat and began frying eggs; she did not once look at him. He sat down at the table and waited.

At last she put the food beside him and poured the coffee; then, without a glance in his direction, she too sat down.

For a long while they ate in silence; the coffee, which she had placed too near the heat, began to boil; but she did not seem to notice and he could not bring himself to get up and push it back. The dying fire crackled in the stove; the sense of waiting was a living presence between them.

It was Emma who spoke at last. She put her fork down and looked directly at him, speaking in a tight, carefully restrained voice.

"What did you do with the baby?"

Chad looked at her, saw the deep lines in her face, the gaunt hollows of her cheek.

"The child was born dead . . . it was a boy."

"I know that. Dr. Matthews told me. What did you do with him?"

"I buried him . . . in the pine thicket up the rise. . . ."

"You took the child up there alone and buried him?"

"Yes."

Suddenly a strange weariness came over her features. She spoke without bitterness. "No, Chad, you didn't bury him . . . to bury a thing you must love it. There's no love in you. You simply dug a hole and put our baby in it . . . that isn't the same thing. . . ."

"Emma . . ."

"No. Let me finish. I've got to say this now. All the time I was lying in bed, I could hear you . . . cooking your meals, cutting wood, doing the chores . . . going, coming, living your life as if nothing had happened. After a while it got to where I dreaded the sound of your movements more than the thought of dying. At first I waited . . . waited for you to come to me and talk about our baby . . . waited for you to tell me that you were suffering the way I was. Then I thought about you, the way you are, and I knew that you weren't coming. After that, I didn't care . . . I didn't even mind the sounds. I knew then that you can never suffer the way other people do . . . because you don't love enough to suffer. . . ."

She turned her head away and began to cry, a soft, whimpering sound, forlorn and defeated.

For a time they simply sat in silence, waiting for nothing. At last Chad stood up and walked to where she sat; but he did not touch her.

"I'm sorry, Emma," he said. "I know I let you down . . . but I didn't know what to do or say. I wanted our son to live . . . when Dr. Matthews brought him into the kitchen and told me he was dead, something died in me too. But that didn't change anything . . . you've got to begin there. I didn't really love the thing he was holding in his arms, because there wasn't anything there to love. Everything dies, Emma . . . or it never lives at all. People who grieve for what's gone are really grieving for themselves . . . for something they wanted and couldn't have. No man is bigger than this world . . . you take whatever the world gives you and you live with it and you say this is right, because there isn't anything else you can do. . . ." He paused, waiting for her to speak, but she said nothing. Slowly, tentatively, he put out his hand and touched her shoulder. "Maybe there'll be another son," he said softly.

He felt her shoulder grow tense beneath his hand; then, suddenly, her whole body shook with sobs; helplessly, he watched her; then she brushed his hand aside and ran out of the room.

For a time he could hear her crying in the back room; at last the sound ceased. The coffee pot sputtered on the stove; he pushed it away from the heat and went to the back porch. He sat for several minutes without moving; then he stood up and walked back through the kitchen and down the hall to the bedroom.

Emma was lying on the bed, staring up at the ceiling; she had stopped crying. He walked to the edge of the bed and stood looking down at her.

"Emma, we can't live with the memory of a dead son."

"I know."

"And we can't let bitterness take away what we have left."

"No."

"Try to understand. I love you."

Her voice was distant and childlike. "Yes, I want to understand," she said. "And I'm not afraid any more." She held out her hand; he took it and sat down beside her.

For a long while neither of them spoke; then, without looking at him, she said, "I love you too."

CHAPTER 17

SUMMER PASSED AND fall came with a sudden rush of color. From the back well porch, Emma watched the trees turn (almost overnight it seemed): the burnished reds and browns, the deep sun-tinted purple of the sumac, the brilliant yellow maples dancing in the first crisp winds of autumn.

Chad saw her there one afternoon as he came down from the bluff, his ax across his shoulder. She waved and he waved back; the sight of her, her hair blowing loosely around her face, quickened something inside him. He walked on, remembering the long, painful days and nights they had shared since the death of their child; remembering Emma's unspoken, tight-lipped courage, the nights she had slipped out of bed and gone to another part of the house to weep alone, knowing at last that a part of the pain—the persistent, deep-rooted part that came back at night—could never really be shared at all. Remembering, finally, how much she had changed, how suddenly she had become a woman, conquering in the end her tragedy with an abiding reserve and containment that had been no part of the girl he married.

Emma ran down the steps and up the hill toward him, shouting something as she came. The wind caught at her dress; she held it down and looked at him, laughing. He stopped and waited for her at the bottom of the path.

When she reached him, he held out his hands, and she took them, looking away, almost blushing, like a schoolgirl on her first date. He smiled, thinking that out of her sadness she had grown incredibly beautiful.

"It's been a fine day," he said.

She looked up at him and smiled. "It's been a wonderful day," she said. "I've never seen the trees so pretty. I started to come to the bluff and watch you work."

"Why didn't you?" he said. "Somehow I kinda thought you might."

For a moment she watched him, studying his face.

"I'd like to go up there now," she said.

"To the bluff?"

"Yes. I want to see where the baby is buried." She noticed the change in his expression. "It's all right," she said. "I've wanted to go for a long time . . . but somehow I couldn't. I've been thinking about it the last few days . . . I know now that it's all right. . . ."

He said nothing for a moment; then he nodded. "If that's what you want," he said. "Do you want me to come with you?"

"Yes, I want you with me."

Together they walked back up the path, still holding hands. Chad led her past the first clearing and on to a thin grove of pines at the base of the bluff. The slight mound of earth was still there, marked by a small stone. For a long while they stood beside the mound, saying nothing. It was Emma who spoke at last.

"Did you see him?" she asked quietly.

"Yes, I saw him."

"Was he a pretty baby?"

"Yes. He was a fine boy."

She glanced up at him and smiled, a faint, reticent smile, assuring him that it was all right.

"When I was carrying him," she said, "I used to worry about whether he'd have all of his fingers and toes. For your sake, I wanted him to be strong."

"He was a fine baby," Chad said again.

They stood a moment longer, looking at the grave; then Emma took his hand.

"Let's go on to the top," she said. "It seems like years since I've been up there."

They walked on; at the clearing on the bluff, they stopped

and looked back toward the valley, strangely still in the gathering dusk.

"This is where I used to come when we lived in the house," Emma said. "I used to sit right over there on that rock. Sometimes I'd spend a whole afternoon here, thinking about the time I'd leave the basin and go off in the world somewhere to live. It's funny. It never occurred to me that I'd live out my life in the basin." Suddenly she turned to Chad and put her arms around his waist. Looking up at him, she said, "That's just what I want now . . . to spend the rest of my life here . . . with you. I love this farm, this hill, our house. I've been thinking about us all day . . . about the baby . . . and the years ahead. They'll be good years, Chad. I know that now." She put her head against his chest and felt his arms around her. "I want another baby," she said quietly. "Even that, I couldn't face before. I want a son to grow up with us, to love this land the way we do . . . a son who will live here when we're gone . . . whose sons will live here. . . ."

He held her close. In the valley below them, he could see the dark outlines of the house and barn, farther on, against the failing light, the dim ridgy lines of the basin rim. A sense of peace came over him.

"When I first came here," he said, "Will Kelly tried to get me to sell this land. He knew the trouble it would cause for me and the people in the basin. After I'd talked to him, I thought maybe that was the best way. But the next morning we rode down here and stopped our horses, over there where the river road turns, and I looked down at the basin and thought, this is where I'll stay. Even if I have to fight for it, this is where I'll stay." He put his hand under her chin and raised her face toward his. "It wasn't always easy to stay. If I had lost you, I'd have lost this too."

She stood on her tiptoes to kiss him.

"I'd like to name our next son Lance," she said. "Timothy Lance. That was papa's full name. We could call him Timothy."

He nodded. "I think Timothy Lance would be a fine name."

PART III

THE MUSTANG

For this is wisdom: to love, to live, to take what Fate or the Gods may give.

———LAURENCE HOPE

CHAPTER 18

In the spring of 1909, a trade syndicate—which later became the Panquel Millwork Corporation—purchased from the Chekow County Land Commission a three-hundred-section tract of land, extending from the upper rim of Big River basin to the heavily timbered lowland regions just north of Daiker's Pitch. The effects of this transaction were felt throughout the river bottom country—and it brought with it the end of a way of life. The privately owned farms in the basin were not, of course, a part of the original purchase, but within a month after the sale, two well-dressed gentlemen with bulging briefcases (agents of the syndicate) were visiting the gumbo people and offering such fabulous prices for the land that few could withstand the temptation to sell. Even those who were at first reluctant to give up their farms, were, in the end, compelled to face the truth: that life in the basin would never be the same again. Some of the river people remained to work for the Panquel Corporation, but most of them found the prospect of steady employment unappealing and either returned to Daiker's Pitch or migrated to other unsettled regions beyond the mountains.

By July work crews were clearing the land along the river above the bend, and a week later the first heavy-wheeled wagons creaked over the old river road, loaded with machinery and equipment. Piece by piece the mill went up, covering at last almost five square acres of land, an awesome city of spinning wheels and strange sounds. By mid-August the valley was filled with the whine of the big saws and the high, urgent shouts of the yard bosses. One by one, the gumbo people departed, shaking their heads sadly, wondering how the basin could have changed so much in so short a time.

In another way, Gipson, too, was affected by the birth of the Panquel Millwork Corporation; the streets now rumbled with a never-ending train of heavy lumber wagons; the boardwalks were cluttered by a sourceless stream of strange faces: big, scowling men who wore tin hats and seemed always to be shouting; heavily rouged women with hard mouths who laughed too much and spoke in coarse, strident voices; children who, from all outward signs, belonged to nobody, running in packs through the streets, ill trained and undisciplined.

Gipson's reaction to this new prosperity was generally one of uneasiness. From the beginning, the older citizens complained of the noise, the dust, the eternal clamor. Beneath the outward sense of well-being, some read more ominous signs. The mill, they argued, would bring only the riff-raff with it, people by nature homeless who could not be expected to concern themselves with or take an active part in the welfare of the community. It was true, they agreed, that the new industry had got rid of the gumbo rats, but compared to these people, the gumbo rats were a minor problem. Why already they were talking about voting in liquor; that would mean dance halls and, in due course, all the other foul vices of a godless community. It was something to think about, they said, shaking their heads knowingly, they'd all live to see Gipson unfit for decent folks.

The Panquel Corporation's strongest backers in Gipson were the merchants, who, for a time, did a booming business; new store-rooms were built and stocks extended; prices were raised and display windows set up; even when word leaked out that the company ultimately planned to construct its own commissary, the air of prosperity and high living was undampened.

And so, in Gipson too a way of life ended. Some of her citizens, like the river people, sold their homes and moved away; those that remained either adapted themselves to the increased tempo of industrial living, or sat in the shadows of their porches, murmuring dire prophecies and waiting for their fulfillment.

At his desk in the land office, Will Kelly sat musingly, watching the steady flow of wagons and people along main street. Last night there had been another meeting at the Baptist church—which Will regularly attended—to discuss, as Brother Hemstead rather vaguely put it, "the future of Gipson." It was another in a long series of such meetings, and, like the others, had been a long-winded, tiresome affair. The mill, of course, was the problem but those who opposed its coming into Gipson didn't have the foggiest notion what they were going to do about it; in fact, there was nothing they could do. Will had sat wearily through the meeting, hoping that he wouldn't be called upon to speak. But before the meeting ended, everyone had been asked to make a statement; at last Brother Hemstead had asked him to "take a stand."

Take a stand, indeed. There is nothing to take a stand about, he had told them; the mill is here, and it will remain here until the Panquel people decide to move it; a thousand meetings like this one won't change that. So, we'd better make the best of it. I realize that most of you have owned property in Gipson for a long time, some of you still have growing children to consider, you want the town to stay the way it's always been. Maybe that's natural. But the change is already here, and I'm afraid we'll all have to change with it. Up to now, I've tried to keep my opinions to myself; feelings are high and everybody is thinking in terms of himself and what's good for him, but I suppose this is a good time to get my own viewpoint on the record: I think the mill is good for Gipson. There'll be some problems, sure . . . and we'll have to deal with them as they come up . . . but in the long run it'll mean more money and a better way of life.

Then he had sat down; and he had known from the silence that followed his speech, the accusing glances that were cast in his direction, that his words had sounded traitorous to the group. Well, maybe so. He had not been altogether honest in what he said; it had simply seemed the most sensible thing to say under the circumstances. Remembering the meeting now, he had to smile. What they had not known was that, personally, he would probably lose more at the hands of the new corporation than any of them. There was already talk of disbanding the local land office, whose purpose, after all, had now ended; in fact, the function of the land office had been for some years in question. Of course, the Panquel people had already suggested that his knowledge of the river country and the river people would make him a valuable agent and buyer for the new corporation; but up to now the suggestion had been pretty tentative, and even if they did come up with a concrete offer, he was not sure that he would accept. After all these years, it would be hard to work for somebody else; being your own boss could get to be a habit.

Will sighed inwardly and turned away from the window; if I had told the church committee how I really feel, he thought, they would have elected me Chairman of the Board; I haven't been fishing since the damned Panquel Corporation moved in here.

He was checking some leases a few moments later when a big man with heavy, hawklike features entered the office. Mr. Stanley, the manager of the Panquel Corporation, moved with an air of unfinished business; he spoke in a sharp, clipped voice and wore always a slight frown of impatience. Still, Will liked him; their relationship, which in the beginning had been professionally quite close, was altogether pleasant, and Will had decided long ago that his tight-lipped, almost dictatorial manner, was really an adopted pose that hid a kind and understanding nature.

"Afternoon," Will said, pushing the leases to one side. "We haven't seen much of you lately."

"No. I've been up in St. Louis working out some details with the home office." Mr. Stanley sat down. "You go ahead with your work . . . I can wait." He managed to make it sound like a concession, as if he were a man unaccustomed to waiting.

"Nothing here that's urgent," Will said. "Just a routine check, I can do it any time."

Mr. Stanley took a cigar from his shirt pocket, elaborately removed the wrapper and clipped the end, then lit it. This is no social chat, Will thought; he's come for a reason.

Abruptly Mr. Stanley said, "There's some talk going around that they're going to close the land office . . . anything to it?" He was watching Will closely.

"That's the impression I get," Will said, deliberately adopting a casual tone. "Although I haven't been officially notified, there's no longer any real function for a land office now that the Panquel Corporation has bought up the river bottom."

"We'll need more land than we've got to make this venture pay off," Mr. Stanley said. "It doesn't take long to cut off timber once you get rolling."

Will felt that he was expected to make some comment but he could think of nothing to say so he reached for his pipe.

After a moment, Mr. Stanley said, "That's one of the things I wanted to talk to you about. While I was in St. Louis, the company authorized me to hire another buyer for the mill. We all feel that it would be wiser to select a local man, someone who knows the country and the people." He sent a puff of smoke into the air. "Naturally, I thought of you."

Will struck a match and lit his pipe, holding the match against the bowl until it had burnt out; he smiled to himself, thinking, this is turning into a smoking duel.

At last he said, "I'm flattered . . . although I'm not at all sure that I'm the man for the job."

"We think you are," Mr. Stanley replied with brisk authority. "The job would involve some travel, of course, but it has a number of rewarding features. Generally, you'll be your own boss; the company will give you a list of leases it would like to obtain and you will take it from there." He

169

paused a moment, then added, "It pays sixty dollars a week to start."

Will glanced up, then nodded his head slowly. Stanley had, of course, used the sixty dollars as a clincher; it was just twice what Will made as land agent.

"Sounds fine," Will said. "I'd like to think it over a day or two. . . ."

"Of course. Take your time. Naturally we'd like to get a man as soon as possible, but a week or two won't make any difference one way or the other. Let me know as soon as you've reached a decision." He stood up and turned toward the door, then stopped and turned back. "There is one other thing," he said. "How well do you know Chad Walters?"

Will leaned back in his chair and puffed his pipe thoughtfully. The question did not come as a surprise; he had heard that the Panquel people had been unsuccessful in their attempts to buy Chad's farm. Now, he smiled.

"That's a pretty tough question," he said. "I don't really know how well anybody knows Chad Walters . . . he's that kind of a man. I suppose I know him as well as anyone else . . . better than most, I guess. I think he trusts me . . . with Walters that's where friendship begins. Why?"

Mr. Stanley looked at him for a long moment. "I think you know why," he said. "When we moved into the river bottom, we were told that the basin farms could be bought from the owners. That was important to us, and, as you know, the project has gone well. We've had to pay a little more than we expected to, but that's all part of the bargain. The only farm left, of any size, is the Walters place. Our agent, Mr. Bascomb, has talked to Walters several times—in fact, he's been authorized to pay Walters twice what the land is worth—but up to now he hasn't made much headway. I'm going down there to see him myself . . . I just thought you might have some information that would help me close the deal."

Will glanced up at the Panquel manager, his eyes amused. "Have you met Walters yourself?"

170

"No. All of our contacts have been made through Bascomb."

"Do you know anything about him?"

"Only what I've heard . . . I know that he isn't a river man."

"That's right, he isn't. And he isn't like any other man you've ever known. You asked me for information that will help you make a deal with him for his land. I'm afraid I don't have that kind of information; nor does anyone else. But I know what his life in the basin has been like, and I know what he's been through . . . if it will help, I can tell you about it."

"All right," Mr. Stanley said, sitting down again. "That's exactly the kind of information I want."

Will tapped the bowl of his pipe against the heel of his hand, remembering a day that seemed now so long ago.

"Eleven years ago Chad Walters came to Gipson and walked into this office. He came to claim a piece of land—the farm he's living on now; it had been left to him by his father. I tried to talk him into selling the place then. I knew he'd have trouble in the basin, trouble adjusting to the river people and their ways. But I didn't have any better luck than Bascomb's had. Anyhow, Chad moved into the basin and settled there. The next few months were hard ones for him; hard enough to break a smaller man. The river folks tried every way they knew to run him out. That same year he married Emma Boone, one of the gumbo women. Maybe in time the river people would have forgiven the rest of it, but they could never forgive him for that. But somehow they managed to get along. The next summer Emma gave birth to a stillborn child. That and a lot of other things were too much for her. She had a breakdown. I watched them for the next two years, trying to understand each other, trying to understand themselves. There was a time when I was sure they wouldn't make it. Then they had another child. A boy. He'll be eight next month, and in him they've found a way. Sometimes when I'm down there I take a meal with them. They're a fine family. Emma and Chad love the land in a way that the gumbo people could never love it. They've worked together, and suffered together, and what's left is theirs. They talk about leaving the farm to the boy and that hope is a part of what they live for."

Mr. Stanley sat for a long while without saying anything. Then he said, "You don't think he'll sell . . . at any price?"

"I'd bet on it."

"All right." Mr. Stanley stood up. "That sounds pretty final."

"Is it really so important to buy him out?"

"From a professional standpoint, yes," Mr. Stanley said. "Naturally, the company would like to own the entire basin. From a personal standpoint, I can't see that it matters much. Anyhow, I'll have to drop by and make him a token offer . . . that's my job."

"Sure."

"Maybe you'd like to go along?"

"Officially?"

Mr. Stanley smiled. "No. As a friend."

"All right . . . any time."

"If you're free, we can drive down in the morning."

"Good. I'll be ready."

"Even if we can't buy his land," Mr. Stanley said. "He sounds like the kind of a man I'd like to know."

CHAPTER 19

DAWN BROKE OVER the river in a dull grey light that revealed
the slow-stirring wisps of fog clinging to the water's surface.
The raucous croak of a heron broke the stillness, followed
almost at once by the labored flap of wings as the bird took
flight.

Out of the fog the prow of a flat-bottom fishing boat appeared, moving slowly through the turgid water. On the
front seat a boy sat, cross-legged, his dark lean face intently
watchful, peering into the river mist; behind him a man
sculled the boat silently through the water, moving the oar
back and forth in a figure eight, scarcely disturbing the surface. His eyes were on the boy.

"We should be about there," he said, his voice loud in the
stillness.

"We just passed the sandbar," the boy replied, still staring
into the fog. "We're about even with the trees now."

"All right, keep a lookout," the man said. "I'll veer closer
to the bank."

He swung the bow of the boat to the right and suddenly
thought of Emma. She would be worried, of course; she
was always worried when Tim was out of her sight. They'd
talked that out long ago, but it didn't keep her from worrying. Well, she had her woman's rights; and cause enough
to worry. But the boy ought not suffer on that account; he
had his own way to go. He loved the river, and already knew
more about it than most men. And he knew when to talk and
when to keep quiet, that was *more* than most men knew.

"The tree's just ahead," the boy said. "Swing her closer
to the bank."

The river bank loomed suddenly through the grey mist.

Chad saw the tree roots and steered the boat toward them. Tim was lying on his belly now, reaching for the trotline.

"I've got it," he said.

"All right." Chad lifted the oar out of the water and placed it in the boat. "Pull your end around and I'll give you a hand."

Using the line as a leader, Tim swung the bow around until Chad could grasp the trotline from his seat in the stern; then together they moved slowly across the stream, lifting the hooks clear of the water.

Some of the hooks had to be rebaited, but there were no fish. Then, suddenly, in the deeper water near the far bank, the surface roiled fiercely as Tim lifted the line. Startled, still lying on his belly, he threw it from him, then quickly grabbed it again.

"Looks like we got us one," he said, obviously trying to control his excitement.

Chad moved forward in the boat. "Let me hold the line," he said. "You go ahead and lift him out."

The fish, a five pound cat, fought viciously but Tim braced himself, his lips pressed tightly together, completely absorbed in the struggle.

"Get a finger in his gills," Chad said. "Get him in the boat before you take the hook out."

Tim pulled the fish into the boat and a moment later had him safely on the stringer; he held it out at arm's length. "He's a big one, ain't he, papa," he said, grinning proudly.

"He's a nice one all right. And the way he fought, I'd say he hadn't been on that hook long either."

Tim studied the fish. "What'd you say, about ten, twelve pounds?"

Chad suppressed a smile. "Well, yeah. . . . I'd say about ten."

There were only two hooks left on the trotline and both of them were empty. Tim rebaited them carefully, then dropped the line back into the water.

"Too bad we didn't bring our poles," he said. "I wouldn't be surprised if the fish were biting good this morning."

"Well, that wouldn't be fair," Chad replied. "We promised your mother we'd be back in an hour. Saturday's her day, you know. I expect she'll want to drive into Gipson after a while."

Tim considered the comment judiciously for a moment. "I was just thinking what we might do next time," he said. "A promise is a promise."

As they drifted slowly back down the river, Tim sat on the front seat, facing his father. Released now from the code of silence which dominated the principle of serious fishing, he chattered incessantly on a variety of unrelated subjects: the new mill, which was an eternal fascination; a lark's nest he had discovered the day before in the meadow below the house; the talk going around that the merchants of Gipson were going to form a Tradesday committee. Tim didn't quite know what that meant but he had heard Billy Martin say that there would be horse races every Saturday, and maybe even a fair ground.

"That'd be something, wouldn't it papa?"

"That'd be a fine idea."

"Did you ever see a horse race, papa?"

"Not a real horse race. But I've seen men run their horses against each other."

For a moment Tim said nothing; then he asked, "Was that when you lived out west . . . before you knew mother?"

Chad smiled. "Yes, that was before I knew your mother."

Tim leaned slightly forward, his face serious. "Did you have a horse then, papa? When you lived out west?" His dark face waited for the answer, and Chad knew that it was some-how especially important to him.

"I've had several horses, son. Out west a man's nearly got to have a horse."

"Working horses or riding horses?"

"Riding horses," Chad said. "Out where I was people didn't do much farming. Mostly, it was a cattle country."

"Mother says you were a real cowboy." Tim said it with obvious pride. When Chad made no reply, he said, "Were you?"

Chad smiled. "Well, I rode after cows. . . . I guess that makes you a cowboy."

"Did you ever race?"

"When I was younger I did." For a time he said nothing more; then he saw that the boy was waiting for him to continue. "I used to work for an outfit in Nevada that raised horses," he said. "Good strong quarter horses that could run half a day at a time. Sometimes, late of an afternoon, when the hands came in from work, we'd gather at a place called deadwood basin and run horses for two or three hours."

"Did you win, papa?"

Chad laughed. "Well, sometimes I won and sometimes I lost."

Tim persisted. "I bet you won more times than you lost, though."

Chad thought that over gravely. At last he said, "I'd say I won a few more than I lost."

For several minutes Tim said nothing, but Chad knew that he was thinking. The river fog was rising and the first sun rays broke through the trees, casting a diffused yellow light on the surface of the water.

At the cove where they kept the boat, Chad steered in to the bank. Tim scrambled out and pulled the boat up on the sandy beach.

Together they walked across the ridge toward home, Tim carrying the fish they had taken from the trotline. He had said nothing for half an hour; now he stopped and looked up at Chad.

"Papa, I want a horse worse than anything," he said, the words coming in a rush. "Billy Martin says they plan to have horse races for boys our age at the Tradesday. Do you think we could get a horse, papa . . . do you think maybe we could?"

Chad put his hand on the boys shoulder and smiled. His request was a natural and just one. "Sure," he said. "We'll have to get you a horse. Maybe we can get in to Gipson this week and talk to Mr. Connie about it."

Tim opened his mouth to speak, then closed it again. A broad grin lit his face. Finally he said. "That'll sure be fine, papa . . . I've always wanted a horse."

They walked on. A moment later Tim said, "We'll have to get a horse that can run, papa. I aim to win most of those Tradesday races."

"We'll have to keep that in mind, all right."

Tim smiled. "I bet mother'll be surprised."

Chad glanced down at him. Until now he had not thought of Emma.

"It might be better if we don't say anything to your mother about it right now," he said. "I expect we'd better wait a few days and see what happens."

"We could just go ahead and get the horse," Tim said, "and then surprise her."

"I guess we'd better just do that," Chad said thoughtfully.

Emma waked from a fitful sleep. She had stirred earlier, when Chad and Tim got up; had lain, only half awake, listening to their movements, their whispered voices, the sound of diminishing footsteps as they left the house; then she had dozed again.

She had been dreaming. She had been alone with Tim in a place she had never seen before. It was a forest, with huge, towering trees that hid the sun and sky. Then she had lost Tim and had become frantic. Rushing through the forest, searching for him, she had seemed unable to call his name, although she was sure that he would hear her if she could only speak. Finally, she had reached a river and had seen a man sitting on a log; for an instant she thought it was Will Kelly, then she saw that it was someone she had never known; she tried to tell the man that she had lost Tim, but she could not utter a word. Desperate, she began to cry. The man on the log said something that she did not understand, and when she looked at him again, it was Chad. Then she had waked up. . . .

She lay quietly for a moment; she felt strangely guilty about the dream; even now, fully awake, she distinctly remembered that in the dream she had responded to the identity of Chad with the old, indefinable aversion. It simply wasn't fair to him! There had been a time, during the months after Tim's birth, when she had lived with dreams; dreams that always seemed to express a faint distrust of Chad. She had told Dr. Matthews about them and he had explained that such "psychological tendencies" were not unusual after her experience with the first baby. Still, the dreams were disturbing, particularly since there was no reason for them. She was perfectly willing to admit that the fault lay with her rather than Chad. He was a perfect father to Timmy. The boy obviously idolized him and had already begun to assume his way of speaking, his way of doing things, even his facial expressions. In fact, that was a part of the problem. As Timmy grew older it was only natural that he should spend more and more time with Chad; Emma had known that this would happen and had carefully set about conditioning herself to it; but she had been less than successful. She could still remember the day she had watched them (with sinking heart) as they left the house with their fishing tackle, going for the first time to the river where they were to spend so many hours together; in time, she had told herself, it will be easier for me; I simply must be reasonable. But the fear remained, ready to leap at a thousand conclusions when they were ten minutes late returning. But the fears were a part of a pattern which she refused to accept as a reality. It was not that she wanted to change anything; she didn't. Timmy was growing up as he should, a happy, healthy boy who was doing the things a boy should do. And he was learning more from Chad than the art of fishing. Once, when they had returned late from a fishing trip, Timmy had come to the kitchen to show her their "catch," and had remained to help her set the table after Chad had gone to the living room. After a time, he had said, very matter-of-factly, "Mother, papa knows everything, don't he?" She had looked down at him for a long moment, at his young, believing face; the question had seemed neither childish nor unreasonable; there were times when she had felt exactly the same thing, times when she had known that she did not understand Chad simply because she lived by limitations that he did not have; at such times, he was a little frightening. To Timmy she had replied, "Yes, son, your papa is a very smart man."

Now, her thoughts were interrupted by the sound of their footsteps on the back porch. Quickly she jumped out of bed and wrapped a robe around her. They were waiting when she reached the kitchen.

"It looks like you overslept," Tim said.

"I sure did," she replied. She glanced at Chad and he smiled at her. "First thing I know, you and papa will be looking for another woman to take care of you."

The statement was made to Tim and it embarrassed him. Looking at Chad, he said, "No we won't, will we, papa?"

Chad shook his head. "I'm afraid she's stuck with us now," he said. "Tell her about the fish we caught."

"Did you catch a fish?" Emma asked, reaching for the tea kettle.

"A ten-pounder," Tim said. "Come on, I'll show you."

They went to the back porch together and Chad could hear Emma admiring the fish. A moment later she returned to the kitchen.

"Timmy took the fish to the wash-house," she said. "He wants to clean it himself."

"He can manage."

Emma sat the kettle on the stove, then turned and looked at him. "Some ten-pounder," she said, laughing.

Chad smiled. "I didn't have the heart to tell him any different," he said. "When you're Tim's age, they all look like ten-pounders."

She walked to where he stood, remembering the dream. Impulsively, she put her arms around his waist and laid her head against his chest.

"I've just been thinking," she said. "Instead of going into town today, why don't we go on a picnic . . . maybe down to the cove, below Samson's header?"

"That sounds fine," he said. "I'll take a picnic over going to town every time."

She looked up at him and laughed. "I'm very happy, Chad . . . I just wanted you to know."

He pulled her close and she felt loved and safe and utterly

at peace with the world.

"I want you to be happy," he said quietly. "You and Tim are what I live for. When you're happy, I am."

Emma sat with her back against the trunk of a tree, her eyes closed, listening to the slow sounds of the river. Overhead, the leaves stirred faintly in a thin breeze; somewhere, farther down, the raucous screech of a bird shattered the stillness. She opened her eyes; beside her, Chad lay on his back, his hat over his eyes. A hundred yards downstream she could see Timmy, perched in the forks of a tree, his fishing line dangling in the water.

"I could stay right here forever," she said.

Chad didn't move.

"Did you hear me?"

"Yes. You said you could stay here forever."

"Well . . . I could," she said.

His head nodded slightly under the black hat. "Me too."

Suddenly she leaned toward him and took the hat away. "I love you."

He put his arms around her and pulled her down to him. For a time they lay without moving.

At last, she said, "Everything seems so right here. It's like we're the only people in the world . . . you and me and Timmy. I guess that's the way I want it." She raised herself on one elbow and looked directly at him. "Is that wrong?"

"No, it isn't wrong. But it isn't the way things are, either."

"Oh you," she said. "You always sound like you're preaching a sermon or something."

He laughed. "I guess I do sound a little like a preacher sometimes," he said. "Maybe that's what I should have been."

She mussed his hair, laughing with him. "You should have been just what you are," she said. "My husband . . . and Timmy's father."

"I'll settle for that."

She laid her head back on his chest. "For the first time in my life," she said, "I'm really living for something. For you and Timmy." She sat up again. "Am I a good wife?"

"You're a wonderful wife."

"Do you really mean it?"

"I really mean it."

"All right, then, I'll tell you something. I think you're a wonderful husband."

Suddenly Timmy shouted and they both stood up. He was holding his fishing line up, showing them the small perch he had caught.

"That's a fine one," Chad called. "Maybe you've hit a school."

Timmy shouted something and turned back to his bait bucket.

Chad looked down at Emma and smiled.

"How big would you say?" she asked gravely.

He thought a moment. "About a five-pounder," he said, and they both laughed.

They sat down again and for some time said nothing. At last Emma said, "Do you think Timmy will want the farm when he grows up?"

Chad turned and looked at her. "I don't know," he said. "I hope so."

"So do I. I think about it sometime. I think about the time we'll be old and Timmy will be married and have children of his own. I used to worry about getting old, I thought it would be the most horrible thing in the world. But it isn't that way any more. Getting old will be fun. We'll build a smaller house up on the bluff and let Timmy have the big one. I want him to have this land and love it the way we do. I want us to be together always."

"Maybe it will work out that way," he said quietly. "If that's what Timmy wants."

"He will," she said. "I'm sure of it."

He looked at her, wanting to explain that life was never that simple, wanting to tell her that you could never be sure of anything, that you could not make the world exactly what you wanted it to be. He put his arms around her waist, remembering what she had said earlier.

"Do you have any objections to kissing a preacher?" he said.

CHAPTER 20

CONNIE LIPSCOMB, a shabby, corpulent man, sat in the littered office of the livery stable and commiserated with himself over his bad fortune. The things had not gone at all well
for him since the Panquel Corporation moved in; and his
disappointment was keener because his expectations had
been so high. Months ago, in the early planning stages of
the new mill, he had been led to believe—had, in fact, been
told by one of the officials—that the new industry would
need someone to purchase moving stock. He had been further
led to believe that he would receive strong consideration for
the enviable post and had envisioned the time when he
would travel commodiously to St. Louis and Kansas City on
regular buying trips, purchasing mules and horses for the
company. However, as matters turned out, the official who
had so generously promised him "special consideration" had
proved to be a rather minor member of the firm without any
real authority, or even much knowledge of what the corporation needed. The Panquel people had not hired a purchasing
agent for moving stock; in fact, Mr. Stanley had told him as
recently as last week that no such position was anticipated.
The company had brought in all the livestock it needed, he
said, and replacements would be secured locally. Well, Connie thought philosophically, I'm no worse off than I was—
but certainly no better off either.

He stood up and left the office, turning through the breezeway to the corral out back. At the end of the breezeway a
negro boy sat on a pile of feed sacks, asleep. Connie nudged
him with his foot.

"Earn your pay, boy," he said brusquely. The boy stirred,
opened his eyes and blinked slowly. "Get a shovel and clean

out these stables," Connie said. "This place smells to high heaven."

The boy stood up slowly, blinked again, then trudged off toward the feed room at the other end of the breezeway.

Connie watched him a moment, then grunted and walked out back.

There were only four animals in the open corral: a big-footed bay mare, a team of bony, grey mules that he had bought from a negro share-cropper east of town, and the mustang pony. Connie leaned against the rail fence for a moment, appraising the stock. He grunted again and shook his head. Not much to work with. He could move the bay mare easy enough, someone around town always needed a garden horse; the Panquel Corporation might take the mules if they were fed up; he made a mental note to feel Mr. Stanley out on the subject. The mustang was another matter. A lean, tawny sorrel, full of fear and bad manners, he stood now at the lower end of the corral, his head high, his feet wide apart as if ready to bolt at the first sound. On his hip was a brand, something like a Lazy-H; the horse had come from Texas, range bred, and only half-broken. Connie had bought him at an auction in Pemberton for fifteen dollars and had thought it a shrewd investment at the time; now, he was not so sure. There wasn't much market around Gipson for a crazy mustang. Maybe he could take him back to Pemberton . . . get his money back anyway. . . .

Behind him he heard voices, someone talking to the negro boy. He turned away from the corral and saw Chad Walters and his boy coming through the breezeway.

"Howdy," he said amiably. "You men are out mighty early this morning."

Chad nodded. "We've got work waiting for us at home," he said. "Just dropped by to see what kind of stock you've got on hand. Tim's in the market for a horse."

Connie had no wish to overstate his case; Walters knew horses. "Well, the picking is pretty slim right now," he said, nodding toward the corral. "That bay mare and the Texas pony is all I've got on hand."

Tim had run ahead to the corral fence and was peering now through the railing.

Chad and Connie joined him and for a time no one spoke.

Suddenly the mustang whirled around, staring wide-eyed at the spectators; then he snorted, flung his head high and dashed to another corner of the corral where he stood trembling, his ears pressed flat against his head.

Tim glanced up at Chad; Chad was watching the mustang.

The bay mare ambled across to where they stood and stretched out her head, nibbling congenially at Tim's fingers. Tim withdrew his hand and looked back at the mustang.

"That's a mighty pretty horse, ain't it, papa?" he said.

"He's a good *looking* horse," Chad agreed, "but there's a lot more to horses than looks."

"That pony came from Texas," Connie said, quick to note the first stir of interest in Tim's voice. "Range bred . . . tough as they come. . . ." Chad glanced at him, his face grave. "Course, he needs some more breaking," Connie amended.

Chad looked back at the mustang. After a moment he said, "Sometimes range ponies won't take breaking . . . it depends on how long they've run loose. How old is he?"

"Well, I couldn't rightly say . . . I got him over at Pemberton . . . fellow I bought him from said he was a four year old."

Chad smiled. "Didn't you look to see?"

The question annoyed Connie; the truth was, he had tried to check the mustang's mouth and had almost been trampled for his trouble. "Well, the fellow I bought him from is reliable enough . . . I've bought horses from him before . . . never caught him in a lie yet."

Chad turned to Tim. "I guess we'd better look around, son."

Tim said nothing but his disappointment was evident. After a moment, he looked again toward the corral.

Chad said, "We're going to have enough trouble as it is, convincing your mother that you need a horse. I'm afraid she wouldn't think much of that mustang."

Without looking around the boy said, "We could break him, papa." Then, as if sensing that he had used the wrong words, he added, "All he needs is taming down a little . . . He looks mighty fast. . . ."

Chad smiled. He watched the mustang; the boy was right, the pony could run. Emma, of course, was the problem; but then she would object to any horse. If the pony could be gentled. . . .

Connie, with the horse-trader's instinct for a prospective sale, said, "If you're interested, Mr. Walters, I can make that pony worth your money. It just happens that I got a pretty good buy on him myself . . . there ain't much market for a range horse in Gipson . . . might as well turn my profit to you."

Tim watched Chad expectantly; Chad stared across the corral for a long while; then, without looking at Connie, he said, "How much?"

Connie's mind clicked, weighing the chances for a substantial profit against the possibility of losing the sale altogether. It would be a mistake to over-price the mustang; Walters had already taken his measure. Still, it would be a mistake to sell him at cost if there was a chance to . . .

"Twenty-five dollars," he said. "That's what I give for him."

There was no reaction from Chad; nor did he turn around. Connie inched to the left, trying to see his face; it was hard to trade with a man if you couldn't read his expression.

Tim watched his father; Chad said nothing; Connie nervously jingled the two dimes in his pocket and waited; the bay mare ambled away across the corral. What seemed like several minutes passed.

Connie thought, If I don't close the sale now, I'll never close it. If I thought he was trying to smoke me out, I'd stick till hell freezes over. . . .

"Tell you what I'll do," he said. "If the boy wants the pony, give me twenty dollars and take him on . . . I'll take the loss myself."

Chad turned from the corral. He was almost smiling and

ankle-deep dust. The mustang hit the end of the rope, swung around for an instant, then bowed his neck and ran on, dragging Chad behind him.

Tim shouted excitedly and tried to see through the cloud of dust that boiled up over the corral. Connie licked his lips and climbed to the top of the rail fence, unconsciously caught up in the drama.

The mustang fought viciously, dragging Chad almost the length of the corral before he stopped and whirled to face him. Chad kept the line taut and continued to speak to the horse. As the dust settled, the man and the mustang stood facing each other, the rope between them; then Chad moved slowly forward, walking his hands along the lariat. The mustang rared up, pawing the air with his hooves; he tried again to whirl away; then, abruptly, he lowered his head and waited, as if admitting defeat.

Chad placed his hand on the mustang's mane and with a twist of the rope made a halter which he slipped over his head. A moment later he turned and led him across the corral to where Tim and Connie waited.

"Looks like you've took all the fight out of him," Connie said appreciatively.

Chad made no reply. He stopped the mustang and felt carefully along his legs and back; the animal tolerated the inspection with complete docility. Methodically, Chad looked at his mouth and teeth, but said nothing. He's been handled, he thought, but not enough to take the meanness out of him. Maybe the meanness won't come out; sometimes a range pony that had run wild too long was beyond breaking; anyhow beyond breaking gentle enough for a boy Tim's age. Still, the horse was young, he had good legs, a good chest; and he had enough sense if he'd just use it. . . .

He turned at last to Tim. "Well, what do you think, son?"

The boy grinned broadly, caught between his childish enthusiasm and the instinctive tendency to restrain his feelings. "I'd say we've found us a horse, papa . . . wouldn't you?"

Chad nodded slowly; the presence of Emma hovered in the back of his mind. Well, she'd just have to get used to the idea; the boy needed a horse.

"It looks that way," he told Tim. To Connie he said, "If you won't be needing that rope for a day or two, I'll just take it along."

"Sure," Connie said. "Bring it in the next time you come to town . . . don't make a special trip, there's another one around here somewhere."

Chad led the mustang to the corral gate and across the open yard to the breezeway. He took a worn billfold from his hip pocket and handed Connie a faded, brown twenty dollar bill.

"Much oblige," Connie said, accepting the money. "You made a mighty good trade. It's my loss, but the boy's got what he wants . . . that's what I was thinking about."

Chad nodded and spoke to Tim. "We'd better be getting back, son," he said. "Your mother'll be wondering what happened to us."

Connie followed them outside to the hitchrack where Chad had left his wagon and team. The mustang, at the first sight of the open street, flung his head up and glared about him wildly, every strange sound a potential enemy. Suddenly, snorting his protest, he reared and swung back toward the breezeway; Chad yanked hard at the halter rope, pulling him up short; then, again, he spoke to him, not words but a soft, regular pattern of sounds. Finally, tense and trembling, the mustang followed him outside.

"I expect you'd better drive the team," Chad told Tim. "I'll lead the mustang till we get out of town."

Tim scrambled up to the seat and took up the reins; he made a wide circle in the middle of the street, then Chad clucked to the mustang and followed behind the wagon.

Connie stood in the open breezeway and watched them. After they had disappeared beyond the buildings on main street, he turned back to the office. I should have held out for twenty-five, he told himself; chances are, he'd a paid it.

Emma went again to the front porch and scanned the river road beyond the valley. She admonished herself for playing

Connie had the uncomfortable feeling that he knew exactly what the mustang had sold for in Pemberton.

"Do you have a lariat?" Chad asked.

"Sure . . . there's a couple around here somewhere." Connie turned and walked toward the breezeway. "Jabal!" The negro boy appeared almost at once. "Find me one of them lariats . . . I think there's one up by the feed room."

He waited while the negro boy went to fetch the rope; he had the unpleasant feeling that Walters had out-traded him. He shouldn't have come down on his price; Walters would have paid it. Still, you couldn't be sure. . . .

The stable boy returned with a lariat; Connie took it from him and walked back to where Chad and Tim were waiting.

"This one's got a little manure on it," he said, slapping it against the corral fence, "but I reckon it'll do."

Chad look the lariat and dropped the shag end on the ground; carefully he shook out the loop, then rewound the slack in his left hand. "That mustang *has* been broke?" he asked, glancing at Connie.

"Well, now I never tried him," Connie said. "But the fellow I bought him from said he'd been range-broke . . . course, that's not the same as being gentle-broke."

Chad smiled. "No . . . that's not quite the same."

He turned and walked to a gate at the lower end of the corral, shaking the lariat loose in his right hand. Slowly he moved toward the corner where the mustang waited, speaking quietly to the panicky animal. The mustang threw up his head, nostrils flaring, and whirled completely around, kicking up swirls of dust. Then, suddenly, he stopped and waited, perfectly still except for his quivering flank, watching the man and the rope. Chad, too, stopped; for a moment he stood motionless, speaking to the horse in a low, persuasive voice. Then he took another step forward. The mustang stood poised for an instant, then, neighing wildly, he bolted, running hard and low along the rail fence. Chad moved; the lariat shot out, settling around the mustang's neck; Chad warped the line across his leg and dug his heels into the

186

the anxious wife and mother, remembering something Chad had once told her: people, he had said, have their own lives to live; you can't live somebody else's and you can't make somebody else live yours. How easy it was for Chad; his rules were simple and true and he lived the way he thought; he was right, of course—and she had tried, *really* tried, to be what he wanted her to be. But when she was alone, her good intentions turned to fears and there was nothing she could do about that. At such times, she realized how completely she had lost herself in Chad and Timmy. The basin life as she had known it, as a girl and, later, as a young woman, even her own family, seemed now remote and almost unreal. She received occasional letters from Mase (he seemed to be doing well in Tennessee; he and Lucy were expecting a child in December, and had asked her to come out for a visit); and she had received one short note from Lewt (he and Ben were working on a ranch now; Ben was about to get married; they liked California and didn't know when they would get a chance to come home); but these were scraps of paper from another world, written by people she scarcely knew, awkward, formal remembrances over which she wept, but briefly and for herself.

She glanced again at the river road, then returned to the kitchen and began preparing dinner. Half an hour later she heard Timmy's voice and the rattle of the wagon wheels against the rocky lane leading down to the barn lot. Hurriedly, she pushed the salt pork away from the heat and went out the back way to the yard. Timmy was waving and she waved back; then, she saw the mustang. Chad had slid from his back and was leading him toward the lot gate. Curiously, her first reaction was a pleasant stir of excitement; the horse was beautiful. Timmy was shouting something but she could not understand the words; she laughed and waved again.

Then suddenly, as she watched, the mustang seemed to explode with fury; whinnying shrilly, he rared high on his hind legs and lunged at Chad, pawing the air viciously with his front feet; caught by surprise Chad fell to one knee and rolled away from the flailing hooves; for an instant the line slipped from his grasp, but he scrambled to his feet and grabbed it again before the mustang could bolt; then he flung one arm around the mustang's neck and clutched him above the nose with his free hand; the mustang tried to whirl away, lost his footing on the loose rocks and slid to his haunches; for an instant Chad and the horse were down, both scrambling wildly for an advantage. . . .

It had all happened so suddenly that for a moment Emma stood on the rocky pathway, frozen, unable even to move. Then she saw Timmy, standing beside the wagon not ten feet from where Chad struggled with the maddened mustang, his arms held protectively across his face. Screaming his name again and again, she rushed down the path. . . .

By the time she reached the wagon the mustang was standing quietly beside Chad; Timmy was looking not at her but at his father, smiling proudly. She fell on her knees beside him, clutching him to her breast, sobbing wildly . . . "Timmy . . . Timmy . . . Timmy. . . ."

He allowed her to hold him for a long while, his head pressed against her, but she felt in his thin shoulders the instinctive restraint which seemed so incongruous in a child. At last he pulled away and looked at her curiously. With the utter, terrifying innocence of youth, he said, "What's the matter, mama?"

Unable to answer, knowing that she could not make him understand the mother's fear that had gripped at her heart, she could only pull him close again.

Finally, trying to regain her composure, she stood up and turned to Chad; in him, it seemed, her frustrations always began and ended; even Timmy's unnatural attempts to be reserved and inturned were simply reflections of the admiration he felt for his father; at times, frighteningly, she felt a barrier between her and Timmy which seemed, unreasonably, to originate in Chad.

Now he stood quietly, watching her, that eternal unapproachable patience reflected in his face; neither condemning nor condoning her actions. Crazily, it seemed that even the mustang appraised her with half critical eye.

190

"Whose horse is that?" she asked, her eyes blazing.

"The horse belongs to Timmy." There was something in the way he said it, the deliberate even-paced tone of his voice, the almost formal intonation, that told her he had prepared for this moment. With an instinct born of experience she curbed her anger; it was Timmy who must be protected, and now he saw her as a hysterical and unreasoning woman; she must be careful not to lose an advantage that could not be regained later.

For a full minute she stared at Chad, trying to think of some way to modify her position without withdrawing her objections, wanting to regain the respect she had lost in Timmy's eyes.

In the end she simply turned away and walked back up the lane toward the house. She listened for Timmy's footsteps behind her, desperately needing at least his forgiveness if not his understanding. But she heard nothing. At the top of the hill she looked back; Chad had led the mustang into the barn lot; now he held the gate while Timmy drove the mules through; Timmy said something as he passed and Chad nodded and smiled.

Miserable and alone, feeling that she had handled the affair badly, Emma went inside and sat down at the kitchen table. If only she had approached Chad quietly, had tried to reason with him; perhaps she could have won him over. That possibility now was remote; she had already taken her stand. Keeping the horse was, of course, out of the question; even a gentle, well-trained horse would have been bad enough; whatever could have possessed Chad to buy that vicious, untamed beast she could not imagine.

A moment later she heard their voices as they approached the house. Hurriedly she moved to the stove and began stirring a pot of beans. It was Timmy's voice now, the words spoken rapidly, forgetting to control his excitement, "How long do you think it will be before I can ride him, papa? 'Bout how long would you say?"

And the response, patient, understanding, infuriating, "Oh, not long . . . couple of days maybe . . . we'll work

191

with him late this afternoon and again tomorrow . . . we should be able to tell something by then."

Emma pressed her lips together, thinking: I must remember not to say anything; later I'll talk to Chad alone.

After dinner Chad and Tim went down to the new sawmill to get some scrap lumber for a hog pen. Earlier that week, the new manager, Mr. Stanley, and Will Kelly had driven out for a visit; Mr. Stanley had mentioned buying the farm, but he did not press the point when Chad told him that he did not plan to sell. Surprisingly, the manager appeared to admire and understand Chad's point of view, and he seemed genuinely fond of Timmy. When he left, he urged Chad and Timmy to pay him a visit, and it was then that he had told them they were welcome to the piles of scrap lumber that littered the millyard.

Emma washed the dinner dishes, then went to the bedroom to rest. She lay quietly for some time, staring up at the ceiling. Perhaps she had been unreasonable, she told herself; but she didn't *mean* to be unreasonable, above all else she wanted Timmy's love and respect; she must remember that he was growing up. He was almost eight. Eight years! Where had they gone? So much had happened since that warm, rainy night when she had lain in that same bed, engulfed in an aura of pain and exultation and fear; had seen around her the shadowy remote faces of Chad and Dr. Matthews, blends of lightness and dark in the flickering lamplight; had lain quietly, as she lay now, actually wanting the pain because it seemed a real and necessary part of what was happening to her. And, at last, the pain had become so intense that the exultation and the shadows had retreated and she had waited in a vacuum of blinding agony, suspended between the beginning and the end of all things; then the agony subsided and the faces returned and the shrill plaintive cry of Timmy out of the darkness; and sleep. Later she opened her eyes and saw Chad standing beside the bed; he knelt beside her and held her hands and kissed her gently and told her that they had a son. And from that moment, she had been whole again. . . .

Yes, she must remember that Timmy was growing up; the fears she suffered were a mother's fears and they were hers to bear alone, she must remember that. Chad could tame the mustang; in his lifetime he must have tamed thousands of horses . . . Perhaps she had been unreasonable. . . .

At last she fell asleep.

She was wakened by the piercing, high-pitched squeal of the mustang; startled, she sat up in bed, listening. The sounds came again and again, in quick succession, the pent-up, frustrated protest of a beast outraged.

She jumped out of bed and went to the kitchen; it was still early, she was sure that Chad and Timmy had not returned. She went to the water bucket and drank a dipper of water, then returned to the table and sat down. She could still hear the shrill, agonizing cries of the mustang; she tried to shut out the sound but it seemed now to pervade the entire house; she held her hands over her ears, felt terror return. At last, drawn almost against her will, she went to the back porch and down the steps to the yard. The mustang stood at the far corner of the lot, his head high, his eyes bulging wildly, screaming his defiance; he whirled and charged to another corner, pawed maliciously at the corner post, then dashed back again. The mules and cow were gathered fearfully under the barn shed, watching the mustang with startled expressions.

Emma felt a sudden rush of panic; something had to be done, the mustang seemed bent on escape, even if it meant tearing down the lot fence; he had gone absolutely mad! Terror stricken, yet compelled to act, she ran down the lane to the gate. Suddenly the mustang spun around and ran directly toward her; she tried to scream but was unable to utter a sound; the animal slithered to a stop not five feet from where she stood; the gate between them was closed but the wire loop had slipped off the panel; a touch of his hoof would open it! Emma waited, the terror caught in her throat, unable to move or cry out. The mustang now stood glaring at her, his eyes filled with hatred; he breathed heavily, his haunches and neck lathered with perspiration. It seemed to Emma that he was waiting for her to move; that consciously and calculatedly he planned to kill her.

Suddenly, motivated entirely by fear, her action a reflex rather than a response to thought, she waved her hand at him. "Whoosh!" she said.

The mustang snorted and bowed his neck; he moved a step forward, snorted again; she closed her eyes and waited, terrified beyond sound, as motionless as a stone.

How long she stood there she did not know; it must have been an instant, it seemed like an eternity. Then she heard voices—Chad and Timmy! She tried to call out to them but had no voice; they seemed miles away—perhaps they would get there in time.

An instant later they were beside her. . . .

It was Timmy who spoke to the mustang. "Get on there," he said, waving his hand carelessly. "Hi, mama." The mustang snorted, although the sound was no longer vicious or threatening but almost playful; he turned and trotted away across the lot.

Chad was saying, "Well, we found some scrap lumber we can use . . . we'll have to hitch the mules to haul it in. . . ."

The fantastic moment slid past, so incredible that she would never forget it. She looked at them, her husband and her son. They *really* didn't know how near death she had been. And, with a sudden wave of helplessness and frustration, she realized that she couldn't tell them. They wouldn't believe it . . . they'd never believe it!

Chad was looking at her, his face questioning now.

"Is anything the matter, Emma?" he asked.

She breathed deeply, trying to regain control of herself before she answered; now, oddly, she wanted only to avoid looking ridiculous in their eyes. At last she said, "No . . . nothing's the matter." Then she smiled at Timmy, and turned and walked away from them toward the house.

CHAPTER 21

DURING THE DAYS following, Chad and Timmy spent much of their time at the barn lot, working with the mustang. Emma remained in the house, determined to say nothing more; determined to live with her fear and make the best of it. Her chance had slipped past; Timmy's whole life now was wrapped up in the mustang; morning, noon and night—he talked of nothing else. He had named the horse (rather ironically, Emma thought) "Pal."

At first Timmy said nothing about these daily workouts; Emma simply waited, miserable and often lonely, knowing that she was responsible for the breach that stood between them. Then one day Timmy spoke to her of the mustang, an insignificant comment, offered tentatively, gauging her reaction. With a great effort, she made herself appear interested, asking him questions that would lead to further discussion. After a time he began reporting to her regularly on the events at the barn lot, and mingled with the ever present fear was a sense of gratitude that he had again taken her into his confidence.

Then one morning at the breakfast table, a week or more after her own frightful experience, Timmy told her that he and Chad were going to the river road that day "to teach Pal something about racing."

Emma made herself receive this news with outward calm; she even managed to say, "Racing . . . already? I didn't know you were that far along with him."

"Well, he's still a little skittish," Timmy expanded gravely. "But he'll have to learn sometime. Mr. Kelly says the races in Gipson—" Then he caught himself; neither he nor Chad

had mentioned the Tradesday to Emma; Chad had said they had better wait a while, until Emma had got used to the idea of the mustang. Now Timmy simply left the sentence unfinished and glanced guiltily at Chad.

For a long moment no one spoke; then Emma said, "What races?"

Timmy watched Chad.

"Tim's talking about the Tradesday races in Gipson," he said. "Some of the merchants are working on a plan to get people into town of a Saturday, a big all-day show with barbecue and contests of one kind or another. They have it in mind to make horse racing a part of the show."

"But Timmy is just a boy. . . ."

"Well, they're talking about dividing the races into two groups, one for men and one for boys Timmy's age."

Suddenly Emma felt again that choked, utterly dominated feeling that always came over her when she faced Chad and Timmy as a united front. To make matters worse, her entire relationship with Timmy, the confidence so recently gained, was at stake. Forcing back the objections that welled up inside her, she stood up and went to the stove, returned with the coffee pot and refilled Chad's cup. She did not look at him, but she felt his eyes watching her. She placed the pot back on the stove and sat down again.

She looked at Timmy; he too was watching her, waiting for an answer.

"Well, I didn't know you could train a horse to race without racing him against another horse." She chose the words carefully, wanting to remain neutral at the moment.

Timmy grinned. "Papa's going to race me on one of the mules," he said, mistaking her caution for acceptance. He glanced at Chad and laughed. "That'll be some race."

They ate in silence for a time, all sensing that the issue had not ended. Finally Timmy pushed back his plate and asked to be excused. Emma nodded.

"Want me to catch Pal, papa?" he asked.

It was a moment before Chad answered. In his mind he measured the situation; as the boy had said the mustang was still skittish, but at that he'd come a long way; besides the boy's pride was somehow at stake.

"Might as well," he said. "Run him in his stall, he's easier to bridle there."

"I think that would be best," Timmy said as he walked out.

Now—I must be perfectly calm, Emma told herself; this is my last chance; if I lose this point, I've lost them all.

She looked directly at Chad. "Is it safe to let Timmy catch that animal?" she asked; she was careful not to let her tone condemn his judgment.

"I think so," he said. "He knows the mustang better than I do. Once you know what to expect of an animal like that, you're all right. Tim knows what he will do and what he won't . . . he learns fast."

"And the races . . . you're going to let him ride?"

"Well, I promised him he could."

"Didn't you know I would object?"

"I didn't think about that at the time."

"What *were* you thinking about?"

"My own boyhood, I guess. I was younger than Timmy when I began riding."

"That isn't the same thing."

"Maybe it isn't. But that's what I thought about."

There was a moment of silence between them. Then, in an even, carefully controlled voice, Emma spoke.

"And what if I object now?"

Chad looked at her, trying, it seemed, to read the attitude behind the words.

"Then I'll have to tell him that he can't ride."

"Do you think I'm being unreasonable?"

"No."

"He's my son, too."

"Yes."

There was another pause—then Timmy, shouting from the back yard. "I'm ready, papa . . . I've got old Blue, too!"

Chad sat a moment longer, watching her.

"You don't mind if we go to the river road?"

"No."

He stood up. "If you don't want Timmy to ride in the races that's all right. Don't worry about him . . . he'll get over it."

He walked to where she sat; then he placed his hand on her shoulder. She had needed that; above all else, she had needed that. Without looking at him she put her hand over his.

"I'll have to think," she said. "You go on . . . Timmy's waiting."

She sat perfectly still, listening, as Chad went down the back steps and out to where Timmy waited with the mustang and mule; Timmy's voice, excited and high pitched, his laughter, Chad's responses—and then the sounds, retreating as they rode away.

She stood up and walked to the front door, watching them as they rode across the valley and up the rise beyond. The victory was hers; Chad would not let Timmy ride if she objected, nor would he resent the broken promise. And yet, it was no victory at all; she knew that now. She had wanted so long to be understood, and because she was afraid that she would not be, she had simply remained silent. She had won her point; Chad had understood, but in understanding, he had left her no victory. It was Timmy who must understand, and he had neither Chad's wisdom nor her fears. He had only the immediate desires of a boy, the wish to live by immediate pleasures adopted on his terms because, to him, there were no others. Chad had said that he would get over it; perhaps he would, but at what price? She had won a victory of words—but not of Timmy's heart.

CHAPTER 22

THE FIRST TRADESDAY was held on the last Saturday in September. This was rather late in the year to initiate the enterprise, since it had been agreed that with the coming of bad weather (usually late in November) the operation would have to be discontinued until the following spring. However, as someone had pointed out in a regular session of the Gipson Merchants' Alliance, the Tradesday was, at that stage, an experiment anyhow and its late inception would give the alliance a chance to judge its success as an overall promotional plan.

The idea, of course, was to draw the Saturday shopping crowds into Gipson, which during the past year had lost a good part of its regular revenue to Pemberton on the east, and Delhigh farther south. After the first exciting flush of prosperity, the Panquel Millwork Corporation had proved to be something of a disappointment; economically as well as socially. The population had more than doubled, it was true, but many of the mill people had moved to the basin rather than settle in town; and those who remained had showed an increased inclination to spend their Saturdays (and their money) in Pemberton, which offered the extra enticement of legalized beer. In time it appeared that Gipson had a considerable increase in population with a disproportionate increase in revenue. Then, to make matters worse, the corporation had built a small commissary in the basin which actually undersold the merchants in town.

By mid-summer the Saturday shopping crowd had fallen to less than half of what it had been in previous years; it was during this unhappy state of economic affairs that the

Gipson Merchants' Alliance had been formed and the idea for a tradesday instituted.

The Alliance met regularly, three nights a week, during August and the early part of September. In the beginning, there had been so many differences of opinion, so many conflicting ideas about what should or should not be included in the affair, that it seemed the project was doomed to failure. But during these trying times the Alliance chairman, Mr. Trigby Lutes, had wheedled and coaxed and, at times, tyrannized until an agreement was finally reached on all major points.

It was decided that all business establishments would be responsible for individual displays, the nature of which would be left to the ingenuity of the merchant concerned. Since this display was the merchant's only chance to petition for special attention, some of the ideas were remarkably effective. Mr. Thomas Bridgeman, who owned the Chekow County Hardware, placed a caged turkey in the display window; anyone who bought a dollar's worth of merchandise was entitled to guess at the turkey's weight; at the end of the day, the turkey was officially weighed (to the quarter ounce) and the shopper with the closest guess was awarded the bird, plus a two dollar trade certificate at the store. Mr. Rich Meyers' idea was even more ingenious; he arrived early at his produce store and, with the assistance of a ladder, pasted a penny on the ceiling; anyone who visited the store during the day (no purchase necessary) was allowed to guess at the date on the penny, which appeared to be quite close but was actually so far away that the date was not clearly visible; this scheme provoked much craning of necks and good-natured laughter and was generally so successful that it was later adopted by other merchants; of course, the person who guessed closest to the penny's date was presented a "house prize"—a twenty-five pound sack of All-Lay feed mash.

Ray Grigsby, who ran the saddle shop, gave a new pair of bridle reins to the customer who came closest to the number of dried peas in a quart fruitjar; Mert Dillion let his customers estimate the age of the mule tied to the hitch-rail in front of the blacksmith shop; John Bockman handed out raffle tickets, the stubs of which were placed in a wire basket; at four o'clock his young son, Johnny, drew out the winning stub and the ticket holder was awarded a silver dollar.

These and other such provocative devices were doubtlessly major contributions to the success of the Tradesday, for they promoted a sense of internal competition which pervaded the entire affair.

Aside from the individual displays, the alliance outlined what it called a Main Program, consisting of five "participation events." Tradesday officially opened at nine o'clock in the morning with a guinea chase; the guinea was released (by Mr. Rich Meyers) from the back of his produce truck and everyone was entitled to take part in the chase; the participant who caught the bird and returned it to Mr. Meyers was awarded five dollars in cash (it was agreed to make the initial prize especially attractive in order to encourage early arrivals). After the guinea chase came the pig wrestle, at ten, and the greased pole climbing at eleven. The day reached a dramatic climax in the afternoon with the horse races; the first for boys (age 7–15, inclusive) and, at three o'clock, the adult races. It was with the horse races that a good deal of discussion (and, subsequently, dissention) arose. Reverend Amos Snedley, the Methodist minister and the only member of the alliance who had no commercial stake in the Tradesday, offered the first objection, mainly on principle. Horse racing, he pointed out, by its very nature produced certain evils: gambling, drinking, "religious disobedience." In time it would inevitably attract a certain element which, he was sure, Gipson could better do without. He did not mean to be narrow or unreasonable, they all knew that he was an admirer of fine horse flesh, but that was his thinking on the matter.

The good pastor's objections were forthwith overruled by a vote of the alliance but, as the word got around, other local ministers rallied to the cause and it was clear that something would have to be done. A compromise was finally effected; no horse would be allowed to participate in the races which was not owned by a resident of Chekow County (this, it was presumed, would eliminate the "gambling people"), and Sheriff McKnight was given authority to "arrest on sight" anyone apprehended in the act of "giving or receiving monies" in transactions involving the horse races. This compromise was graciously accepted by the clerical opposition; and thus the main program was completed. Handbills were printed and distributed throughout the county and by late summer a spirit of high excitement prevailed.

Although the alliance looked forward to the opening Tradesday with considerable optimism, they were in no way prepared for the tremendous success it enjoyed. Chekow County, as Mert Dillion later pointed out, "had never seen anything to match it."

The wagons began arriving soon after daylight, at first in small numbers and then in a steady stream; creaking caravans that wound along the dusty roads like columns of ants, from the river bottom, from the mountains north of town, a few even from Pemberton and Delhigh. Anticipating, beyond reasonable hope, such an eventuality, the alliance had designated the area between Bridgeman's Hardware and the Saddle Shop as a wagon lot, and into it the wagons poured steadily; by eight o'clock there was not a foot of available space left and the wagons were tying up under the paw-paw groves below the gin. Members of the Merchant's Alliance left their stores in charge of subordinates and rushed about under the colorful streams of bunting that had been strung along the street, shouting instructions to confused wagon drivers, urging people not to park on main street (which had been set aside for the horse races), and generally enjoying the authority that had been duly invested in them. Gipson seethed in the festive air; people shouted, babies cried shrilly, stray dogs raced through the street, barking insanely at anything and everything; all creating an endless cacaphony of sound that rattled off the buildings in an eternal din.

Into this gala atmosphere came the Walters family: Chad and Emma in the wagon, and Timmy riding behind on the tawny mustang. Catching her first sight of it as they crossed the low rise west of town, Emma felt her breath catch in her throat; it seemed for an instant as if the whole world had gone mad. She watched spellbound as Chad worked the wagon slowly along the street; suddenly she realized that he had stopped. He turned in the seat, speaking to Timmy.

"Hold the mustang on a tight rein, son," he said. "It'll take him a while to get used to this." He glanced at Emma and smiled. "Same as me," he added.

Emma looked at Timmy. He leaned forward, patting the mustang on the neck.

"He's fine, papa . . . I think he'll be all right."

"I think so," Chad said assuringly.

Emma was not so confident. The mustang stood now with his head up, his front feet spread slightly, ready to move in any direction. She leaned toward Chad, speaking above the street noise. "Maybe you'd better ride him until we get settled . . . Timmy can drive the mules. . . ."

Chad nodded, but at that instant Mr. John Bockman walked up to the wagon, his face flushed with excitement; he wore a blue tag on his shirt which said: "OFFICIAL."

"No point in going up town," he shouted up to Chad. "The lot up there is full." He pointed to the cluster of wagons under the paw-paw grove behind the gin. "Some of them's been parking under the grove . . . if you can't get in there, you'll just have to fine a place down by the creek."

Chad nodded, then shook the reins and moved across the street toward the gin. A steady stream of wagons were going that way; one of them stopped, letting him slip into line. He touched his hat to the ladies in the wagon and nodded his thanks to the driver.

There was still some space left at the lower end of the paw-paw grove; Chad pulled the mules in under one of the trees and stopped. Emma looked back; Timmy was directly behind them; he grinned at her and she smiled. The mustang was still nervous but he seemed to be behaving himself.

Chad climbed down and held up his hand to her. She took it and stepped down, carefully holding her dress away from the dusty wheel. Timmy slid from the mustang's back and joined them.

"Ain't this something," he said. "I bet everybody in Arkansas is here." He glanced up at Emma. "Wouldn't you say so, mama?"

She recognized his comment as some kind of overture; although she and Chad had never discussed the mustang in his presence, he had, of course, sensed the conflict. In a way, it was unfair to him.

"I'd say a good part of them are here," she said smiling.

The dust from the passing wagons choked her. To Chad she said, "I'm going to step over here out of the way until you're ready." He had already begun unhitching the mules.

She made her way to a shady spot over by the fence and sat down on the pillow she had brought from home. Watching Chad she wondered again, as she had wondered a thousand times before: what is my relationship to this man; what is he really like; what does he think of me? Even now, performing the commonplace task of unhitching the mules, he seemed to move with a special and exclusive kind of efficiency—that nameless and eternal air of ritual. In the eleven years they had been married, she had never heard him raise his voice, not once, to man or beast; she had heard him laugh, really laugh, less than a dozen times, although it seemed to her that he was frequently amused; she had never known his patience to fail him, not even when Timmy asked the same question a thousand times—not even when she had failed him as lover and bride.

Since the day they had discussed Timmy and the mustang, he had put the entire matter from his mind, leaving the final decision with her. She had tried to speak of it to Timmy, had tried to explain to him the danger of riding in the races; she had desperately wanted him, in terms that he would understand, to know the love that prompted her fears. But this had become an increasingly difficult prospect; Timmy, sensing her constraint, had overruled her tacit objections by an even greater confidence and enthusiasm. In the end, her position of authority became wholly untenable and she had somehow become an unwilling party to this day. Now, in the midst of the surging masses of people, the strange indefinable sense of excitement, a feeling of despair came over her.

Her thoughts were interrupted by the presence of Chad and Timmy beside her; Timmy led the mustang, who seemed now only curious.

Chad held out his hand. "Tim will have to register his horse for the races," he said. "Then we can look around awhile."

She took his hand and let him help her to her feet. "I'll stop at the land office and visit with Will Kelly," she said. "Will it take long?"

"I don't think so. He'll just have to sign his name and stable the mustang till race time."

Together they walked along the wagon lane to the gin. Timmy spoke to Chad.

"Reckon I ought to ride him, papa? . . . let him get used to the crowd?"

Chad nodded. "That might be better," he said. He helped Timmy swing up to the mustang's back. "I expect you'll have to talk to him some," he said.

Emma watched the perceptible tremble along the mustang's flank as Timmy touched him with his heels, saw the eyes, black and ominous, charged with fear and the wildness that could never be tamed out of him. For an instant he refused to move, his front legs stiff and slightly spread. Timmy patted him along the neck and spoke quietly, almost frighteningly the son of his father. The mustang lifted a paw, tentatively struck at the air, then moved away, taut and bouncy. Timmy glanced back and grinned for her benefit.

Chad was watching, his dark face touched with pride. Speaking more to himself than to Emma, he said, "He's got a good way with horses."

"I don't want him to ride!" Emma blurted out the words; it seemed that they sprang up inside her, the pent-up fears of a thousand sleepless nights.

Chad looked at her slowly. "It's a little late for that, isn't it?"

Emma nodded, miserable beyond words, sorry now that she had spoken at all. Of course, it was too late; it had always been too late; from the beginning she had simply been a bystander, without any real authority at all. "I suppose so," she agreed. "I suppose it is."

Chad took her arm and they turned north up main street. "Don't worry about it," he said. "It won't help any."

She glanced at him sharply; only with an effort could she avoid snapping at him. Then, as the quick anger passed, she smiled slowly and turned away. Strangely, the quality in Chad that was most reassuring was the same quality that, at other times, she most fiercely resented. *Don't worry . . . it won't help any;* he had really meant to be kind; it was almost ludicrous; living beyond the simple emotions and passions of normal human beings, he spoke as if these feelings and sensations could be dominated by a voluntary will. People were always saying, don't worry . . . it doesn't help, but somehow they kept worrying. With Chad it was different; when he said worry doesn't help anything, he really *meant* it. Who else in the world said it *that* way?

Suddenly, she felt a little guilty; it was not fair to labor Chad with her woman's fears, not fair to ruin his day . . . or hers. She gave his arm a squeeze.

"Heaven's sake, look at the people!"

The throngs moved along the boardwalks in a surging, shouting, jostling mass. Women carried children too small to walk, the men carried early purchases in bright yellow paper sacks (ordered especially for the Tradesday), holding them high above their heads to protect the contents.

Emma caught a glimpse of Timmy up ahead, riding slowly along the side of the street, letting the mustang pick his way through the wagons and go-carts. Then someone banged against her, mumbled an apology and moved on; she felt

Chad's arm move around her protectively; she glanced up into his face and smiled; then, suddenly, she laughed; he looked a little harassed which was so unusual that it seemed funny. He grinned and shook his head in mock despair.

Timmy was waiting at the hitchrail in front of the land office; he was talking to some men seated on the front porch when they walked up.

A tall, redheaded man was saying ". . . well, I wouldn't be too sure. They tell me that pinto pony Paul Noland's boy is riding is mounted on wheels."

Timmy shook his head noncommitally, then grinned and looked down at his feet.

"Tell you what," the redheaded man went on with pretended seriousness, "if you win I'll buy you a cream cone . . . if Paul's boy wins you have to buy me one . . . how does that sound?"

Timmy continued for a moment to look at his feet, obviously out of his province in this public exchange; then, sounding for all the world like Chad, he said, "I'm not saying he won't . . . but I'm not saying he will either."

The men on the porch laughed and one of them said, "He's a dandy ain't he?"

Chad nodded to the men and spoke to Timmy. "If you're ready, son, we'd better get on over to the livery stable." To the men on the porch he said, "Is Will inside?"

At that instant Will appeared in the doorway, accompanied by Mert Dillion. Seeing Chad and Emma, he smiled with genuine affection, then walked down the front steps to shake hands. "You folks know Mert," he said. Chad nodded and Emma, who had never seen him before in her life, smiled a vague greeting.

"Timmy riding in the race?" Will asked.

"If we can get him registered he is," Chad replied.

"Well Connie will take care of that. I was over that way twenty or thirty minutes ago. He had eight horses entered in the boy's race then." He turned to Emma. "Why don't you wait for them in the office," he said. "We haven't had a good visit in months."

"Well, if it won't be too much of a bother. . . ."

"No bother at all," Will said. "I can't think of any way I'd rather spend the morning." He took her arm and led her toward the steps.

To Chad she said, "I'll be waiting here."

"All right. We'll be back soon as we get the mustang registered and stabled."

At the doorway Emma stopped and watched Chad and Timmy moving across the street; Timmy riding the mustang and Chad walking beside him, his arm resting carelessly across the mustang's rump. Timmy was leaning slightly toward his father, talking seriously, his handsome young face intently absorbed. From time to time Chad nodded a solemn agreement, equally serious, equally absorbed.

Behind her Will too was watching. "I guess it's natural for a man to love his son," he said. "But when they're good friends, that's a rare thing."

Emma looked at him and smiled, curiously grateful. "They're good friends all right," she said, then added, "Sometimes I wonder where I fit in."

Will nodded understandingly. "I expect most mothers wonder that at one time or another," he said.

As matters turned out, her "visit" with Will was rather less than satisfactory. A constant stream of men moved in and out of the office, talking races and horses and the Tradesday in general. For a while Will tried introducing her to everyone but finally, sensing her constraint, he let her sit quietly in the corner, his eyes offering her an occasional apology.

She was greatly relieved when Chad and Timmy returned half an hour later. Chad nodded a greeting to some of the men in the office and Emma could not help noticing when one or two of them said, "Howdy, Mr. Walters." Even with men of his own age and kind, there was a marked restraint, a curious formality. It occurred to her that of all the men she knew, only Will Kelly and Sheriff McKnight called him by his first name. Even Mr. Stanley, rather incongruously it seemed to her, deferred to the formal "Mister."

Chad was speaking to her. "If you're ready we can walk around. . . ."

She got up and walked across to the door, putting her arm around Timmy.

"I'm afraid it hasn't been much of a visit, Emma," Will said. "Why don't you folks come back and watch the races from here . . . I'll save you a place on the front porch."

Chad looked at Emma, who smiled. "Thanks, Will," he said. "We'll try to get back this way about one o'clock."

She thanked Will for "the use of his office," then she and Chad and Timmy left and joined the milling throngs along main street.

During the next two hours Emma almost forgot the races; she could not remember when she had had more fun. They visited all of the stores and Chad insisted that she participate in the individual displays, even making one or two unnecessary purchases in order to qualify her as a "guesser." She had no idea how old the mule was in front of the blacksmith shop, or how many peas Mr. Dillion had put in the quart fruitjar, but she was sure that she had correctly read the date on Mr. Meyer's penny. 1815, as plain as day. Later when she told Chad, he nodded gravely for a moment, then laughed. "You've got better eyes than I have," he said. "I couldn't even see the penny."

Timmy said, "What was the date, mama?"

"1815," she said, shaking her head primly, like a school marm. "Did you see it?"

"I'm like papa," Timmy said. "I couldn't even see the penny."

At noon they returned to the paw-paw grove and ate the lunch Emma had packed before they left home. For a time they chatted casually about the things they had seen and done that morning, laughing as they recalled the amusing incidents they had witnessed—like the old man in Dillions store who thought the jar of peas was for sale and asked how much it was. Then, suddenly, they were not talking or laughing any more; something nameless and dreaded had fallen between them, something that could not be talked about, and they finished the meal in silence.

It was Timmy who spoke at last. He stood up and brushed off the seat of his trousers, then said, "That was a mighty good meal, mama."

"Thank you, darling," Emma replied, somehow unable to look directly at him. She glanced at Chad, met his eyes watching her, then hurriedly began cleaning up the picnic remains.

Another long moment passed, then Timmy spoke again, this time to his father.

"Mr. Connie said the riders were suppose to be at the stables by twelve forty-five . . . wasn't that what he said, papa?"

"That's right. I expect you'd better run along . . . I'll help your mother straighten up here. We'll see you after the race." There was a waiting pause. "Unless you want me to go along," Chad added.

"I'll make it all right," Timmy said. He was watching Emma; she had stopped working and was looking directly at Chad.

"You mean you're not going with him?" she asked, incredulously.

"I'd rather go by myself, mama," Timmy said. "I'll be all right."

She continued to stare at Chad for a moment, then turned away, biting her lip, determined not to fight another losing battle.

Timmy remained where he was for some time, watching her; then he walked across to where she knelt over the picnic remains. She felt his presence beside her but still could not bring herself to look at him.

"Don't worry, mama," he said softly.

She swallowed against the fear in her throat, blinked back the tears that welled up in her eyes; then, with a great effort, she turned to him and smiled. "Oh, I'm not worried," she said, putting her arms around his waist. "You just be careful, that's all."

He grinned, and gave her a quick hug. "I will, mama . . .

don't you worry." Then he was gone, running along the dusty path toward main street.

Emma turned back to the table cloth. She felt Chad's eyes, watching her. Then his slow, patient voice: "I know how you feel . . . but it's his race. It's all a part of growing up . . . I want to help him through the tough spots too . . . but not so much that he won't learn to help himself."

"I know," she said. "I'm all right now . . . here, help me put this basket in the wagon."

A few minutes later they returned to main street and made their way along the boardwalk toward the land office at the upper end of town. There was now a perceptible change in the air, a sense of excitement in the crowd, that she had not noticed that morning. The talk was all of racing and it seemed that everyone had an opinion.

She leaned toward Chad. "Where will the race begin?"

"Down by the gin," he said. "They'll come this way and end at the bank, just up from the land office. We'll be in on the finish. . . ."

She nodded and gripped his arm tighter.

A moment later he said, "There'll be a parade of the riders first . . . down main street to the starting line . . . that'll start any minute."

She nodded again, unable now to analyze her feelings at all; mixed with the fear was a nervous tension in the pit of her stomach that was somehow pleasant. She found herself thinking: if Timmy *should* win, he can use the five dollars prize money for a new pair of shoes . . . he'll certainly need some shoes this winter. . . .

Almost before she knew it they had arrived at the land office; the front porch was crowded with spectators but Will Kelly waved to them and motioned to the chair he was saving at one end; Chad held her arm as they went up the steps and across the porch to where Will waited. The noise now was maddening; both sides of main street from one end of town to the other were lined with people, shouting, laughing, leaning out from the curb, craning their necks to watch for the parade to begin at the livery stable above the bank.

"I brought you a chair," Will shouted above the din of the crowd, "in case they don't get started on time." He held the chair while she sat down.

The tradesday officials were running about in the street, urging the people to stay on the walks, shouting instructions that nobody heard or heeded, clearing the last wagons away.

Then suddenly a hush fell over the crowd, beginning somewhere beyond them and moving in a wave past the land office and along the street toward the gin. Emma could not see; at last she stood up, holding Chad's hand, and leaned out from the porch. The riders had already left the livery stable and were moving down the street toward the land office. Someone blocked her vision for an instant, then moved back. She saw Timmy on the mustang, third in line. Then they were passing directly in front of the spectators on the porch; most of the boys were older, some looked like men. Timmy looked down at the mustang's neck, leaning forward, holding the reins in tight; suddenly he glanced toward the porch and smiled; she smiled back and waved, but he had turned away. She felt Chad's hand on her shoulder and glanced up; he winked at her and nodded.

There were eleven horses in all, most of them heavy-footed animals that had worked in harness all week; two stood out, even she could see that: the lean, nervous mustang and a tall, rangy black mare ridden by the Nolan boy. Too quickly the riders had passed from view. One of the men on the porch said, "Who's boy is that on the mustang?" and somebody behind said, "That's Walters' boy ain't it?" After that two of the men talked of betting but Will Kelly said, "You men save your money," and that ended the discussion. One of the race officials (Mr. Cramer, she thought) was standing in the center of the street directly in front of them, looking toward the lower end of town, holding a red flag by his side. Emma had sat down again but from the chair she could not see beyond the corner of the blacksmith shop; she rubbed her hands nervously along the sides of her dress and fretted inwardly; at last she stood up and moved out to the edge of the porch. Except for the gin itself, the entire street was

visible from where she stood. She felt her breath catch in her
throat and found that she was unable to breathe deeply
against the rising pressure in her chest. . . .

Someone on the porch said, "This is it. . . ."

Mr. Cramer now was holding the red flag above his head,
leaning slightly forward, peering intently down the street toward the starting line. A long instant passed—then Mr.
Cramer thrust the flag downward in an arc and ran for the
boardwalk. . . .

Emma leaned out from the porch and heard the resound-
ing wave of cheers move up the street, rattling and echoing
against the air; she saw first the cloud of dust—then, hurtling
into view, the horses. For an instant it was impossible to
distinguish one from the other, they ran close together,
bunched in a pack, directly up the middle of the street. Then
she saw Timmy, riding in front, the mustang running low
against the ground, the Nolan black running hard on his
flank; Timmy lay flat against the mustang's back, his heels
drumming against his sides. She watched, entranced, as they
came, heard as one sound the pounding hooves and the wild
cheers . . . then, above the din, her own voice, screaming
encouragement to Timmy. She was never able to remember
clearly the exact order of events that occurred during the
next horrifying moments; she remembered only that the
cheers of the spectators became shrieks, charged with terror,
and that her own fear was something alive and moving inside her stomach; she saw the dog, a small, black mongrel,
dash from the curb into the street, barking at the oncoming
horses; saw the mustang break his pace, shy away, staring
wild eyed at the dog, then bolt, running across the street
and into the crowd on the other side. The other horses tore
by, leaving a swirl of dust; across the street somebody, a
woman, was screaming; a man on the porch shouted, "Look
out!" and ran down the steps, followed by the others.
Numb, unable for an instant to move at all, Emma heard
again the shrieks of the woman across the street—then she
was moving with the mass of people, for a time carried along
by the force of the crowd, and then running desperately,

fighting the resistance of it, screaming something, she did not know what.

Suddenly, without knowing how she got there, she was standing at the edge of an opening in the crowd; in the center of the opening she saw Chad, kneeling over the twisted body of Timmy; somewhere, far away, there were still shouts but the circle of faces was perfectly quiet, motionless. A voice said clearly, "The boy should have throwed himself clear . . . I seen the whole thing . . . he tried to hang on and slid underneath the mustang's belly . . . the hooves caught him as he fell . . . I seen the whole thing. . . ."

Emma tried to move, to speak, and was unable to do so; the world spun around her, she heard other sounds, distant, receding; through a blur she saw Chad, lifting the small, crumpled body, moving away through the crowd; she fought for consciousness, felt herself falling, strong arms holding her up. O God, she thought; O God, please. . . .

CHAPTER 23

THE FUNERAL PROCESSION—eight people—moved slowly up the hill through the slow drizzle of rain that had fallen steadily since daybreak. Walking in front were Will Kelly, Sheriff McKnight, Mr. Stanley and Mert Dillion, bearing between them the rough, unpainted wooden box. Following directly behind the pall bearers were Emma and Chad; Emma dressed in a black, woolsey dress, her shoulders slightly hunched against the falling rain, her face pale and lifeless; Chad sensed her presence beside him, heard her footsteps on the damp earth, felt the distance she had placed between them; he did not look at her; he lived, as she did, with the deep pain inside him, and hardened himself against it.

Behind Chad and Emma walked Mr. Bockman and Connie Lipscomb, Connie breathing heavily as the climb steepened, his feet slipping on the muddy path.

Slowly the procession wound across the piney hill and along the rocky ridge that led upward toward the bluff. Somewhere, far down the hill, a wet quail piped thinly; the rain spattered softly against the pines. At last they reached the bluff and the grave that Will and Sheriff McKnight had dug earlier that morning. The pallbearers stopped and carefully placed the wooden box on the ground beside the mound of wet, fresh dirt. Chad and Emma walked to the coffin and stopped beside it. For a long moment they simply waited. Then Will Kelly walked away from the group, to the head of the open grave. He looked downward into the yawning hole, saw the water in the bottom of it and the tiny circular patterns where the rain fell. Slowly he looked upward, into the rain, and felt the cool drops against his cheeks, saw the grey sky beyond. Somewhere up there is a God, he thought; you have to believe that, otherwise there is nothing left—nothing but the pain and aching inside . . . and a man can't live by that.

Still looking upward, the wetness glistening on his face, he began talking.

"God . . . we bring you this boy. We don't know why you saw fit to take him, but you did . . . and we're not saying that's wrong. You know how much hurting you've left behind . . . and I guess you'll know how to take that hurt away when the time comes. It says somewhere in the Bible that you have a special feeling for children . . . that you understand them and know the things they need and want . . . so I guess Timmy'll be in good hands. Look after the boy for us . . . and if it doesn't interfere with your plan for taking the boy this way, try to help his mama and papa understand why it had to be." For a full minute he stood without moving, his face turned into the rain, then he said, "Amen."

He walked back to the wooden box and nodded to the other men; they lifted the coffin at one end and Sheriff McKnight slipped a rope around it, then they slid it forward across the mud into the grave and lowered it slowly to the bottom. The pallbearers looked to Will for instructions. "All right," he said, "cover it up."

Mr. Dillion and Sheriff McKnight took the shovels that had been placed to one side and thrust them into the muddy mound beside the grave. The first shovelful struck the box with a loud spat. Will glanced at Emma. She was staring at the open grave, but without visible emotion. She looked almost detached, as if she had lost all feeling; oblivious, weary, sensitive to nothing, she stood now motionless, watching with tired eyes, seeing only movement without purpose or meaning. He had hoped the funeral might break her; she had not wept a tear since Timmy's death, had spoken quietly about the arrangements, had referred to Timmy's body only as "that little boy." Now the hurt was locked inside her and he knew that she was not a woman who could live with so much pain. Beside her Chad, too, looked at the grave. His suffering was visible, touching every feature of his face; and yet, he was the stronger.

No one moved or spoke until the grave was filled; then Will glanced at Chad and nodded. Chad took Emma's arm. "We'd better go now," he said. She allowed him to lead her away, down the pathway toward the valley. She did not once look back, did not speak a word.

When they reached the house, she went inside, leaving the others standing in the rain by the well porch.

Chad watched her go, then turned back to the men. "I'm sorry . . . she's torn up . . . she doesn't understand it yet. . . ."

"Of course," Will said. "Is there anything else we can do?"

"I don't think so . . . not now. Thanks for coming. . . ."

The men nodded, stood a moment longer, waiting; then turned and walked around the house.

Will remained behind. "Take care of her," he said.

"I'll try, Will . . . I'll try. . . ."

"I know that." He waited a moment longer. "Come see me," he said, then turned and walked away.

"Sure . . . we'll do that," Chad said behind him.

Chad stood for a long while on the back porch, looking up at the dark sky. How can you be strong, he thought, when your own strength is gone? How can you help someone else when you don't care any more yourself? Maybe like Will said, you had to believe in God, maybe that was the answer. If you just knew what He was.

At last he walked into the kitchen and across the hall to the living room. Emma was seated in the chair by the window, looking out at the falling rain. He walked to where she sat and stood wordless beside her, unable to communicate his own grief, knowing that it would help her to know that he too suffered.

It was Emma who spoke at last, spoke in a quiet, distant voice, perfectly controlled.

"I'm going away."

"Emma . . ."

"No. Talking won't help now . . . I'm going to Tennessee where Mase is. . . ."

"We've been through this together before . . . it takes time . . ." He broke off, knowing that he was not saying what needed to be said, knowing that whatever he said she would not listen.

For some time neither of them spoke. He wanted to kneel beside her, to hold her close to him until the fear and heartbreak had passed. But now the words must come first . . . and there were no words.

Another moment passed.

"You can take me to Gipson in the morning," she said. "Early . . . I'll wait at Will Kelly's office until Mr. Dickson takes the mail to Pemberton . . . I can take a train from there." And then she stood up and walked out, leaving him alone in the dark room, with the rain drumming against the roof.

And so, the next morning he hitched the mules to the wagon and drove up the lane and saw her waiting under the mulberry tree in her fresh gingham dress and knew that it was too late.

They rode in silence down the rise, across the meadow strip that stretched away to the river, then on across the first piney ridges beyond. At the rim of the basin they turned west, down the old river road that led to Gipson.

And he looked at her and remembered that day so long ago when he had taken her, his new bride, to the house his father had built for the Indian woman. . . .

EPILOGUE

LONG YEARS LATER Will Kelly would remember that day; would remember the first glimpse of the wagon, a quarter of a mile away, crossing the rise at the lower end of town; would remember watching as it moved slowly up main street toward the land office; would remember even the street itself, strangely empty at eight in the morning.

In point of time, the incident would always be associated in his mind with the other, purely official, matter: the announcement the day before that the land office would be closed the first of the month. He had expected the notice and had not been at all disturbed when Mr. Bockman, as chairman of the city council, had brought him the word. But now, seeing Chad and Emma, a nameless sense of melancholy came over him. Watching them he thought: I saw the beginning; I saw the long suffering between; and now I am watching the end. The world was too much for them after all; too much for Emma, anyhow. And who can blame her?; unless you understand, unless you know—or *think* you know—why things happen the way they do, life loses all meaning. For her, there is nothing left; nothing but Chad, and she understands him least of all.

The wagon pulled in to the hitchrail and stopped; Will stood up; neither Chad nor Emma had looked directly at him; they did not look at him now.

Chad climbed out and held up his hand; Emma looked down at him, and for an instant something changed in her face; it was a flicker, nothing more; she took his hand and stepped down, then walked past him and up the steps to the land office.

She nodded to Will and smiled, a faint smile without warmth or meaning.

"It looks like I'm always asking a favor of you," she said. "If I won't be in the way, I'd like to wait in the land office until the mail wagon runs." She paused, looking away. "I'm going to Pemberton . . . to catch a train," she added; embarrassed, reluctant words, uttered almost as a matter of duty.

Will opened the door for her. "You're always welcome here," he said, aware that he had spoken in a curiously formal tone; sensing his inadequacy. What could you say? What could words mean now?

Emma walked inside and sat down, folding her hands in her lap. Will waited at the door for Chad; when he walked up on the porch, he said, "Hello, Will," and went inside.

Will followed him into the office. He walked to his desk and sat down; now he resented the intrusion; why should he be subjected to the pain and heartbreak? Why should he be asked to share the suffering?

Although there was an empty chair beside Emma, Chad remained standing by the door. He watched Emma; she sat very still, knowing that he watched her, refusing to meet his eyes.

A long moment of silence passed. Then, speaking to Emma, Chad said, "When you've had your visit out . . . come on home."

To Will it seemed that the words were torn from him; the words of a strong man who was compromising himself; the difficult, halting words of a child.

Emma did not move or raise her head.

"You go on back," she said. "I'll wait here for the mail wagon."

It was an answer to his question; which needed no answer at all. It was her way of saying: I am not going to visit, I am going to stay; a dismissal, a final judgment.

Chad did not move. Will looked away. He thought: for the first time in his life, this man is afraid of losing something; and he cannot face the thought of living without it.

After an interminable time, Chad spoke again.

"Well, I'll go on back then. I'm sorry . . . about the boy . . . about everything."

Still he waited; unable to say more, unable to go. At last he said, "You take care of yourself." Then he walked out.

They heard his footsteps cross the porch and descend the steps; a moment later, the creak of the wagon; and then the sound of the wheels against the gravel street, diminishing; at last, no sound at all.

The clock above the office door ticked noisily. Emma had not moved; Will watched her; she glanced up and smiled faintly, then looked again at her hands.

"So you're going away," Will said.

She nodded but did not look up.

"Maybe it's none of my business," Will went on. "Maybe it is . . . at least you and Chad have always meant something to me that I didn't realize until now. You've meant the courage and the hope and the love that makes this mixed up world worth living in. Chad is a strange man. I knew that the first time I saw him. And I know he isn't easy to live with; but that's because he knows more about living than the rest of us. You said once that you'd be happier if you knew he needed you . . . he needs you now. Maybe I know better than you do how much losing Timmy meant to him. I saw him waiting in the doctor's office the day Timmy was killed. I saw the hurt in his eyes, a hurt deeper than you or I will ever know. I watched him yesterday at the funeral . . . last night I lay awake for hours, remembering his face. I saw him just now, begging you not to go away, begging you with his eyes because he could not tell you with words how he felt . . . it was a terrible thing to see. . . ."

Emma sat with her head bowed; she was crying; quietly weeping for the memories she had lived with so long.

". . . but it isn't Chad I'm thinking about now," Will said. "It's you . . . it's you who failed to make the marriage work. When you and Chad came to the office today, I resented it; I resented the fact that you had brought your problem to me. Now I know why. I didn't want to face the

truth . . . I didn't want to admit that there was a problem
. . . to admit that I was wrong. I guess we're all like that
. . . and yet we've got to face the big problems sooner or
later. I didn't want to face the problem of you and Chad
because it's easier not to. I told myself that what has happened between you is no concern of mine . . . but that's
not true. It is my problem because I believe that your love
for him, and his for you, is a good thing for this world; if
love is destroyed, the world will have lost a very important
battle. If people like you and Chad can't win, then life is
stronger than men. I don't want to believe that."

Will stopped talking and leaned back in his chair; he
was very tired; he wanted to get up and walk out of the office
and go away; he was tired of fighting Emma . . . and himself. He heard Emma crying softly, the tick of the clock
above the door, the drone of a fly against the front screen.

How long they sat there he did not know; at last Emma
raised her head, her face streaked with tears; she had stopped
crying.

She spoke quietly, looking away from Will, toward the
open door.

"You told me once that things would change after I married Chad, that I'd have to change with them. I guess I never
knew what you meant. I tried to keep things just the way
they were . . . tried to live everybody's life but mine . . .
Lewt, Ben, papa, Mase . . . even Chad. . . . I tried to make
them what I wanted them to be. I know now that you can't
do that. . . ."

She looked at Will and smiled.

"Now," she said, "I want to go home."

Will nodded, feeling the quiet peace inside him.

"I think that's where you belong," he said. "Come on, I'll
take you back."

On the long ride back to the basin Emma sat silently.
Sometimes she looked at Will and smiled and the smile was
something that could not be said in words.

They reached the rim of the basin before noon and turned

222

down the road that led across the pine ridge. Crossing the meadow beyond, they saw Chad; he stood on the front porch, watching them.

At the foot of the rise, Emma touched Will's arm. "If you don't mind, I'll get out here."

"Sure." Will patted her hand. "You folks come see me."

"We will . . . soon."

She climbed out of the buggy and turned back to Will. "Someday I'll tell you how wonderful you are."

He nodded, then watched her, first walking and then running back to Chad's arms.